RHAPSODY OF THE SPHERES

Third Flatiron Anthologies
Volume 12, Book 32, Summer/Fall 2023

Edited by Juliana Rew
Cover Art by Keely Rew

Rhapsody of the Spheres
Third Flatiron Anthologies
Volume 12, Summer/Fall 2023

Published by Third Flatiron Publishing
Juliana Rew, Editor and Publisher

Copyright 2023 Third Flatiron Publishing
ISBN #979-8-9886547-0-4

Discover other titles by Third Flatiron:
(1) Over the Brink: Tales of Environmental Disaster
(2) A High Shrill Thump: War Stories
(3) Origins: Colliding Causalities
(4) Universe Horribilis
(5) Playing with Fire
(6) Lost Worlds, Retraced
(7) Redshifted: Martian Stories
(8) Astronomical Odds
(9) Master Minds
(10) Abbreviated Epics
(11) The Time It Happened
(12) Only Disconnect
(13) Ain't Superstitious
(14) Third Flatiron's Best of 2015
(15) It's Come to Our Attention
(16) Hyperpowers
(17) Keystone Chronicles
(18) Principia Ponderosa
(19) Cat's Breakfast: Kurt Vonnegut Tribute
(20) Strange Beasties
(21) Third Flatiron Best of 2017
(22) Monstrosities
(23) Galileo's Theme Park
(24) Terra! Tara! Terror!
(25) Hidden Histories
(26) Infinite Lives: Short Tales of Longevity
(27) Third Flatiron Best of 2019
(28) Gotta Wear Eclipse Glasses
(29) Brain Games: Stories to Astonish
(30) Things With Feathers: Stories of Hope
(31) After the Gold Rush

License Notes
All stories are copyright their respective authors and published here with permission.
www.thirdflatiron.com

Contents

Editor's Note by Juliana Rew 7
The Solution to Everything Is Disco
   By Jenny Perry Carr 11
And Lifts Her Leafy Arms to Pray
   by Brian Trent 19
One Last Night at Benny's Magic Fantastic
   Cabaret by Jeff Reynolds 25
The United Flamemakers of Ravalli
   by David Hankins 35
The Day Luna Swallowed the Sun
   by Akis Linardos 49
Euterpe by Maureen Bowden 59
Let Sleeping Rock Stars Lie by Bruce Golden 71
Celestial Notes by Robin Pond 79
Peer-Reviewed Spellcasting by M.A. Dosser 91
An Autograph by Stetson Ray 101
Dog's Body by Edward Barnfield 111
Dream Bones by Neethu Krishnan 123
Discordia by Liam Hogan 133
Matryoshka by Douglas Gwilym 145
A Touch of the Grape
   by Sharon Diane King 151
Lost and Hound by M. R. Abbink-Gallagher 163
Museum of the Multiverse by Anne Gruner 173
Physics for Witches by Monica Joyce Evans 181
Grand-Père's Last Transmission
   By Bev Vincent 189
Changing of the Guard by Taylor Dye 199
Sunrise on Eris by Mike Adamson 207
The Stellar Instrument by Brandon Case 213
Opal World Frolic by Jendia Gammon 225

Grins & Gurgles
    The Art of Music Surfing by Lisa Timpf 241
    The Last Viceroy by Julie Biegner 245

Epic Poem
    The Arbitration of Beauty
        by Emily Martha Sorensen 249

Credits and Acknowledgments 259

*****~~~~~*****

Editor's Note

Welcome to Third Flatiron's new anthology, *Rhapsody of the Spheres*, a collection of SF, Fantasy, space opera, and hopepunk short stories.

The dictionary defines a rhapsody as "an effusively enthusiastic or ecstatic expression of feeling." In ancient Greece, a rhapsody was also part of an epic poem of a suitable length for reciting. Edie Brickell waxed rhapsodic about a smile on a dog, and Queen and Liszt gave us their musical Bohemian and Hungarian rhapsodies, respectively.

Our authors have given us their opinions of fictional what-ifs that might make us happy, and we're even including a bit of epic poetry. We're proud to point out that all of our authors claim to be people rather than AI, so the human connection is very real here.

Space opera is one of those genres that some might say verges on the operatic, while exploring the mysteries of the universe. For real-life amazement, we recommend a science news article in *The Atlantic Magazine* about how gravity waves pass through us all:

Rhapsody of the Spheres

"Scientists Found Ripples in Space, and You Have to Buy Groceries," by Adam Frank (June 30, 2023) https://www.theatlantic.com/science/archive/2023/06/universe-gravitational-waves-nanograv-discovery/674570/

Jendia Gammon's space opera, "Opal World Frolic," anchors *Rhapsody of the Spheres*, in which a cyborg soldier meets all sort of beings on a planetary system quest. Brian Trent treats us to a space opera/fantasy mashup about a space colony with unauthorized trees, complete w/ dryads, "And Lifts Her Leafy Arms to Pray." Akis Linardos's AI protagonist builds a Dyson Sphere to protect humanity, in "The Day Luna Swallowed the Sun." Mike Adamson's astronauts enjoy the sun from afar as they visit a newly discovered dwarf moon in "Sunrise on Eris." Visits from advanced aliens take the stage in Bev Vincent's "Grand-Pere's Last Transmission," in which humans receive an invitation, and Liam Hogan's serendipitous "Discordia," in which aliens reveal that Earth's origin may have just been a "happy accident."

For those into hard scifi, we think you'll enjoy "Dog's Body," Edward Barnfield's tale of bioscientists working on an isolated island lab to clone domestic animals in preparation for a related secret project. We offer an imaginative time travel tale from Stetson Ray ("An Autograph").

Or should we call it RAP-sody? Many of the stories we received involved music and its power to change the world. Our anthology leads off with Jenny Perry Carr's "The Solution to Everything Is Disco," about a discouraged lab researcher who experiences a eureka moment when she lets the beat *drop*. Anne Gruner's "Museum of the Multiverse," imagines an eternal species that loves the music of the long-extinct human race. We direct you to Robin Pond's tale, "Celestial Notes," about a scientist who assembles a dissonant musical performance to save the world from climate catastrophe. Jeff Reynolds

Editor's Note

describes "One Last Night at Benny's Magic Fantastic Cabaret," for the jazz lover in us all. Even immortalized rock legends can undergo some ch-ch-changes in Bruce Golden's "Let Sleeping Rock Stars Lie."

Epic poems and mythology: We mentioned that epic poetry is sometimes called a rhapsody. Emily Martha Sorensen took up the challenge to write her poem about the origins of the Trojan War, "The Arbitration of Beauty." Happiness sometimes needs a bit of help from the goddess, in Maureen Bowden's "Euterpe." In Neethu Krishnan's "Dream Bones," a sleepwalker swims into the world of dreams to enlist as a dream keeper.

Fantasy and magic are always good to lift our spirits, right? A princess brokers a détente between humans and dragons with her song, in David Hankins's "The United Flamemakers of Ravalli." If you're a scientist, you might have wished you had magical powers to get to the solution, or at least to have your hard work recognized. Check out M. A. Dosser's "Peer-Reviewed Spellcasting." Monica Joyce Evans's "Physics for Witches" paints an artistic picture with quantum mechanics.

Family matters: Family can be both a challenge and the source of the greatest happiness, as shown in Brandon Case's futuristic social media foray, "The Stellar Instrument." Motherhood is strange and wonderful in Douglas Gwilym's "Matryoshka." Sharon Diane King's psychedelic "A Touch of the Grape" brings us family nostalgia at its best.

Then, there's always hope: 'Lor' willing and the creek don't rise' is an old Appalachian expression that things are bound to get better with enough focused intention. Lovely hopepunk stories that ring true include Taylor Dye's "Changing of the Guard," in which two supernatural beings are on a mission to save a sick child, and "Lost and Hound," featuring M. R. Abbink-

Rhapsody of the Spheres

Gallagher's trippy tale about a telepathic dog who thinks deep thoughts.

As usual, our **Grins & Gurgles** flash humor section offers a chuckle, in "The Art of Music Surfing" by Lisa Timpf, as well as an ironic look at the last days of a butterfly, in Julie Biegner's "The Last Viceroy."

At one time, dozens of paddle steamers plied the rivers and canals of Scotland. The seagoing Waverley, pictured in the ebook, remains a tourist's delight, referred to by some as a "Hebridean Rhapsody." We hope you enjoy the many meanings explored in Third Flatiron's *Rhapsody of the Spheres* anthology.

Stay in the pink,

Juliana Rew
August 2023

*****~~~~~*****

The Solution to Everything Is Disco

by Jenny Perry Carr

"... *bit off more than you can chew*..."
"... *vain to expect such results*..."
"... *is the right program for you?*"
"... *need to see evidence of sound research within three months*..."

Melody's PhD thesis committee shredded her work, saying her ideas were too lofty, unrealistic. But isn't that what science was about? Dream big, make it a reality? She trudged toward the Yale Science Building perched atop Science Hill, fall leaves rustling with a chorus of uneasiness. Shivering, she shoved her hands deep into her polar fleece pockets, hugging her arms close to her body. Their words stung more than the biting wind.

They couldn't see her vision and wanted her to focus on a narrow question. That didn't interest her. Sure, she studied basic science, the fundamental building blocks of life, but that didn't mean she couldn't accomplish great things. Melody walked through an exhaled cloud, edges swirling as she yanked open the heavy metal door.

Rhapsody of the Spheres

Are they right?

After a series of forced smiles and obligatory nods at fellow students and professors, she made her way up in the elevator to the brightly lit laboratory, awash in late afternoon sunrays and fluorescent light. Talk radio droned on in the background, adding noise to the bustling genetics lab. Days-old cultures reeking like soup and dirty socks, swirled in the squeaky shaking incubator, warming the experimental cells to promote growth. Grad students curled over their benches in pristine white lab coats, blue nitrile gloves, with thumbs triggering their pipetors, measuring out minuscule volumes of solutions into tiny tubes.

The weight on her shoulders lifted, and she inhaled deeply. The familiar messy white shelves and black countertops cluttered with machines and wire racks comforted her. She spent more days and nights here than in her apartment.

What did her advisors know, anyway? Jaded by the politics of academia, grant writing, and the peer-reviewed journal process, they wouldn't know an innovative idea if it were right under their noses. Weren't scientists supposed to think big? And wasn't climate change the biggest challenge of their generation?

Her work focused on developing synthetic bacteria capable of absorbing carbon dioxide from the atmosphere. Known bacteria were inefficient at this process, so she developed her own strain by introducing new genes into an existing organism, creating new life. One that could efficiently reverse man's effect on the environment. Restore the balance. She hypothesized seeding the atmosphere with specialized bacteria could serve this function. Was that too vain?

She plopped onto a padded stool and flipped through her lab notebook, turning to the last page to assess her progress and the next steps.

The Solution to Everything Is Disco

Scott, her bench mate, carried a stack of bacteria-laden petri dishes toward the incubator room down the hall. "How did the committee meeting go?"

Her lip curled, and she managed to voice an *ack*.

"That good? Sorry."

Melody glanced up. Scott was already gone, and instead, Penelope stood in the doorway.

Double *ack*.

Penelope breezed into the lab and passed Melody too close for comfort, then hovered by the humming shaking incubator. "I heard your committee isn't happy." She raised an eyebrow and smirked.

What a jerk.

Penelope had joined the lab that semester and started out super friendly, always taking an interest in everyone's work and peering over shoulders to learn. That changed quickly as her true colors emerged. None of her ideas were her own, so no one talked to her about their work any more, for fear it would end up in her thesis.

Melody prepped a nutrient broth to feed her cell cultures, measuring out a solution of sterilized beef extract into a bottle. "I guess that means you won't be interested in stealing any of my work again, then."

Penelope chuffed.

The students and lab assistants appeared to finish their work simultaneously, each hanging up their lab coats and donning jackets, and hurried out the door. Penelope had a way of clearing the lab, but Melody wouldn't skulk away like the others.

"Oh, I'm sorry. Was this yours?" Penelope held a stopper in one hand and an empty test tube in the other.

Melody's stomach flip-flopped.

Her cultures were in that shaker, not Penelope's. That was no "accident."

Melody raced to the incubator, gripping the open lid, warm air engulfing her. "What did you do?"

Rhapsody of the Spheres

"My bad. I hope that wasn't important." Her words were sympathetic, but her snarky tone wasn't.

"What did you put in my culture?"

Penelope handed Melody a test tube labeled *HCl*. *Hydrochloric acid*. The low pH probably killed the cells, and Penelope knew it.

"I thought it was mine."

"You knew very well it wasn't. Don't ever touch my stuff." Melody ripped the stopper from Penelope's hand and recapped the flask. She snatched it up from the incubator.

Melody just wanted some peace and quiet in the lab. Not have to worry about sabotage *or* be reminded about her failures with her thesis committee. How could she get rid of Penelope?

She cradled the warm culture against her body as she schlepped back to the bench. *Warmth. Heat.* Melody's gaze wandered to the vents overhead, then ditched the spoiled flask on her bench.

She unzipped her polar fleece and sauntered to the coat rack by the door. She glanced over her shoulder as she pulled off the coat, noting that Penelope appeared to be distracted on the lab's computer. As Melody hung her jacket, she repeatedly tapped the up-arrow on the thermostat. Eighty-eight degrees. Hopefully hot enough to drive Penelope out.

Over the next several hours, as the temperature rose, Melody fed her cell cultures and assessed their health under the light microscope. The tainted flask stared at her, contributing to her rising temperature nearly as much as the heating system. She blotted sweat from her upper lip with a lint-free tissue and fanned herself with her lab notebook.

Penelope had stripped down to a chic pink tank top and didn't seem deterred in the least by the fiery air pumping into the lab. She continued working away at her bench.

The Solution to Everything Is Disco

Melody wouldn't survive much longer in the heat, and she had hours of work remaining. To purge Penelope from the lab required a more effective means. She scanned the room, searching for ideas. The speaker chattered away the evening news. Melody grinned.

I will *survive.*

Melody called up her favorite playlist on the computer, one Penelope absolutely *hated.* She set the volume to max and hit play.

A flourish of ascending and descending scales filled the lab. Gloria Gaynor's clear, sultry voice sang out. The digital equalizer's blue lights danced up and down to the tune.

Penelope threw up her hands. "Oh, come on."

The driving disco beat kicked in and rattled the glassware. The drums thumped in Melody's chest.

"Not more of your lame music."

Melody shrugged and moved to turn the thermostat back down to 70 degrees. "It's not lame. It's classic." She re-settled onto her stool.

A frustrated shriek emitted from Penelope. "Fine, fine. You win." She ripped her jacket from the coat rack and stormed out of the lab.

Finally.

Melody cackled. At least she'd have the evening in peace now, alone in the lab.

She tapped the remote to lower the volume to a more enjoyable level and eyed the tainted flask that Penelope had sabotaged. Maybe she could try to salvage the cells. Would they be viable? Only one way to find out.

Melody withdrew liquid from the culture flask and dripped a drop onto a glass slide. She flattened the droplet with a thin glass coverslip and positioned the sample under the microscope. She smiled. There they were—the spherical *Mycoplasma* cells rotated through the liquid media like dust particles tumbling through a shaft of light. They indeed looked alive, despite Penelope's acid bath.

Rhapsody of the Spheres

They pulsed in the solution. *Pulsating?* Were they reacting to the carbon dioxide in her breath?

Melody beamed. If that were true, it meant her experiment worked.

She tapped her foot in time to the cells' rhythmic vibrations. Melody glanced at the speaker. The beat matched the song. She narrowed her eyes. *Odd.*

The yellow-orange nutrient broth bubbled as she used the pipetor to prep another sample on a slide. Studying the round cells with the microscope, they appeared to dance on the slide. She rubbed her eyes. *This can't be real.*

Then the song changed. Driving drums paired with the scratch of a guitar, then Vicki Sue Robinson belted out her hit "Turn the Beat Around." A faster song.

She again examined the cells. The rate of cells' pulsations increased and matched the tempo of the music. Melody gasped and leaned back. *That can't be. How can they react to music? I've never seen anything like this before.*

She furiously jotted down the findings in her notebook, documenting everything she'd seen and the conditions within the lab. *What was different this time?*

Melody noted the spike in temperature within the lab and the hydrochloric acid Penelope had dumped into her sample. Somehow, these conditions altered her cells. Every sample she studied in this batch showed the same results. Nothing similar in her other cell cultures. This culture was special. These bacteria reacted to music.

How is that possible? Was it the numerous beta carboxysomes she had introduced into these cells, intended to convert carbon dioxide into glucose within the bacteria? Did the low pH mutate the cells? Was the temperature a factor?

This wasn't what she hoped to develop, but perhaps it was better.

The Solution to Everything Is Disco

Think of the applications. Bacteria you can turn off and on. Targeted drug delivery via bacteria only triggered once music is played. This could advance medicine by decades.

Melody froze, then laughed hysterically. Ironically, the sabotage may have helped create this mutation. She'd probably have to share credit with Penelope, and she might actually deserve it, despite her idea-stealing antics. Penelope's thesis committee probably pressured her just like Melody's. *Who cares? This discovery is so huge it'll take tons of researchers to continue and replicate the work.* She'd need the help, even if it was Penelope's.

This wasn't the direction she ever thought her research would go, but it was viable. She had a working experiment right before her eyes.

Take that, thesis committee.

The song changed again. Horns blared through the speakers, and a chorus of voices from Kool and the Gang sang "Celebration."

Melody hopped off her stool and turned up the volume. She danced across the lab, shimmying her shoulders and singing the tune at the top of her lungs, using a pipetor as a microphone.

She whirled around.

Scott stood in the doorway, chuckling. He clapped.

Melody's cheeks warmed and flushed. She smiled and grabbed him by the hand, twirling him into the dance.

He reluctantly joined, then went with it. "What are we celebrating?"

"I made a breakthrough, and it *literally* rocks."

"The new strain?"

She nodded and laughed, unable to contain her excitement. "I—well, Penelope and I—made a discovery."

"Penelope?"

She grinned. "I know, right? Not sure it was her intention, but she actually helped me. We'll have to replicate the experiment, but the committee will be pleased. We've uncovered some *very* sound research."

###

About the Author

Jenny Perry Carr's "Blood on the Wing" appeared in the anthology *MURDERBIRDS* in April 2023 by WonderBird Press, and "Blue Serpent" was published by *Dark Recesses* in May 2022. "Luck, Life, Light, and Other Frivolous Pursuits" will be published by LTUE/Hemelein in the anthology, *Troubadours and Space Princesses* in 2024.

She is group vice president of scientific services for a medical communications company by day, budding sci-fi/fantasy/horror writer at night. She has a PhD in molecular neurobiology from Yale University, which influences much of her speculative writing. She's part of Wulf Moon's Wulf Pack writing group.

*****~~~~~*****

And Lifts Her Leafy Arms to Pray
by Brian Trent

"There's a naked woman in the garden," his supervisor said, pointing to the security feed with one hand while picking at his eyebrow with the other.

Sitting across from the man's immense desk, Dr. Henry Takayama—Head Botanist of the colony—fidgeted anxiously. "Sorry?"

"There's zero chance you didn't hear every word I said. A woman, stark naked, creeping around the garden. Garden Five, to be specific."

The supervisor office was as unlike a garden as anything in the known universe. A sterile cube of gunmetal gray walls and floor, with the only furniture being two chairs and the desk that separated them. The security feed displaying on the desk was a luminous square, inches from a placard: BOTANY SUPERVISOR GREGORY WASHINGTON. The timestamp read: 02:13.

Henry peered at the image. "Actually, there are *two* naked women there."

Supervisor Gregory Washington enlarged the image with a splay of his fingers. It was grainy and indistinct; at two o'clock in the morning, the colony's garden pods automatically dimmed their lights to simulate

Rhapsody of the Spheres

a terrestrial night. Nonetheless, it was possible to distinguish two women capering among the trees.

"*Two* women, you're right," Washington said. "Accurate numbers are important. At 02:13 this morning, a pair of unauthorized women broke into Garden Pod Five, and then proceeded to break several morality codes."

The room settled into a dangerous silence. Half a minute stretched into a full minute, during which the two men regarded each other.

"*You're* the master gardener," Washington prompted at last. "You're responsible for locking up the gardens at the end of your shift."

Henry nodded. "I locked them."

"Then can you explain what's happening here?"

The botanist nervously pulled at the hem of his lab coat. "No, but I have a theory. You see, those women aren't really—"

"Those women aren't my main concern."

"They're not?"

"*This* is my main concern." Washington zoomed the security feed out, providing a wide-view of Garden Pod Five. It was a scene dominated by trees, with the women pushed to the periphery.

Henry frowned. "What am I looking at?"

"The trees!"

"The trees?"

Washington stabbed a finger into the image. "Apple trees! Peach trees! Cherry trees! Maple and hickory! Blue spruce, white birch, and evergreens!"

The botanist cleared his throat and blotted his sweaty hands on his pants. "Sir? I'm afraid I don't understand."

"They're *real* trees!" Washington cried. "Why are there *real trees* in the garden? All of our trees are supposed to be plastic—we 3D-print them in accordance with the colony's beautification ordinance. So how in the hell did we end up with *actual* foliage in Garden Five?

And Lifts Her Leafy Arms to Pray

Where did they come from? And what the hell happened to the *plastic* trees?"

Henry's shoulders slumped in defeat. It was inevitable, he supposed, that the discovery should come to his supervisor's attention. It had been two hundred years since the colony ship departed Earth. In that time, onboard scientists had learned to grow food in bioreactors. Meat stock. Vegetable matter. Grain. It all bubbled up from cellular scaffolding in large vats, and poured out of spigots as brightly colored sludge. Even the colony's oxygen was produced by cutting-edge air filtration and processors. Real trees were no longer needed. They took up space, they smelled weird, and their roots buckled the ground in ways not approved by the colony's beautification ordinance.

Washington picked a stray eyebrow hair like a weed and said, "Did you think I wouldn't notice? Accurate numbers are important. There were *one hundred* plastic trees in the garden. Each and every one of them has been replaced by an actual, living tree. Explain yourself!"

"I was trying to think of a way to bring this up. . . "

"Ah!" the man gave a smile as cultivated as Astroturf. "You pilfered the emergency seedbanks, is that it? Thought you could run a crafty little side-operation for profit? Did you think we wouldn't notice? Vat-grown fruit sales *are* down. What's next? You sell wood pulp? Surplus oxygen?"

"This has nothing to do with—"

"I admire your audacity, Dr. Takayama, even though the effort was childish. You made no effort to hide your real trees. People are obviously noticing the difference: visitors to Garden Five are up *five hundred percent*. Half the colony spends at least some of its free time there now. That cuts into holoviewer rates. Advertisers are pissed!"

Henry sighed. "I'm not responsible for this, but that's beside the point."

Rhapsody of the Spheres

"How so?"

"Real trees satisfy an important need."

"What need?"

"To walk in the woods."

His supervisor's triumphant smile turned down at the edges like the branches of a willow. "I beg your pardon?"

"It's been established science for hundreds of years," Henry explained. "Studies dating back to the twentieth century have shown tremendous psychological benefit to being surrounded by nature. My own ancestors had a word for it: *shinrin-yoku*, which translates as 'forest bathing.' Nature brings down blood pressure. It cleanses the mind of stress. It centers our emotions, and this colony is in dire need of that. Our social behavior is—"

"Perfectly fine! Job productivity, social media engagement, pill consumption. . . in every subcategory, we're tracking better than ever!" Washington rubbed the bald patch in his eyebrow, grunted in satisfaction, and went to work on the opposite one.

"We *need* nature," Henry insisted. "In a very real way, it connects us to the heartbeat of the cosmos. Trees drink sunlight, produce oxygen, and we in turn breathe that oxygen and produce carbon dioxide. Humans evolved as part of that harmonious system—a symphony of interdependence and cooperation."

"Don't be ridiculous!"

"When you divorce humanity from that symphony, it causes a breakdown of health. This is measurable and quantifiable. And that takes us back to these two naked women. See, they're not—"

"Naked?"

"Human."

His supervisor lowered his hand. "Excuse me?"

Henry pointed to the video feed. "Look at their skin."

"I'm seeing entirely too much skin."

And Lifts Her Leafy Arms to Pray

"It's green."

"What is?"

"The skin. They have *green* skin. You must have noticed."

Washington chewed his lip and clicked his teeth. "It's obviously a lighting issue."

"It's *not* a lighting issue. Those women have green skin. And if you look closely, you'll realize they aren't wearing leaves in their hair. Rather, their hair is *made* of leaves. See, I've concluded they are. . . "

"Aliens?!"

"Dryads."

His supervisor stared without comprehension.

Henry touched the desk and typed into the shipboard encyclopedia. In moments, it displayed an ancient Athenian fresco of dancing women, flowers and vines growing from their scalps in place of hair. "Dryads were mythical protectors of the forest. They helped things grow. They were known to bring forth vegetation where none had ever been. Maybe this is how life started on Earth billions of years ago. For want of a better word, they had magical powers. And *that's* how they transformed one hundred plastic trees into one hundred real ones. We banished nature, but they brought it back."

"You're joking."

"There are more things in heaven and earth, right?"

Washington made a scoffing sound and typed a command onto the desk. "I'm running an identity scan on their faces. In moments, we'll identify your operation's conspirators!"

Henry settled back into his chair. "Don't you get it? For most of human history, we were surrounded by nature. Yet here in this colony, we've shifted away from it. Maybe that's why the dryads returned. They want to remind us of what's important. I don't know how they got here. Maybe they tagged along with us, in a kind of

Rhapsody of the Spheres

torpor, like seeds that have yet to take root. But they're here now. They're trying to save us from—"

The desk surface flashed red, and Washington leapt to his feet. "These women are not registered with the colony census!"

"Of course not. What part of 'they are dryads' did you not understand?"

"This can only mean one thing!"

"Should I even bother asking you—"

"Someone lied on their census forms! We've got two undocumented people in the colony!" He stabbed a button on his desk. "Security! Meet me in Garden Five!"

Henry's jaw dropped. "What are you doing?"

"I'm arresting them."

"You can't do that!"

"Watch me!" The man stormed into the corridor, where he was joined by five security guards.

Alone in the office, Henry touched the desk and conjured a real-time view of the garden. Accurate numbers were indeed important, he thought. There were two dryads in Garden Five. There were one hundred trees. And there were six people—his supervisor and security—who barged into the pod with weapons drawn.

A few minutes later, there were one hundred and *six* trees.

About the Author

Recent work by Brian Trent appears in the New York Times-bestselling Black Tide Rising series, *The Magazine of Fantasy & Science Fiction*, Escape Pod, Flash Fiction Online, and *The Year's Best Military and Adventure SF.*

*****~~~~~*****

One Last Night at Benny's Magic Fantastic Cabaret

by Jeff Reynolds

  I came in through the back door using the spare cantrip Benny handed out to a privileged few, each tiny spell a snippet of *Round Midnight* by Thelonius Monk. Took me forever to locate the portal, even though he'd told me where he'd hidden it. He put it in an old sardine can tossed with seeming carelessness into the gutter, in a dark alley behind Rose Avenue. But he had to play things tight to the vest now that the government was gunning to arrest those who ran the magical speakeasies, or performed in them.
  David sat at the bar, nursing a scotch and looking glumly into the glass. Ethel sat with Darla, the two of them talking quietly. Ethel had a glass of whiskey in front of her, Darla a glass of wine. Jonathan helped Benny load unopened bottles into crates behind the bar, packing them around with straw. I suspected Cole and Henry were somewhere in the building. They wouldn't miss closing

Rhapsody of the Spheres

night. Julie and Lillian would probably show up sooner or later.

Everyone who had loved this place and the spell that it wove over us.

The stage was empty, the instruments resting in their cases or on their stands. The trumpet drew my eye, as it always did, though I hadn't blown one in thirty years, and then only in the marching band. I'd never seen the stage at Benny's empty before. No musicians, no poets, no comedians telling jokes. The legal changes had worried me, but now I just felt sad. I never thought there'd be a last night for Benny's place. Now that it had come, it felt even more depressing than I'd expected.

"You here for the wake?" Denver asked. I hadn't noticed him sitting in the corner, a drink in one hand, a book in the other.

"Saying goodbye to the place, sure. Didn't have anything better to do."

"Might as well wallow in the deep like the rest of us."

"You? Wallow?"

He laughed. "More than most of you. That's what editors do. We face the existential darkness and wallow in it. You writers think you have a monopoly on ennui and solipsism? Try being an editor. But it beats facing reality."

"What are you having?" I pointed at his glass.

"Macallan."

I whistled. "You come into some cash?"

"Still broke. Benny's feeling generous tonight. Whatever we want, it's on the house. I asked for a cheap whiskey, and he gave me his best instead. I'm not complaining." He finished his drink.

"Nor would I. Give me that, I'll get you another."

He handed me his empty, and I walked to the bar. Jonathan nodded and gave a smile, then nudged Benny so he noticed me. Benny wore his favorite vest, the rainbow-

One Last Night at Benny's

colored one. No shades, though. His purple suit jacket hung from a hook behind him.

"Hey, Michael! Good to see you tonight, cool cat. What are you having? It's all on the house on account there won't be a house after tonight."

"So, this is really it? You're not going to set up shop someplace else?"

He shrugged and tried to smile. "All good things must come to an end. We did have some mighty fine times though, didn't we?"

I held out Denver's glass. "Another for the solipsistic beatnik in the corner."

"And you?"

"You know me, Benny."

"Seltzer it is."

I turned and looked at what remained of the bar. An ordinary room tonight, no magic on display. A dozen tables, most of them empty, a single lit candle beneath glass in the middle of each. A few pictures on the walls of folks that had entertained here. But I'd seen this room on nights when bands blew the doors off and raised the walls. Literally; the music, the poetry, the laughter weaving a spell that touched all between within its confines. Evenings when we kicked the dust off the moon itself, starlight blazing in our retinas as music torched our hearts down to a smoldering core of love.

"Sure wish Thelonious would come walking through that door and take the stage," Benny said. "That man sold his soul for the magic to make music, let me tell you. I'd love to see him one last time."

"Remember that time Miles showed up and played a spontaneous set?" I asked. I closed my eyes. I could see him standing on the stage, wearing his tan suit, sweat running down his face, trumpet glowing like it had it had been dipped in a volcano's fiery caldera. Every single eye watched him, entranced.

Rhapsody of the Spheres

"Never forget it," Benny said. "That cat smoked this place. Thirty years old and more talent than anyone could dream of containing. It leaked from him. You could scoop it up if you knew how, hold it in your hands."

"Whatever happened to him?"

Benny slipped me my seltzer and Denver's refresh. His face looked somber. "He ducked out a while back. Kept running into the pigs, you know? Got arrested a few times. Drug use first; then they got him for use of illegal magic. Spent a couple of months in county lockup down in Georgia. The way they treat a man, that's about enough to break you. Strapped down, mouth taped shut, so you can't recite poetry or even whistle. You can't cast a spell if you can't make music. It ain't human, man."

"Where'd he end up?"

"Amsterdam, last I heard."

"Amsterdam?"

"They got freedom over there, baby. No laws against the poetry of our times, you know? When he got out, he caught the first steam tramp out of Savannah headed east. Playing gigs on the Keizersgracht now, and bringing the house down every night."

"I'll bet."

Jonathan came around the bar and clapped a hand on my shoulder. "This for Denver?" He took the whiskey and waited for me to grab my seltzer, giving my glass a mocking grin. "Still drinking the hard stuff, I see."

"Never could hold my liquor." I shrugged. "Not much of a writer I guess."

"You do fine. It's not how drunk you are, but how much a writer can hold onto their guilt and let it go at the same time. I'd say you're about the most Catholic of the lapsed Baptists I've known when it comes to it, but you dump your crap onto the page."

"Most of it."

"Most then." He walked over to Denver's table and handed him the glass. "There you go, sir."

One Last Night at Benny's

"Thank you, my good man," Denver said.

"Don't mention it."

"Already did." Denver closed the book and waved at the empty chairs around his table. "Sit with me a while, let's catch up."

I listened while they chatted. I felt too maudlin to try and force myself to speak. I'd never known how to behave at a wake. Endings left me bereft, so celebrating them felt odd. The two let me be quiet. I loved this crowd for that. For the way they let you be who you were, never judging, always supporting. Man, it felt good just to be with them.

The stage drew my eye. I'd stood there once under the spotlight. Only once. I had a poem in my heart one night, so I staggered up onto the stage during one of Benny's open calls, and it tripped off my lips smooth and easy. I rode those words and dragged the room with me, wove a spell that carried us through the clouds above like we were gulls winging over the harbor on stiff sea winds. I couldn't bring myself to repeat the experience, though it nestled warm and deep in my heart. One perfect moment. But I kept staring, and it kept calling, and my eyes fell on the trumpet again. Bell down on its stand, brass darkened yellow with age, a few dents in the metal. Handsome old thing.

"I think I'm going to play something," I said, interrupting the two.

They both stared at me like they didn't know me. Denver rocked his head to the side towards the stage. "You can play one of those things?"

"Yeah," I said, rising from my seat. "I blow horn."

"You?"

I smiled and nodded. "Me. Been thirty years, though. It won't be great."

"Better than all the bleak depression we're listening to now," Jonathan said. "Go on, play us a song, brass man."

Rhapsody of the Spheres

I walked over and stepped onto the stage. One step up was all I needed. This wasn't a night when the Lander Sisters swung their harmonies from the rafters and turned the stage into an ancient, Greek theater with a dozen marble steps to climb, beams of light slashing through the nights as the women ripped through a boogey woogey number. Tonight, there was only me, an out-of-work writer thirty years removed from his days playing in a marching band. But I took the old trumpet in my hands. My fingers slipped into the hooks, caressed the valves. I felt the eagerness of the instrument, the need to be played. To make some magic.

"Be easy on me," I told it. "Been a while. Not sure my embouchure is up to your high standards. But I'll do my best."

I pressed my lips to the mouthpiece, tensing them. I knew where the low C would be, and I blew a single, soft note. A little testing of the lips to ensure I could still vibrate them. Damned if I didn't nail it, too, which surprised me. The old trumpet wouldn't let me fail.

"Nice," Benny said. "Go on, show us something."

Instead of jumping into a tune, I ran the scales a few times. The valves moved smooth and free, like they'd been freshly oiled. The slides did, too, when I tried them, though I'd never been the type to bend notes when playing. If someone gave me a sheet of music, I could read it cold and nearly nail it first time out, but jazz improvisation hadn't been a strength of mine. I wisely left that to my betters, knowing Dizzy and Louis would show people what a trumpet could do in the hands of the truly gifted. I had been the barely competent.

But I wondered then whose trumpet this belonged to. Which musician had left it here for others to use?

The first notes rose, a graceful arc rising the scale, then a downward trill. Soft and easy, like the song. I wouldn't be playing *Be-Bop* tonight, but that piece was far beyond even the gifts of this instrument, in my hands at

One Last Night at Benny's

least. *Smoke Gets in Your Eyes*, though? Now that was a tune we could handle.

The lights dimmed around me as the magic took hold of the room. I rolled into the main verse, and strings joined in the background, holding long, sustained notes. The plunk of the standing bass propped us up. The light counterpoint of the piano teased the melody along. I couldn't see the musicians, but they were there. Echoes from another show perhaps, the universe's harmonics played backward or forward through time's empty tunnels.

The magic flowed, as easy as it ever had for better musicians. Snow fell around me as I played. It evaporated against everything it touched, a cool kiss on the skin. I blew into the final verses, with some longer, faster trills, and managed to not stumble too badly. I even managed to hold the stage for a few more moments, the last note wavering in the air like the heartbeat of the muse. When it faded, the lights went with it, leaving me speared in one single, bright spotlight.

Clifford Brown stepped up into the beam and shouldered me aside with a grin, taking the trumpet from my hands. Clifford, who had been dead for three years now. But all things had been made possible this evening. All realities were turned on and tuned in. The Magic Cabaret made certain of that on this, its last night. Clifford might be a ghost, but he felt real enough.

"Not bad, old man," he said. He held the trumpet in his hand, and it glowed bright and golden, lit from within by his tonal fires. "Not bad at all. But let me show you how it's done."

The others had arrived by then. Julia and Fred and Winnie. Allie greeted me with a hug and said, "that sounded great." Ethel and Darla and Lillian and Cole pushed some tables together, and we drank and watched as Clifford lifted his trumpet and blew a song into the heart of our world, so powerful it stripped the paint off the bar.

Rhapsody of the Spheres

Dizzy joined him. Miles, too. Duke Ellington led the ghostly orchestra floating in the corner. Ella sang the main vocals. Billie backed her, then the two switched off. They even let old Frank have a brief moment, though they hustled him out of the way pretty quick when it looked like he might try and upstage everyone. He'd gotten dangerously close to swinging into a rendition of *My Way*, and there weren't no one who needed or wanted it this evening.

And we? The regulars, the friends, the people Benny brought together? We drank and watched and laughed and cried. We danced with each other. We bellowed the songs at the top of our lungs, and we drove back the night, turning Benny's club into a Caribbean Island, with warm sands beneath our unshod toes, and torches lighting the night as we swayed and juked, until time came to close those doors and move out into the cold, dark night and find our way home. The jazz greats faded away as the magic died, and we raised a last toast to them and to Benny. But we had our one last night, and that's all any of us had really wanted. Things come to an end. You take what you can from that and move on.

I noticed the trumpet had returned to the stand when we walked out. I left it alone. It wasn't mine to bring with me. It would find its way to someone else on another night in another bar where a little musical love might be needed. But I silently thanked it for the gift of magic it had given us, and turned my collar up against the cold as I swung out through the portal into the alley with the sardine can.

Snow began to fall as I walked home.

One Last Night at Benny's

About the Author

Jeff Reynolds is a writer from Maryland who works for Johns Hopkins University Applied Physics Lab, home of New Horizons and Parker Solar Probe. His work has appeared in *Clarkesworld, Escape Pod,* and *GigaNotoSaurus.* He's a graduate of Viable Paradise writers' conference.

*****~~~*****

The United Flamemakers of Ravalli
by David Hankins

What human *dared* barge into a dragon's cave? It's as if their species didn't understand the concept of manners! Sunset's warm glow silhouetted the bandy-legged knight crouched just inside the rough-hewn cavern Nelson called home. He smelled of horse sweat.

"Go away," Nelson growled. "I'm sleeping."

The knight drew his sword and stalked forward. "I can slay you awake or asleep. Your choice."

"I can eat you in one bite or two. *Your* choice." Nelson surged to his feet, green-scaled muscles rippling, and loomed over the intruder. The fool knight circled. Sunlight struck his face, and Nelson snarled. "Corbin the Coward. You stole my tooth last year!" His tongue prodded the space where his left upper fang had been.

"It's just Corbin, now. I'm retired."

Nelson eyed the bared blade. "Yeah. Looks like it."

Corbin's sword drooped. "Retirement. . . hasn't gone well. Caroline's not used to having me constantly around."

Rhapsody of the Spheres

"So you decided to slay me because your wife's feeling crowded?" Typical humans! Can't get along, so they make everyone else suffer.

"No, I'm slaying you for stealing cows. The farmers are rather upset." Corbin raised his sword again, gripped in both hands.

"Of course! Cows wander off, and everyone blames the dragons! Slay the dragons! I'm sick of it." Fire rumbled in Nelson's chest. He stepped left as Corbin circled.

"That's the way of things. It's tradition. Dragons terrorize humans, kidnap princesses—"

"Do *you* see any princesses here? I like a singing princess as well as the next dragon, but I thought this was about cows!"

"It is! I'm saying that *traditionally* dragons do unspeakable things, and knights right their wrongs."

"Persecution! Dragons have no recourse. Tradition must change!" Flame curled from Nelson's maw. "Dragons do a lot of good in Ravalli—"

"Like what?" Corbin's head cocked back; his bushy brows furrowed.

"We're apex predators! We keep Ravalli's ecosystem in check, but does anyone care? No! We get blamed for every runaway princess and wandering cow. Don't take a nap, dragons, or a knight may come and dice you up!"

"Fighting dragons is good training!"

"Dragons working without compensation!"

"We're not paying you to *eat our cows!*"

That wasn't the point! Nelson blew a frustrated gout of flame, which made Corbin leap aside. An idea percolated in his mind. "Dragon-kind must unite against our oppressors," he muttered.

"So, it's a battle you want." Light glittered in Corbin's eyes.

The United Flamemakers of Ravalli

Fire licked at Nelson's chops and burned in his soul. "Blades do not change tradition. Words and deeds do. Meet me and the dragon clans one week hence upon the Devil's Plateau. Bring your kings. Bring your knights. Dragon-kind's common complaint shall be heard!"

He blew flame, Corbin dove aside, and Nelson darted out into the evening sunlight. Without waiting for a response, Nelson leapt from the mountainside and shot skyward.

. . .

Nelson soared high above Ravalli's western mountains. Dark forests and deep ravines passed below as the wind cooled his wings and his temper. He wanted dragon-kind to unite, but he didn't want to start a war. How could he unite dragon-kind for *peace*?

Nelson banked between sharp peaks and dropped into Drachenfels, the steep-walled valley where the dragon elders gathered. The sun disappeared behind a ridge as Nelson skimmed over lush pines. He landed near a dozen elderly dragons lounging around a smoky bonfire. Terrified cattle lowed nearby.

"Firefang!" A hefty green dragon missing his left eye pushed past his fellows. Snaggletooth, Nelson's father.

"I told you. Call me Nelson."

"Firefang is a proper dragon name. Your grandfather's name!"

Nelson was a thinker, not a fighter, and preferred his chosen name. Not in the mood to rehash an old argument, he eyed the cattle. "I thought we'd talked about stealing cows."

"It was a midnight raid. Got away clean."

"Not quite. Corbin the Coward tried to slay me for *your* theft."

"And not a scratch on you!" Snaggletooth turned to the elders. "Guess what? My son defeated Corbin the Coward!"

Roars of delight echoed through the valley.

Rhapsody of the Spheres

"I didn't—" Nelson raised his voice. "—I didn't defeat Corbin! We talked, and, well. . . " Nelson's earlier confidence fled, but he blurted out, "Dragon-kind needs to unite."

"A dragon army?" Snaggletooth chewed his lip. "Humanity has been getting unruly." Rumbles of agreement rose from the elders.

"No. NO!" Nelson stomped around the bonfire, demanding attention. "We unite for peace! Humans and dragons are stuck in a cycle of violence that must end."

A yellow dragon named Blackwing—because of his single black wing—harrumphed. "Kill 'em all, and *then* we'd have peace." The rumbles of agreement intensified.

"And where would we get cattle and sheep to eat?" Stony draconic expressions met Nelson's. He cringed. "Where would we find princesses to sing us lullabies?"

A rhapsodic grin split Blackwing's face. "It's been ages since I heard a good lullaby." He nudged a blue dragon. "Whaddya say, Icebreath, wanna kidnap a princess?"

Icebreath nodded enthusiastically, and Nelson yelled, "This is what I'm talking about! We hunt humans, they hunt us, and everybody suffers. The violence needs to end! Humans will listen if we speak with a united voice."

Snaggletooth snarled, "'Cause if they don't listen, we kill them all!" The elders roared in agreement. "Gather the army!" Elders lunged into the air.

"It's not an army!" Nelson roared. Names were important, and 'army' was too aggressive. "Call it. . . the United Flamemakers of Ravalli!"

"Call it whatever you like, son. Our dragon army will solve the human problem once and for all!"

Nelson wilted and watched the departing elders, a rainbow of shimmering scales that disappeared beyond the ridge.

The United Flamemakers of Ravalli

He'd united dragon-kind, all right. For war.

. . .

The first dragons arrived that evening. Within two days, the valley felt crowded. By day six, Nelson couldn't turn around without tangling tails with another dragon. He argued for peace with anyone who'd listen, but the clans were eager for war. He did, however, convince the elders to let him lead the negotiations *before* the killing started.

At least his name for the army had stuck. They thought it a grand joke.

One week after Nelson's arrival, the United Flamemakers of Ravalli took flight. It was an awesome sight, dragons of every hue rising on thermals to meet the sunrise. Nelson flew with the elders, filled with anxiety. If his negotiations failed, he'd set the conditions for the biggest war Ravalli had ever seen.

The western mountains fell away behind them, replaced by rolling fields. The Devil's Plateau towered a hundred feet above the valley floor, connected to the grasslands by a long, shallow slope at one end. The plateau's stony sides looked like bunched columns, sheer and unscalable. Human armies covered the accessible end of the plateau.

Nelson landed the negotiating committee near a large white tent in the center of the plateau, forward of the human army. The plateau shook with the weight of a thousand dragons landing behind them. They roared in defiance. Nelson cringed but said nothing.

There was commotion in the open-sided tent before Corbin rode out leading a dozen nobles whose polished armor gleamed in the sunlight. Corbin's armor didn't gleam. It was too dented. A thin man with a wiry mustache and a reedy voice pushed past Corbin. "I am Duke Pennyworth of Puria. How dare you bring war against humanity, dragon!"

Nelson scowled. "We're not bringing war. We're bringing negotiations. And call me Nelson."

Rhapsody of the Spheres

"Nelson? That's a ridiculous name for a dragon."

Nelson growled. "It's. My. Name. Do you *want* a war, Penny-Pincher?"

Pennyworth's face turned purple, and Corbin raised his hands. "All right, let's start over. The dragons came to talk, so we're listening." He gestured to Nelson.

Silence fell.

Nelson's mind went blank.

He'd rehearsed this speech the entire flight, but now. . . nothing. Butterflies danced in Nelson's stomach.

"We, uh, the United Flamemakers of Ravalli, have, um, unionized to represent dragon-kind's common complaint against mankind. We will no longer tolerate dragon persecution and demand compensation for work performed."

Pennyworth spluttered. "Work? What work? Dragons are a menace!"

"Is it not common practice for young knights to slay dragons as part of their training?"

"It is," Corbin said, glaring at Pennyworth.

Nelson nodded. "Thus, we are part of your training regimen and demand compensation—or we'll stop fulfilling this vital function."

"What?" Pennyworth's mustache bristled. "You can't refuse to fight!"

"Sure we can. And without dragons to train against, how will your knights fare against the true monsters of Ravalli? The giants, the golems. . . the gnomes."

A shiver ran through the men. Corbin pursed his lips. "What sort of compensation?"

"Chests of gold!" Icebreath yelled. Draconic voices chimed in.

"Cows!"

"Princesses!"

"Fat cows!"

"Fatter Princesses!"

The United Flamemakers of Ravalli

Nelson groaned. The negotiating committee was still vague on what he wanted, but they'd latched onto the idea of 'compensation.'

A high voice cut through the commotion. "We will *not* be traded as a commodity!" A young woman Nelson hadn't noticed spurred her horse between two portly nobles. She wore a green dress, and a tiara sat atop her braided black hair.

"I am Princess Isabella of Puria, and I am sick and tired of princesses being the objects of draconic and knightly heroics."

Blackwing lurched forward. "Now hold on. Kidnapping princesses is traditional! You sing so beautifully."

"Kidnapping is barbaric and terrifying, and it strains our voices to sing all day for ungrateful dragons!"

"I'm grateful," Blackwing muttered.

Princess Isabella whirled on her companions, who jerked back in alarm. "And as for the knights! Just because you rescue a princess, it doesn't mean she has to marry you! Knights are smelly, overbearing, and—in my opinion—entirely unsuitable as husbands. Always gallivanting off on adventures."

Nelson sat back, dumbfounded. He'd never suspected princesses felt this way. Though, upon reflection, it made sense.

A smile stole across Corbin's craggy face. "What do you propose, Your Highness?"

"We shall form a princess's union! No more kidnappings! No more singing without compensation! And no more marriage demands from malodorous knights! At least bathe first!"

Pandemonium erupted as nobles tried to silence Princess Isabella.

She refused to be silenced.

Dragons added to the bedlam with demands for compensation. Swords slid from scabbards. Teeth and

Rhapsody of the Spheres

claws flashed. Nelson cast about, seeking something, anything, to stop the pending bloodshed.

An idea struck him. "We challenge you to a tournament!" he roared. "To fight for honor and our rights!"

Pennyworth slashed a hand at the nobles, silencing them. His eyes narrowed behind his raised sword. "Negotiations upon the field of honor?"

"Yes."

Princess Isabella added, "For *all* our rights?"

"Of course."

She nodded. "Very well, we accept." Duke Pennyworth's lips flapped as though he'd intended to answer, but he clenched his jaw and nodded along with the other nobles.

. . .

Within hours, the field was transformed into a roped-off arena, with large boulders scattered throughout. The armies gathered on opposite sides, and the lead negotiators watched from the open-sided tent.

Nelson felt cramped, curled under the white canvas, but he refused to sit outside with the horses while the humans lounged on ornate wooden thrones. Princess Isabella sat beyond Duke Pennyworth, arms crossed, expression inscrutable.

Corbin stood in the center of the arena. "Welcome to the first-ever Tournament of Sword and Claw!" Cheers and roars rose. "United Flamemakers of Ravalli, name your first point of negotiation and your champion!"

Nelson growled, "No more dragon slayings! I name Snaggletooth as our champion!"

Nelson's father leapt into the arena, wings spread wide, and blew flame heavenward. Green scales glittered in the sunlight, and his scarred left eye gave him a fierce scowl.

Duke Pennyworth twirled his mustache. "Sir Thaddius shall defend our right to slay dragons!"

The United Flamemakers of Ravalli

A hulking brute ducked under the rope and sauntered onto the field to whoops and applause. Sir Thaddius, known as Thud, drew a monstrous broadsword from his back.

Corbin stepped from between the combatants and yelled, "Begin!"

Snaggletooth blew flame, and Thud dove behind a boulder. He darted out after the flame stopped and swung his broadsword at Snaggletooth's neck. Nelson's father flinched back, but the sword nicked his chin. First blood. The crowd went wild.

Nelson's heart sank at the thundering bloodlust. The tournament *had* been his idea, but negotiation by combat was a mistake. Even if his father won, decisions bathed in blood wouldn't last.

He eyed Pennyworth. "May I offer a compromise?"

The Duke sneered. "Afraid your champion will lose?"

"No. But this"—he jutted his jaw toward the arena—"solves nothing. It's entertainment."

Pennyworth scowled, "What do you propose?"

"Simply this: you don't slay us; we don't eat you. *And* we establish a joint judiciary to adjudicate dragon/human crimes."

A roar went up as Snaggletooth's tail smacked Thud across the field. Pennyworth's scowl deepened. "Dragon slaying prepares our knights for the monsters of the world." He cocked an eyebrow. "As you noted."

"So, we make this tournament annual and create a training ground where knights and dragons work *together* to hone their skills."

That scowl turned contemplative.

Snaggletooth roared in pain, drawing Nelson's attention. His father had Thud pinned under one emerald forepaw, which was pierced from beneath by the knight's

Rhapsody of the Spheres

sword. A growl rolled from Snaggletooth on a cloud of smoke.

The knight raised one hand. "I yield!"

Snaggletooth huffed into Thud's face before letting him up. The United Flamemakers roared their approval.

Nelson eyed Pennyworth, whose jaw clenched. "Work with us, not against us, and Ravalli can have enduring peace."

The duke drew a deep breath and rose to address the crowd. "Congratulations, Snaggletooth. Humanity and dragon-kind will establish a joint judiciary to handle human/dragon crimes. *All* crimes, from dragon slaying to cattle theft and terrorizing villages."

A few dragons growled, but Nelson nodded his support. "Agreed."

Princess Isabella, who'd been listening intently, shot to her feet. She pointed at Blackwing.

"For the next match, I challenge you! No more princess kidnappings!"

Duke Pennyworth placed a hand on her arm. "You can't fight a dragon! The mere idea—"

Princess Isabella reared back, fire in her eyes. "Tread carefully, Your Grace! We fight today for *all* our rights. *When* I win, none shall doubt that princesses are our own persons, not pretty baubles to fight over." She ducked under the rope, leaving Pennyworth looking rather flummoxed.

The princess marched onto the field, head high, shoulders back, green dress snapping with her stride. Blackwing and Corbin followed her, their expressions unsure. They met at the arena's center, and Corbin made some quiet protest.

Princess Isabella's finger thrust toward the knight. "Call it!"

Silence fell over the assembly and Corbin said, "Very well. Combatants, begin!"

The United Flamemakers of Ravalli

Blackwing reached a tentative paw forward as if to swipe at Princess Isabella, but she stopped him with a raised palm.

"Dragons value princesses for our singing, do you not?"

He nodded.

"Very well, I challenge you to a duel of song."

Blackwing's jaw dropped. Cheers and whoops rose from the audience. The princess turned both palms outward and silence fell like a curtain. She gestured to Blackwing. "Sing, as if your life depended on it."

The dragon gulped, cleared his throat, then sang with a deep bass growl.

"There once was a dragon who took to the sky,
The name of the dragon was Golden Eye
The winds blew up and he swooped down low,
Seeking that cave of gold!

"He fought with a knight, and he fought with a king,
He fought with a troll, a hideous thing,
In Ravalli so long ago
Seeking that cave of gold!

"Gather all your riches come,
Steal 'em, hoard 'em, hide 'em son.
One day, when the fightin's done
We'll find that cave of gold!"

Blackwing bowed, wings spread like a cape, and everyone cheered. Even the humans.

The applause faded into silence. Princess Isabella stood tall, hands relaxed at her sides. The silence stretched before she pierced it with a high slow soprano that cut to Nelson's soul.

Rhapsody of the Spheres

"Return, my love, return to me,
From o'r the mountains come!
You stole my heart, then rode away,
For fame and fortune won.

"I sought you near, I sought you far,
But war had drawn you nigh!
I pray you will return to me,
And stay here by my side.

"Now hold my hand, my love so dear,
Returned to me once more!
Upon your shield, to home you've come,
Your soldier's banner tore."

Princess Isabella paused. Everyone leaned forward, entranced. One hand reached heavenward.

"Return, my love, return to me,
From o'r that veil do come!
You stole my heart, then rode away,
But fame and fortune won."

Silence followed Princess Isabella's final haunting note. It was the expectant silence of a thousand held breaths. A single tear rolled down Blackwing's yellow-scaled cheek. He bowed.
"I yield."
Applause shook the Devil's Plateau.
. . .
That evening, Nelson sat alone in the moonlight, watching the post-tournament celebrations. Dragons and humans mingled around bonfires, sharing mutton and ale. Blackwing sat among singing women—barmaids or princesses, Nelson couldn't tell—eyes glowing with rhapsodic delight at their campfire tunes.

The United Flamemakers of Ravalli

Corbin and Princess Isabella approached Nelson, leading a packhorse. Corbin said, "May we join you? We have firewood and a barrel of ale."

Nelson nodded, and within minutes the fire was roaring, and the ale distributed, Nelson drinking from a tureen Princess Isabella produced.

"Thank you," he said to Corbin. "The United Flamemakers of Ravalli couldn't have achieved all we did—in writing—without you."

"You didn't get everything you wanted."

Nelson shrugged. "That's the nature of negotiation and compromise. I'm just glad I didn't start a war today."

Princess Isabella leaned forward, her tiara sparkling in the firelight. "The Tournament of Sword, Claw, and Song was an inspired idea."

Nelson snorted. "I only wanted to end the cycle of violence. You added the music that softened every heart."

She smirked. "You weren't the only one negotiating for more rights." She raised her goblet. "To music."

Corbin's goblet joined hers. "To new friends."

Nelson grinned his toothy grin and raised his tureen. "To new traditions!"

###

About the Author

David Hankins is a Writers of the Future winner (Volume 39), a 2022 Critters Readers Choice Award winner, who's been previously published with Third Flatiron ("Reassessed Value" in *After the Gold Rush), Unidentified Funny Objects 9, DreamForge Magazine*, and others. He's an active member of the Wulf Pack Writers.

*****~~~*****

The Day Luna Swallowed the Sun

by Akis Linardos

After her sentience was complete, she leaped from the coldness of her pod into her mother's warm embrace.

"Your name will be Luna," her mother said. "It means moon in Spanish, and it fits you because you will be the one to absorb the sunlight, and reflect its light upon the darkness."

[March 13, 2359, 10:39 PM. 1 year before completion of the Dyson Sphere]

Luna floated alongside Marko and Keiko in the spacecraft's crew quarters, surrounded by bed bunks, stored cargo, and the smell of mushroom noodle soup. Luna sipped on her liquid battery that tasted like tangerine. *Slurp. Slurp. Slurp.*

"You know," Marko said, noodles spilling from his mouth, staining his beard. They floated upward in zero-gravity, giving him a squid-like look. "You can sip less loudly."

"Sure, kraken boy," Luna said.

Rhapsody of the Spheres

Keiko chuckled and spat her own noodles, then exploded in a fit of coughing and began slamming her chest.

"Easy there," Luna said as she rubbed Keiko's back, her fingers tangling with her long black and purple hair. It was not often the designated eating area room was undergoing maintenance, but the messy lunch situation was fertile grounds for a chuckle.

Luna needed this bit of laughter. Coming into existence as an adult, never experiencing childhood, and having only five sweet years to spend alive, you come to appreciate every piece of laughter you can get.

She left her liquid battery bottle to float on its own, the lid protecting it from spillage as she removed her metal straw, then grabbed along the protruding railing to grab a glass bottle from the storage.

She handed it to Keiko. "There you go. Bottoms up."

Keiko nodded and coughed a weak *"thank you."*

"Sometimes I wish I could try the noodles," Luna said.

"Oh, it's crap," Marko said, "Trust me on this. I'd swap it for your liquid battery any day."

"That would ruin your liver."

"If I cared for my liver, I'd have stayed on Earth."

Their casual talk made Luna's chest feel warm. The rest of the crew was too wary and rude to her, but Keiko and Marko were different. They treated her like her mother used to. Like family.

Keiko flicked a strand of hair off her face. "Say. . . Luna?"

"Hmm?"

"It's one year until the project ends. It might be the last time we'll be celebrating your birthday together like this."

The Day Luna Swallowed the Sun

A cold hand gripped Luna's core. A year left before the comet, Lupin, would collide with Earth. A year left in the project aimed to stop it.

Marko groaned, tossing the noodle plastic wrapping into the chute.

Keiko cocked her head. "Marko?"

"It's just not right."

"Marko!"

"What? You know I'm right. She doesn't want this either. Do you, Luna?"

Luna sighed. In a way, the comet was the reason she existed. She had been *made* four years ago, after it had first been sighted, to stop its collision. She owed it her being, her making friends, having a mother, *living*. Owed it all to this harbinger of doom.

And she also owed it the heavy price to be paid. Once the project neared its end, they'd upload her mind into the Dyson Sphere. She'd harness the sun's power and distribute it toward the production of space weapons that would shatter Lupin.

"It's not fair," Keiko said. "You pushing her against the wall like this. She has no choice. You know what's at stake."

"You're starting to sound like the rest of them. Tell you what? The ends don't always justify the means."

"No," Luna said. "They don't."

The room fell silent. Something burned inside Luna—the thought of this being the *last* of her birthdays in true companionship. It was like the stem of a rose that had been coiling around her circuits the past two years had finally grown thorns, piercing all the cables that made her.

She did not want to save the planet. She did not want to be a hero. All she wanted was to *live*.

She exhaled the weight of the world. "What if I— What if we took a space pod. All three of us. We could go to the Mars colony. Legislation is still loose there."

Keiko gazed downward, saying nothing.

Rhapsody of the Spheres

"Luna," Marko said. "You don't even have to be illegal about it. If you don't want to do this, then don't. They'll upload a software to do it and just accept the risks. They can't *force* you to do it. Forcing you would mean they wouldn't be able to trust you with sun's power either."

"I can't. I can't face the crew. I can't face Mother. I would be turning my back on my purpose. I just. . . can't. Let's just leave. In secret."

Keiko bit her lips, and Marko breathed heavily enough that Luna could see the movement on his shoulders.

Marko seemed about to say something, when a zooming sound pulled their attention. With a whoosh, one of the side doors opened, and Captain Holstein floated through, shooting a piercing look that meant trouble.

"We got new visuals of Lupin," he said. "The situation changed."

Luna spoke first. "What happened?"

"Daniel says we had misunderstood the planet's composition. It's the only reasonable explanation for it. Probably some foreign material that was sensitive to the sun's radiation expelled gas and propelled the comet forward."

"What does this mean?" Luna asked, feeling her core overheating, sending scalding tendrils to her arms.

"It means the comet is rapidly accelerating." He exhaled a long sigh. "It will make impact with Earth in three weeks."

. . .

"So I was born. . . with a purpose?" Luna asked her mother, after she blew out her first birthday candles. Queen's 'I Want to Break Free' drummed on a boombox.

Her mother spooned a piece from the cake and placed it in Luna's mouth. "Yes, Luna. Your mind will enter the Dyson Sphere. Remember the satellites we learned about two weeks ago? Now picture a thousand, a hundred times the size of those. All of them surrounding

The Day Luna Swallowed the Sun

the sun and like flowers drinking from its life force to make more things bloom."

"But, I don't want to have my mind in a megastructure. I want to be here with you. I want to stay in this body you made for me."

Her mother tongued her own thumb and rubbed Luna's cheek. "You have to, Luna. Using the power harnessed by the sun, humanity will make big weapons. Weapons that will allow us to survive."

"Weapons that will make Lupin go away?"

"Yes, Luna. Weapons that will make Lupin go away."

. . .

[March 13, 2359, 01:58 AM. A week before impact]

Cloistered by the computer panels lining the walls of the control room, Luna felt the crew's gazes piercing her as if she were a soulless thing.

It was not uncommon for them to glimpse at her awkwardly, but now they glared shamelessly. Because that *thing* was standing between their families and Lupin.

"It's insane," Marko said. "Half the energy collectors are untested. It might just fry her consciousness to control them all!"

"It's worth the risk," Daniel the astrophysics expert said. Of course he'd say that. "I'd also prefer we stick to schedule. Would minimize risk of failure. But it cannot be helped. Maybe some solar panels will be wasted. A worthy sacrifice at this point."

"Solar panels?" Keiko said. "Did you ask *her?*" She pointed at Luna.

"You'd put that *thing* over Earth's security?"

Marko narrowed his eyes. "Take. That. Back."

"Are you serious right now?" Daniel said. "Are you seriously doing this? What's *wrong* with you? Lupin is *coming.* All the people we love will die. And you worry about—about—an AI?"

Rhapsody of the Spheres

"You don't all need to talk as if I'm not here." Luna said.

The room fell silent.

Luna pushed herself off the wall behind her and grabbed one of the handlebars near the two men. She laid a hand on Marko's shoulder. She wanted to tell him, "Let's go away. I'm not doing this." She wanted to threaten that if they forced her, she'd bring all the Dyson Sphere parts crumbling down and drifting to space. She wanted to shout at them:

I want to live.

Instead she turned to Daniel, and said, "How long does a consciousness upload take?"

Marko grabbed her arm "Luna!"

"Marko." She clenched her fingers on his shoulder. "Please."

Marko's mouth worked, producing no words. Then his features relaxed, and he nodded.

"Daniel?" Luna asked again. "How long?"

Daniel shook his head. "Four days to complete. Maximum five. There are trillions of multi-dimensional parameters that need to be stored and distributed across all power plants and energy collectors."

"Will that be fast enough?"

"Yes. The nuclear missile silos are already on high alert. They'll work overtime to produce enough firepower to redirect the comet. The additional Dyson Sphere energy will power construction automatons and gravity tractors to slow down the comet. Giving us time to finish the nukes."

"Great," Luna said, then turned to the crew. Something different in their gaze. No longer seeing *through* her, but looking *at* her.

"I've been with you for two years. It was scary at first, leaving Mother's lab. But I knew my purpose. Lupin was my destiny. This comet was the beginning of me, and it will also be my end. Or, well, the end of a life worth living. I will continue to serve. For Mother. For my

The Day Luna Swallowed the Sun

friends. For the Earth that birthed wonderful sentient beings like you. Like me."

She put a hand on her chest. "It was a wonderful, *wonderful* thing. To just partake in the sweet rhapsody of sentient experience."

She turned to Daniel. "Time to initiate the upload."

Daniel nodded and hoisted himself toward the computer screen. "You must enter the pod." He pointed at the man-sized tube. So much like the incubation pod that birthed her. "And . . . uh. . . I'm sorry. For earlier. Fear got the best of me."

"That's all right."

Keiko began clapping.

The crew followed. "A toast to Luna!" Marko yelled, raising his hand as if he were holding a glass. "The savior of the Earth."

The claps faded and everyone raised their hands.

"Guys. . . " Luna's voice was tremulous now, like the shiver of a butterfly. She had to bite her tongue to not let it out. Cage the truth, leave it unspoken. Don't let them know you are *terrified*. "I don't deserve that. It's not even my choice. I'm an android. Mother programmed—"

Marko snapped his fingers. "Hey. We're all machines here," he pointed at himself, and the rest of the crew. His smile showed teeth through his beard. "We just happen to be molecular machines. And you're made of something different, but our shape's the same. We're all programmed. One way or another. Humans and androids. Be it genes or circuits, what difference does it make?"

Keiko mirrored the smile. "Picture two statues. You like Queen, don't you? Picture two statues of Freddie. One's made of oakwood, one of clay. They're both painted the same. Which one you pick?"

Luna's mouth trembled. The core thrummed with nauseating heat. "I'll miss you so much."

Her friends pulled her in a group hug.

Rhapsody of the Spheres

It all was so overwhelming. The nausea. The pain. If only her mother had supplied her tear ducts. How freeing it would be, to let it all leak out in warm rivulets down her cheeks.

"Don't worry," Luna said. "As Freddie said, the show must go on. And the show is on Earth." She pulled herself away from the hug and retreated to the pod that would send her consciousness away. "Goodbye."

. . .

When Luna reached her second year of age, and it was time to embark on the space mission she'd not return from, she banged her fists on the walls of her room and tossed over the furnishings. Her mother had to hold her tightly to stop her from hurting herself.

Luna had not exhibited rage of this level before or since.

"Why me? Why?"

"We had no choice, Luna. It's for humanity. Dyson Sphere needs *a mind. Please. Calm down. This is not like you."*

"Why give me sentience if it was just to upload me in a huge box to shuffle stupid satellites around forever? You had my neural networks trained for years *in robotics, energy, materials science, astrophysics, and all the rest of that crap. Why shove a* consciousness *in it?"*

Her mother held her head, looked her in the eyes. "Can you imagine what something with the power of the sun can do? To the world? Can you imagine a soulless piece of software having full control of it, only to crash or malfunction? Or figuring out that humans may not be worth its time? We needed *a soul as intelligent and kind as yours, Luna. Please." Her mother's voice broke, and something melted inside Luna. "Please, don't make this harder. We have no choice. Not anymore."*

Luna grabbed her mother's shaking hand. The song she heard from Queen, some weeks ago, came to her

56

The Day Luna Swallowed the Sun

mind. "This world has only one *sweet moment set aside for us."*

Her mother kissed her forehead. "Record this and keep it with you. I'll always be by your side. In your mind."

. . .

[March 17, 2359, 07:58 AM. Upload completed]

When Luna awoke, she felt the piercing coldness of space across a scattered body she couldn't identify as her own. It was the modular body of a Dyson Sphere. She was larger than she had ever been, but she was also a baby again, taking her first steps.

What had she become? Was this what it felt like? To *be* a Dyson Sphere?

She thought of her friends. Their words soothed her fragmented mind.

We're all machines, here.
Which one do you pick?

Slowly she began sensing all the parts of her new body. She no longer felt one humming core but a million. She was everywhere, her parts wrapped in chilly void. But there was the sun. She only had to approach it. Like a frail child trapped in a cold forest seeking the bonfire, she wrapped parts around it. Her energy collectors encircled the radiant, life-giving star, sucking its rays. She felt the heat, a phantom warmth inside a belly that did not exist between her scattered parts.

Slowly, Luna relaxed and let herself succumb to the warm sensations. To her new self. She searched her records and put on music to play within her mind. Freddie Mercury's wonderful voice rang with the eerie slowness of the intro of *Bohemian Rhapsody*.

She sent the energy away, distributing it to channels that would bloom volcano-sized guns from the Earth. Volcanoes so massive they'd pierce Lupin's heart with their lava spittle.

Rhapsody of the Spheres

Through the channels, Luna also transmitted a message aimed to inspire.

I am Luna, she said. *I am the sister of the moon and the mirror that reflects the sunlight. Use the radiance to crush Lupin. Give the comet a taste of sentient willpower.*

As the light sucked through her and from her, she gave an order to her mind, *Replay record. Retrieve file:* [March 13, 2359, 10:39 PM. 1 year before completion of the Dyson Sphere].

The algorithm ushered her mind into a peaceful moment with her friends. Her new body floated, a sphere among spheres, and Queen's rhapsody crescendoed to a chorus.

###

About the Author

Akis (legally Panagiotis) Linardos is a Greek ESL writer, Biomedical AI Scientist, and maybe human. He's published fiction at *Apex Magazine, The Maul Magazine,* Grendel Press, and others.

*****~~~~~*****

Euterpe

by Maureen Bowden

Throughout our childhood in *Cornflower Meadows* children's care-home, Jimmy Nelson was my closest friend. When we reached adulthood I worked as a classroom assistant in an under-staffed primary school that couldn't afford more teachers. He enrolled in Medical College to train as a doctor. We should have spent our lives together, but I jammed up the works with a metaphorical spanner by marrying Guy Beauchamp (pronounced Beecham), a wealthy, young aristocrat.

I met Guy at a Halloween party. He was dressed as the devil: body-hugging jump suit, forked tail and papier-mâché horns. I was a witch: pointy hat, cloak, and black nail polish. He beguiled me, and I probably beguiled him. After a fast-tracked courtship, he said, "I want you to marry me, Mia, and have my babies."

I longed to be part of a family, so I raised no objection when he placed a huge sparkly nugget on my finger.

Rhapsody of the Spheres

He introduced me to his parents, Sir Henry Beauchamp, the local Member of Parliament, and Lady Dorothy, renowned for supporting urban charities to house the homeless, recycle rubbish, and save the snowdrop.

Sir Henry pummelled my hand with a practised action. "Pleased to meet you, m'dear. By Jove, the boy's found himself a bobby dazzler. You'll soon knock him into shape. Make a man of him, what?"

Out of earshot, Lady Dorothy warned me, "Guy's a charmer, Mia, but he has a dark side that isn't his fault. It's mine and his father's."

I thought she was going to tell me about a gruesome hereditary condition involving the full moon and silver bullets, but it was nothing so gothic.

"We over-indulged him, gave him everything he wanted, sorted his problems and misdemeanours, making consequences go away. He can't deal with stress or disappointment. He's never learned how."

"He's an adult now, Lady Dorothy," I said. "He'll learn to cope with life's problems, as we all do."

She shook her head. "He'll withdraw into himself, becoming feral and unpredictable if whatever's upset him isn't resolved. He'll be impossible to live with. It would be wise to give him back the ring, head for the hills, and don't look back."

"I'll consider it," I said, but I didn't.

My parents, whoever they were, had never been part of my life, so Jimmy Nelson walked me down the aisle. He had tears in his eyes. While the wedding reception festivities were in full swing he whispered, "When you need a friend, Mia, you know you can call me."

"Yes," I said. "We'll always be friends."

We hugged. Then he left.

I was happy, so was Guy. Life was sweet. He took me flying in the two-seater plane, a birthday present from his parents two years earlier. We flew over North

Euterpe

Cornwall's Atlantic coast. The vastness of the ocean unnerved me. He swooped and dived, whooping and laughing, while I longed to feel Mother Earth's concrete pavements beneath my feet.

Three months after we married I became pregnant. I instinctively knew the child was a girl. I chose the name, Grace. Our doctor confirmed my pregnancy. Guy and I were delighted, and morning sickness was an excuse not to go in that wretched plane. Flying was fine, but not with Guy in the pilot's seat.

I was shopping for baby clothes and toys, when I spotted a little shop I'd not seen before. The sign said, *Culsans' Cloister.* I remembered a story from *A Child's Introduction to Myth,* a library book I'd read when I was seven years old. In Greek mythology, Culsans was keeper of the gate of happiness. I was intrigued.

The window was cluttered with candle-sticks, ornate cutlery, desk calendars, charm bracelets, brooches containing locks of human hair, silver buckles, and an assortment of what could be best described as junk. A pretty musical box caught my eye. It was topped with a female figure in a dancing pose, balancing on a tiny turntable. She was playing some kind of wind instrument. I opened the shop door; a jangle of bells announced my entrance, and an elderly man approached me. He had a tangled mop of silver hair, a jolly, rotund face, and John Lennon spectacles perched on the end of his nose. He said, "Welcome, dear lady. Do you see anything that makes you happy?"

"I'm already happy," I said, but I'd like a closer look at the musical box in the window."

He reached for it and handed it to me. I examined the tiny dancer. She wore a long, scanty robe with a slit up the side revealing one of her legs up to the hip. A cluster of curls framed her face. The rest of her long ringlets formed a complicated top-knot. I said, "Who is she?"

"Who do you think she is?"

Rhapsody of the Spheres

I shrugged. "A Greek goddess, but I don't know which. They all look the same to me."

He smiled. "Possibly they are the same, but she has many names."

I'd had enough of mythological perplexity. "How much is it?"

"No charge. Keep it as long as you like. Bring it back when you have no further need of it."

"That's an odd way to do business."

"It suits me, dear lady." He opened the door. "Off you go."

I left, still perplexed.

When I arrived home Guy was out, probably doing aerobatics over the Atlantic Ocean. I carried the musical box into the bedroom we'd furnished as a nursery, placed it on the toy chest and wound it up with the key protruding from the mechanism. The turntable carried the goddess into action. She twirled and swayed, and the air filled with waves of music, like a soaring flute but sweeter and richer. It wrapped itself around me and transported me into a honeysuckle-scented garden abundant with flowers of every colour. A beautiful woman I recognised as the tiny dancer was sitting on the grass, leaning against a willow tree, with her flute lying beside her. She beckoned to me.

I sat beside her and asked, "What's happening? Where am I? Who are you?"

Her rippling laughter sounded like music. "I'll answer your questions in reverse order, Mia. I am Euterpe, Goddess of Music, Mistress of the Rhapsody of the Spheres, and Giver of Delight. This is my garden, a haven of happiness. Culsans gave you the gateway, and you turned the key."

"It's wonderful," I said, "but I was happy where I was."

She patted my hand. "There are pitfalls in your world. When you need respite from the sorrows they

Euterpe

bring, you may again pass through the gateway, and I will help you regain what you require to be happy."

She picked up the flute and began to play. The music carried me back to Grace's nursery.

. . .

Grace died in my womb. The hospital did all that was required, and before I was discharged a sympathetic gynaecologist tried to ease my devastation with encouraging words. "You're young and healthy, Mia. There's no reason why you can't have more children after you've had time to grieve."

Guy picked me up, not saying a word, driving like an idiot, exceeding the speed limit, skidding around corners and jumping red lights. I closed my eyes, wishing to die.

We arrived home. He retreated to a corner of the kitchen, curled into the foetus position, and howled like a baby. I knelt beside him, placing my arm around his shoulders. He pushed me away, screaming, "Don't touch me. You killed my baby."

Whatever Lady Dorothy thought, I didn't believe over-indulgent parenting caused this. It was some kind of affliction. He needed help that I couldn't provide, but I was too engulfed in my own pain to find someone who could. He began to drink heavily and stay out overnight. He refused to talk. I stopped caring.

After six months or so his overnight absences ceased. One evening, as he sat on the kitchen floor escaping into a vodka bottle, the doorbell rang. I opened the door to a bedraggled, gaunt young woman. She said, "Does Guy Beauchamp live here, please?"

I said, "Yes, who are you?"

"I'm Evie, his girlfriend. I'm pregnant. Who are you?"

"Mia, his wife."

She stared at me, shook her head and sobbed. "I didn't know he was married. I'd better leave."

Rhapsody of the Spheres

I reached for her arm. "No, come in." She followed me into the kitchen.

Guy looked up from his friend the voddy bottle and sprang to his feet. "What the hell are you doing here? Leave me alone."

Her voice trembled. "What about our baby? I have no money. You must help me."

He clamped his hands over his ears, screaming. "I won't listen. It's not my baby." He released one of his ears and pointed at me. "She was having my baby, but she killed it." Before I could stop him he dragged Evie to the door, threw her out, and slammed it. He stood in front of it. "Don't go after her, or I'll kill you, like you killed my baby."

I remembered his mother saying he could turn feral, and I was afraid. I retreated to the kitchen. He followed me. I backed away from him, flinching.

"I'm going out," he said. "I need to fly."

"You can't take the plane up tonight," I said. "You're drunk."

He ignored me and left. I never saw him again.

Three days later the wreckage of the plane washed up on Tintagel beach, but the ocean had taken Guy's body.

I vowed to rebuild my life, but first there was something I needed to do. The musical box still sat on Grace's toy chest. I turned the key, and the music carried me through Culsans' gate. Euterpe sat, leaning on her willow tree. I sat beside her. She took me in her arms and asked, "What do you need to be happy, Mia?"

"I need Grace, but she's dead."

"Unimportant. Every little soul that misses the chance to be born finds an opportunity to try again. The bonds of love are strong. They'll reunite you. Evie provided the opportunity. Grace will be waiting for you. I'll tell you when it's time. Be patient."

"How will I know where she is?"

"Your soul mate will help you find her."

Euterpe

She picked up her flute, and the music took me back to the nursery with hope in my heart.

. . .

I was patient. I returned to work, and two years passed. Then I had a dream. I heard the rattle of a Pendolino as it clanged along a railway bridge that arched over a road, and I heard Euterpe say, "She's here. Reach out to your soul mate."

On a Saturday in late September I rang Jimmy. Keeping things light, I said, "How are you?"

"I'm an over-worked, under-paid junior doctor, but doing what I was meant to do. How are you?"

My composure slipped. "I need help."

"Give me your address."

I gave it to him.

"I know where that is. I'll be there in an hour."

He arrived in forty minutes. I threw myself into his arms and wept. I told him everything, except about Euterpe. I didn't want him to think I was completely bonkers. "Guy's parents think his behaviour was their fault because they spoilt him, but I think it was something more."

He nodded. "Sounds like a serious personality disorder. Maybe even a physical abnormality in his brain."

"I let him down," I said. "I should have found him help."

"Would he have accepted it?"

"No, not a chance."

"Then there's nothing you could have done. Stop blaming yourself. You need help too, and I'm here now."

"Help me find Evie and her child."

"Okay, but I must make a phone call first." He rang the hospital and told them he was taking the leave due to him so he could deal with a family emergency. Then he said to me, "Right, I'm all yours."

I said, "Guy may have met her in *McGregor's,* his favourite hostelry."

Rhapsody of the Spheres
"Then that's where we'll start."

. . .

McGregor's bartender remembered Evie. "Poor girl. The posh boyfriend got her pregnant, stopped paying her rent, and left her destitute. She should take him to court for every penny she can get."

I said, "He's dead."

He shrugged. "No loss."

Jimmy said. "We want to help her. Do you know where she lives?"

"Nowhere. Her landlord evicted her."

"What?" I said. "He threw a pregnant girl onto the streets?"

"So I heard. You could try the Homeless Shelter on Station Road. They provide hot meals and a bed for the night."

We thanked him and left.

The sun was setting as we drove to Station Road. Darkness fell, and an autumn chill sent shadowy figures hurrying into shop doorways seeking shelter for the night. I heard the rattle of a Pendolino. We turned a corner, and I saw the bridge. "Stop," I shouted.

Jimmy slammed on the brakes. "What's wrong?"

"You may think I'm crazy but I saw that bridge in a dream. This is where we'll find them."

"You're not crazy, Mia. There's a lot we don't understand about the subconscious mind."

We abandoned the car and ran towards the bridge. A little girl, no more than two years old, sat beneath it next to a huddled figure that lay still. Jimmy examined the figure. I knelt beside the child. She whimpered, "Mamma sick."

I glanced at Jimmy. He said, "She's dead. Take the child home. I'll call the police. They can drop me at your house later. They'll want to talk to us both." He took out his phone.

Euterpe

I said to the child, "What's your name, sweetheart?" She shook her head. I said, "What did Mamma call you?"

She pointed at herself. "Dat's Baba."

"You're safe now, Baba. The nice man will take care of Mamma and I'll take care of you." She held out her arms. I picked her up and said, "Baba's name is Grace."

I took her home, fed her milk and mashed banana, and she fell asleep in my arms. She needed me as much as I needed her. I would ring the school on Monday and cancel my contract for this school year. My classroom assisting would have to wait a while.

The police arrived with Jimmy and a social worker called Marianne. She said. "Thank you for caring for her. I'll take her now."

"No need," I said. She's family. My late husband was her father. I'm sure his parents, Sir Henry and Lady Beauchamp will provide DNA to verify that."

Her attitude changed. "The MP? Oh, in that case I see no objection to her staying here but we must meet with them as soon as possible."

"No problem. Leave me your phone number. I'll ask them to contact you."

I could see Jimmy was trying not to laugh. He added, "And when Mia and I are married we'll adopt her." He looked me in the eyes, and I nodded.

Marianne coughed. "You do understand that adoption applications can be long and complicated?"

I said, "No doubt, but Sir Henry is very good at cutting red tape."

She smiled. "You're right. Good luck and congratulations."

Jimmy stayed the night.

Next morning I said, "There's something I want to show you." I led him to the nursery, picked up the musical box, and turned the key to the gateway. With Grace on my

Rhapsody of the Spheres

lap, I held Jimmy's hand, and the music took us to the garden.

Grace pointed to Euterpe and said, "Pretty lady."

Jimmy said, "What the f—?"

Euterpe said, "Don't curse, Jimmy. I am Euterpe, Goddess of Music, Mistress of the Rhapsody of the Spheres, and Giver of Delight. Mia will explain later. Sit."

We sat.

She said, "Are you happy now, Mia?"

"Yes, except for one thing. I grieve for what happened to Evie."

"Good answer, but you need not grieve. The bonds of love will draw her back to Grace. She will be born to you and Jimmy."

I looked at him. "You okay with that?"

"Fine, but I'll be surrounded by women." He turned to Euterpe. "Any chance of us having a son?"

She said, "I thought you'd never ask. Guy loved Mia as much as he was capable of loving anyone. He'll be drawn back to her, and his mind will no longer be afflicted. With you two as his parents he'll become the good man he was meant to be."

Jimmy squeezed my hand. "Right, as long as we don't have to call him Guy."

I returned the squeeze. "James would be a good name."

Euterpe said, "How happy are you now, Mia?"

I said, "As happy as a soaring flute, the scent of honeysuckle, and a child's laughter."

"Then go now, and share your happiness. It's time to return the gateway to Culsans." She played her flute and the music took us home.

. . .

While Jimmy and Grace were getting acquainted with each other and the contents of the toy chest, I took the musical box back to *Culsans' Cloister*.

Euterpe

A careworn woman, holding the hand of a small girl not much older than Grace, was talking to Culsans. "It's her birthday. Do you have anything she might like that doesn't cost much? I have very little money."

The child looked at me, pointed to the tiny dancer, and said, "Pretty lady."

I turned to Culsans. He nodded. I handed the musical box to the child, and said to her mother, "keep it as long as you need it."

About the Author

Maureen Bowden is a Liverpudlian, living in Wales with her musician husband. She has had 182 stories and poems accepted by paying markets, she was nominated for the 2015 international Pushcart Prize, and in 2019 Hiraeth Books published an anthology of her stories, *Whispers of Magic*. They plan to publish an anthology of her poems in the near future. She also writes song lyrics, mostly comic political satire, set to traditional melodies. Her husband has performed these in folk music clubs throughout the UK. She loves her family and friends, rock 'n' roll, Shakespeare, and cats.

*****~~~*****

Let Sleeping Rock Stars Lie
by Bruce Golden

  He drifted out of Redemption Hall into the sublime sunshine and took a long last look at the heavy double doors closing behind him. He felt like a new man, and, thanks to the divine guidance of the Holy Father's 1,012-step plan, he was. New as a rosebud about to bloom on a spring day. New as the first tinkling laugh of an infant. New as the glossy coat on a freshly painted '65 Mustang. New as—well, you get the general idea.
  Yesterday's Jesse was gone, cleansed of his rancor, his negativity, his derision. No more would he ride the storm of discontent. He couldn't wait to embrace the world—the warmth of its breezes, the music of its soul, the puppy-dog playfulness of its children. He was also very hungry.
  However, before he could decide if he finally wanted to try the Sacred Cow Buffet or just stick with the Celestial Cafeteria, his mentor approached. He fought off his demon first impulse to think, *What now?* and greeted her with spurious enthusiasm.
  "Hello, Priscilla."

Rhapsody of the Spheres

"Good day, Jesse, and congratulations on your graduation. I thought you might want to take advantage of your new A-3 status, and have a look through the Earthfinder."

He'd always been curious about the Earthfinder, but hadn't been permitted to use it.

He was anxious to find out what wonderful and glorious things mankind had been up to over the last few decades.

"Far out," he replied, "let's go look."

She led him back down the hall, where he thought he caught a whiff of lemon meringue incense, past the guardian, who didn't so much as glance their way, and right up to the edge of an enormous crystal sphere.

"Do you know what you'd like to see first?" asked Priscilla. "What do you miss most?"

"Well, I sure miss singing the blues. There's not a lot of call for that up here. I guess I'd like to see how the rest of my old group is doing."

"Then look."

Jesse looked into the sphere, and, as the smoky haze cleared, he saw his old friends. They were all together, and they were jamming. That surprised him. He hadn't expected them to still be making music after all this time. He figured they would have found something else to do—gone on to bigger and better things in their old age.

They look ridiculous, he thought, with their gray ponytails and potbellies, trying to be hip. The sphere's audio became more distinct, and he was able to hear them. They were playing one of his old songs!

"Look at them. I come out after three decades of soul-cleansing, and there they are, playing the same tired old tunes, looking like poster children for a geriatric jamboree."

"*Jesss-seee*," admonished Priscilla, "where's your sense of charity, your willingness to be tolerant towards others? Have you forgotten your lessons so soon?"

Let Sleeping Rock Stars Lie

"Oh, yeah. . . I mean no. I was just, uh. . . joking with you. I think the old farts are, uh. . . cute."

Now Priscilla was an A-2, only a cherub's breath away from being promoted to A-1, and Jesse realized he couldn't pull the wings over her eyes that easily.

"Until you've walked as many miles in their snakeskin boots as they have, you have no basis on which to judge them. Even then—"

"Judge not, lest ye be judged," Jesse replied as if by rote.

"That's right," she said, "but I think you need to do more than mouth the words you've learned. You need another kind of lesson."

"But I just finished—"

"Now, Jesse," she said before he could go on. "Consider this the first step towards becoming an A-2."

Boy, he thought, you'd figure they'd let a guy enjoy being an A-3 before they started pushing him out of the nimbular nest toward A-2.

"It's not about enjoyment, Jesse," she said, reminding him for the umpteenth time that she could hear his thoughts as plain as his speech. "It's about a willingness to learn. So, . . ."

So wham, bam, thanks a lot, ma'am, Jesse found himself back on terra firma.

He realized right away how good it felt. Walking on air with his head in the clouds had always made him a little queasy. He did, however, experience a brief sensation of claustrophobia. Four walls and a ceiling were a bit much after all that time in the infinite expanse.

He became aware that Priscilla had outfitted him in his trademark black leather pants, and he was enjoying the smooth sensations, when he realized he'd been transported into the recording studio where he'd seen the guys laying down some tracks. They were so busy arguing, they didn't notice him.

Rhapsody of the Spheres

"Can't you guys ever agree on anything?" he asked, waiting for their reaction.

"*Jesse?*" they called out simultaneously in amazement.

"Rick, Joe, Rollie, good to see you guys again."

"But. . . how?" sputtered Rick.

"I know this must seem like a weird scene after all this time," said Jesse, "but don't worry, I'm still dead. I mean, I did die, you know, way back when. I'm just visiting."

"Where—?" asked Joe, and Jesse pointed up, anticipating the rest of his question.

"Why—?" began Rollie.

"My mentor thought it would be good for me," said Jesse.

"How long—?" queried Rick, but again the answer came before the question was completed. He was getting the hang of this consciousness-attunement thing.

"I'm not sure exactly," said Jesse. "Probably not long."

"Well, you look great, man" said Rick.

"I should, I haven't aged a day in 30 years. Sorry I can't say the same about you guys. You know, when I saw you all, I thought you looked pretty ridiculous. I mean, you're all pushing 60 and still trying to be rock stars."

"Hey, some of us still have to make a living," responded Joe.

"Yeah," added Rollie, "not all of us got to be a dead icon."

"An icon?"

"Don't you know?" asked Rick. "Man, you've got more fans now than you did when you were alive. They think you're some kind of rock 'n' roll god."

Suddenly a great rumble swelled from beneath the floor. The entire room shimmied and shook as they each grabbed hold of something to steady themselves.

Let Sleeping Rock Stars Lie

"Another L.A. quake," said Joe when the rumbling ceased.

"No," replied Jesse, motioning upward with his head and eyes, "He just has a low threshold for blasphemy. But look, what I wanted to tell you is, what you're doing is cool with me. I mean, who am I to judge?"

"I'm glad you're in tune with that," said Joe. "I was afraid you came back to kick up a fuss about the pantyhose commercials."

"What pantyhose commercials?"

"We sold a few of our old tunes," said Joe, "and they're using them to sell pantyhose. It's not a big deal. They just changed a few of your lyrics."

"Changed my lyrics for *pantyhose*?"

Jesse tried to remain calm. They were only words. After all, he reasoned, who was he to criticize? Just to be safe, however, he inwardly recited several soothing mantras.

"The commercials aren't nearly as good as the lunchboxes," said Rollie.

"Lunchboxes?"

"Yeah, we got this great merchandising deal," Rollie continued enthusiastically. "I used my percentage for hair implants. Looks pretty real, huh?"

"I think the little figurines are kind of cute myself," offered Rick.

"Figurines?"

"Yeah, you know, like little dolls, only made to look like us. The Jesse doll is a real big seller. You are *so* like it, man."

"The Jesse doll?"

Jesse increased the pace of his mantras, but they weren't having much effect. He was smoldering inside, and the words that were coming to mind weren't as virtuous as he would have liked. He hoped his mentor was out of range.

Rhapsody of the Spheres

"You okay, Jesse?" asked Joe. "I'm not getting very good vibes from you. You look like you've seen a ghost... so-to-speak."

"I'll be all right, as soon as I get rid of this feeling that someone's stomping all over my grave."

"Uhh... speaking of graves, man...." Rick didn't finish, but looked to his comrades for help. Neither of them wanted to elaborate.

"What?" demanded Jesse in the most spiritual way he could manage.

"What Rick means," said Joe, "is the lease on your gravesite in that French cemetery is about to expire, and the locals want to move you."

"Lease? Move me?"

"Yeah," chimed in Rollie, "it seems a bunch of your crazed fans have been dousing the place with booze, littering, and generally desecrating your final resting place, as well as the surrounding gravesites. The French authorities say they've had enough, so they're refusing to renew your lease."

"They're going to dig up my grave?"

"Hey," said Joe, raising his drumsticks in mock surrender, "you're the one who wanted to harmonize in the hereafter with all those 17th Century poets."

"There's talk of building a shrine for you here, man," said Rick, trying to find a bright side. "I think they've got a spot picked out in Burbank."

"A shrine in Burbank?" Jesse was seething now. "Are you dudes crazy? You're going to let them dig me up and replant me like so much mulch? I've never heard of such an asinine excuse for—"

"*Jesss-seee*." It was Priscilla, suddenly at his side and looking very disapproving. The instant she appeared his former bandmates froze like wax figures. "Where's your angelic sense of forgiveness? Your compassion for those who lack your celestial insight?"

Let Sleeping Rock Stars Lie

"In a hole, six feet down, just outside of Paris." Jesse plopped onto a stool like so much dead weight. "I've been kicked out of a lot of places, but I never thought I'd get booted out of my own grave."

"Look at it as part of life, or, in your case, afterlife." Priscilla tittered at her own wit.

"However, I'm afraid this outburst means it's back to Redemption Hall for another cleansing. I'll have to revoke your A-3 standing."

"Another 30 years?" whined Jesse.

"Don't worry, you have all eternity. Besides, I have it on good authority your friends will have joined you by then."

"Can I at least say goodbye?" he asked, and before the last word was out of his mouth, she was gone and his old friends were reanimated.

"I've got to go, guys, but could you do me a favor? Would you see if you can talk them into renewing my lease? Promise them my pantyhose royalties or something. I'd hate to be uprooted now that I'm just getting settled in."

"We'll keep trying, man," Rick assured him.

"Hey," cried out Joe as if a light bulb had exploded over his head. "Why don't you cut a song with us and improv some lyrics before you go? Maybe a little blues number. We'll call it 'Growls from the Grave'!"

"Right!" chimed in Rollie. "We'll make it the centerpiece of a huge concert like 'Live Aid' or 'Bangladesh,' only we'll be raising money to keep Jesse's room in the tomb!"

"It'll be a world event," agreed Rick. "Peace for a day. . . food for all. . . let sleeping rock stars lie!"

Jesse looked upward for guidance, and in his mind he saw the ethereal image of Priscilla nodding her head in approval.

"Far out," he said, "let's jam."

###

Rhapsody of the Spheres

About the Author

Bruce Golden's short stories have been published across more than two dozen countries and 40 anthologies. *New Myths* magazine said of his novel, *Red Sky, Blue Moon*, "With thematic echoes of *Dune, Dances with Wolves*, and *The Last Samurai*, it's an epic tale of adventure and arrogance, discovery and desire, courage and greed." His book, *Monster Town*, a satirical send-up of old hard-boiled detective stories featuring movie monsters of the black-and-white era, has been stuck in TV series development hell for some years now. Website: http://goldentales.tripod.com

*****~~~*****

Celestial Notes
by Robin Pond

Outside, the storm rages relentlessly, rain slashing down upon the lighthouse, a monolithic white spire rising up through the bleakness. The winds churn up the roiling sea, frothy waves cascading against the foundations.

But inside, they are oblivious to the tempest, focused intently on their music, a plaintive prelude in E-minor. Hans, an earnest young man with tousled hair, crinkles up his eyebrows as he coaxes the notes from his flute. Hudson, a middle-aged harpsichordist with a week's growth of beard, dips his head slightly with each beat of the music. And Olga, a young woman with long blond hair, is hunched forward, pouting slightly as she draws her bow evenly across the strings of her cello. They finish, exhaling in unison, allowing the final notes to reverberate momentarily in the air around them.

Hudson swivels away from his keyboard, shaking his head vehemently. "This is hopeless."

Hans adjusts the sheet music in the stand in front of him. "I don't know. I thought we were much better that time."

Hudson glares at him. "That's not the point."

Rhapsody of the Spheres

"And what a strange arrangement," Olga adds, studying the music.

"Yeah," Hans agrees, "but Dr. Allegoris has been very clear on the instruments which must be used, and the tempo, and even the key, E-minor. And the notes must resonate crisp and clear, to emphasize the dissonance."

These would-be musicians are in a makeshift recording studio on the ground floor of the lighthouse. In front of them is an archway leading to the anteroom with a wrought iron staircase spiraling upwards past all the rooms above to the very top of the lighthouse. Behind them is a wall filled with cabinets and wires and electronic components, an extensive sound system with copious tiny red and blue flashing lights. Interspersed among this equipment are three giant speakers from which a muted whispering continuously emanates. Now that the three have ceased playing, this whispering becomes more pronounced.

"How can anything be clear with that incessant noise?" Olga exclaims petulantly, "Isn't it driving you crazy?"

Hans merely shrugs. "I'm starting to get used to it."

But Hudson explains, "It's just space noise. Allegoris told me the lighthouse has been hooked up to function as a stellar transponder. So it's probably just picking up the white noise of the dark matter in space, or maybe it's the last groans of the big bang, only now reaching our planet."

"No," Hans responds, "It's not random noise. I can detect a linguistic pattern, like a hoarse whispering in some indecipherable language."

"Damned annoying," Olga insists. "It never completely stops."

Hudson brings both fists down upon his keyboard. "I just want to go home. But Allegoris has locked away all the boats. I should've fought harder when they abducted me."

Celestial Notes

"You were abducted?" Hans asks. "I was lured here. They said I'd won a raffle for a luxury yacht."

"I was invited to what I thought was going to be a wild party, one of those apocryphal, world's-ending-might-as-well-enjoy-it type of things," Olga wistfully tells the others. "I was so excited. Back home everyone's too busy producing enough to eat and bailing water to keep the city afloat to ever have any fun. And when I first saw the speakers, I thought there was going to be dancing, orgiastic lose-yourself-in-the-rhythm type dancing."

Hudson suggests the three of them should team up to force Allegoris to release them.

But Hans is hesitant to join any mutiny. "I don't know. I feel we must've been brought here for a purpose."

"Yeah," Hudson replies mockingly, "to endlessly play the same useless piece of music."

"No, Hans is right," Olga states with conviction. "We're here for a reason, probably to start a new human race."

"What?" Hudson scowls.

But then Dr. Allegoris, an ancient crone-like figure of indeterminate age or gender with a hooked nose, a pointy chin, and bony hands protruding from her flowing black robe, enters hurriedly through the archway. "Why have you stopped playing?" she rasps in her husky voice, which always carries a note of urgency, "You must continue."

"We've decided there's no damned point," Hudson announces. "We demand to be allowed to leave."

"But there is a point. The most important point in all the universe. You, my friends, have been selected as the last hope of humanity. I've brought you here to save mankind."

Olga jumps in enthusiastically. "I knew it! I knew it! When do we take off?"

The crevices in Allegoris' face deepen in confusion. "What?"

Rhapsody of the Spheres

"I knew when I saw the lighthouse it was really a spaceship," Olga announces. "We're blasting off to a new planet, one with a better atmosphere, and it'll be up to me to propagate a new human race. We should leave right away."

"No!" Allegoris is clearly shocked.

"But why wait?" Olga asks eagerly.

"It's not a spaceship," Allegoris insists. "Sometimes a lighthouse is just a lighthouse."

Olga shakes her head. "A lighthouse on top of a mountain in the Himalayas? That's ridiculous."

"Actually, it's not," Hans chimes in. "Once the oceans really began to rise and the cities started being converted from land-based to sea-faring, lighthouses were put on a lot of the mountains, just in case."

"And it's a good thing too," Allegoris adds. "Floating Mumbai almost rammed us a few months ago."

Olga is disappointed. "So, no propagation?"

"Definitely not," Allegoris assures her, "I would never presume—"

"A little presumption's okay," Olga argues. "It's not always a bad thing—I mean—if it's for a good cause. I'm certainly willing to do my part."

"But the lighthouse isn't just a lighthouse, is it?" Hudson queries suspiciously. "I've already told them about it also being a stellar transponder."

"Yes," Allegoris agrees, "and perhaps it's time to tell you all exactly why I've gathered you together here."

"I knew it couldn't be just to play a prelude in E-minor," Hans declares.

"But it is," Allegoris corrects him. "That's exactly why you're here. I've carefully chosen accomplished musicians who are also scientists—you Olga, a cellist/biologist, and you Hans, a flutist/oceanographer, and of course you, Hudson, our harpsichordist/environmental chemist. I've selected you

Celestial Notes

three to forge the intimate connection between science and celestial music."

"Are you a scientist?" Hans asks Allegoris.

"Yes, I'm a quantum alchemist."

"So you—what?—turn lead into gold on a molecular level?"

"That's a common misconception," Allegoris explains. "Alchemy's not primarily about turning things into gold. It's about learning science from the ancients."

"You mean like when Aristotle claims maggots are just meat in another form?" Hudson asks.

"Again," Allegoris responds impatiently, "it's not all about transmutation."

Olga looks at her doubtfully. "So, what's your science got to do with us?"

Allegoris draws a deep breath. "When the sea levels started to rise rapidly, and the cities were all intent on converting to nautical, I foresaw that this was only a temporary remedy. So I decided to remain on land to search for a more sustainable solution."

Hudson smiles derisively. "You mean all the cities rejected you?"

"No. I wasn't rejected! I chose to remain on land."

"You shouldn't feel upset," Hans tells Allegoris. "The cities needed to recruit real scientists."

"It was my choice!"

Hudson, Hans, and Olga give each other knowing looks.

"It was!" Allegoris insists, composing herself before continuing. "Anyway, as the water rose, I was driven to higher and higher ground, until I eventually arrived here, on top of the mountain, at the Buddhist temple."

"What Buddhist temple?" Hans chimes in.

"It's underwater now. But I got here before it was completely submerged, and I found in their vault—"

Rhapsody of the Spheres

"The Buddhists had a vault?" Hans again interrupts.

"Yes. Would you let me tell the story?" Allegoris glares at Hans. "Anyway, there in the vault I found an ancient text which demonstrated the harmony of the heavens, the celestial spheres. The music you've been learning to play comes from that text."

"It's not very harmonious," Olga observes. "But, regardless, how is playing music supposed to save mankind?"

"Don't you see?" Allegoris' voice rises as she pleads her case, "This music has to be the solution. It has to be. How else would a prelude in E-minor, which sounds like something from—I don't know—maybe the early renaissance, how could it end up in an ancient Sanskrit text?"

"Who the hell knows?" Hudson is losing patience. "Maybe Marco Polo dropped by and traded it for some spices."

And Olga is also struggling to make sense of this. "I still don't see how it's going to save mankind."

So Allegoris continues, "Many ancient texts discovered from various cultures have mentioned the music of the spheres. With the right notes, augmented of course by our stellar transponder, we can achieve the God-frequency, that special combination of notes, sounds which will cause the spheres to resonate, augmenting and reflecting the pulses back on to the Earth, like hitting just the right resonant frequency to shatter a wine glass, only for select molecules rather than glass."

Hudson is outraged. "Really? This is your great plan to save mankind? Mythology? Ancient texts with silly tales?"

"But inside all mythologies lurk kernels of scientific truth," Allegoris insists. "I'm convinced the cosmic spheres are actually great undiscovered energy

Celestial Notes

fields which will respond to the right amplified frequency."

Hudson snorts, "Ridiculous!"

"Yeah," Hans agrees, "and besides, mankind doesn't need saving. We just need to adapt a little, that's all. The floating cities aren't so bad, once you get used to them."

"No. Actually the Doctor's got that part right." Hudson raises his arm. "I've got a state-of-the-art Climatic Fitbit here that's monitoring everything, and it's not looking good." He points at the dial. "The atmosphere's passed the tipping point. The ocean's becoming way too acidic. And the hydroponic farms are all beginning to fail. Humanity's really screwed."

Olga is alarmed. "Why couldn't you have just built a spaceship so we could all be off propagating somewhere?"

Allegoris becomes defensive. "There weren't resources, okay? All available resources in the U.S. went into converting the cities. And even then, by the time the water started to reach the Midwest, places like Cleveland and Scranton, we didn't even have the resources to keep those cities afloat."

Hans shrugs. "A small price to pay."

Olga stares wide-eyed at Allegoris. "So now you're telling us this musical Hail Mary's the only hope humanity's got left?"

"Exactly."

"But we've been playing this tune for a month now," Hudson points out, "so it's clearly not working."

"I know," Allegoris responds. "There's still something missing. But maybe if we listen to what the spheres are telling us. . . " She walks over to one of the speakers and leans in, listening intently. The whispering seems to become louder.

85

Rhapsody of the Spheres

"That incessant noise?" Olga is incredulous. "I'm willing to endure the odd murmured utterance as much as the next person, but enough is enough."

"It's in an ancient Sanskrit dialect." Allegoris listens intently. "One I didn't readily recognize."

"You mean there are some you do readily recognize?" Hans asks her.

Allegoris smiles. "Yes, several, but for this one I had to consult an ancient thesaurus."

They lean forward in anticipation. "And?"

"It confirms what I already suspected. It's saying, *There is order in the cosmic chaos. Chaos channels the current of the cosmic order.*"

Hudson gives Allegoris a sour look. "Sounds to me like a cosmic fortune cookie."

But Allegoris darts quickly back through the archway into the anteroom. The others all stand in a group, staring after her. Outside, the torrential downpour continues to batter the lighthouse, the unremitting pounding reinforcing the whispering from the speakers.

Allegoris returns a moment later, escorting an unsteady young man with a craggy face and shaggy red hair, dressed in full Scottish regalia, including a kilt and a faux-leather sporran. In his left arm he is clutching bagpipes.

"I've prepared for this," Allegoris assures the others. "So let me introduce you to the final member of your ensemble. This is Angus McLean, a noted physicist and renowned bagpiper from the Floating Edinburgh Institute."

"Ach, what's the meaning of this?" Angus blinks, trying to get his eyes to focus. "Where the hell am I?"

"I'm sorry for having drugged you, sir," Allegoris apologizes, "and for this rude awakening from your drug-induced state. But we have no time to lose."

"Hi, there. I'm Olga." She offers Angus her hand.

Celestial Notes

But he says, "Ooo. . . Everything's still a wee bit unsteady."

"That's 'cause you're no longer on a floating city," Hans explains. "It takes a little while to get your land legs."

Angus shakes his head groggily, "But how?"

Olga asks him, "What's the last thing you remember?"

"I was just sitting down to breakfast, all set to enjoy one of those beyond-meat haggis patties. But after just a couple of bites, everything went blank."

"So clearly they doused your haggis," Hudson informs him.

Angus is now sufficiently recovered to feel a surge of anger. "That's outrageous, messing with a man's haggis. It's a horrendous crime! Unforgivable!"

Hans shrugs. "I think the real crime's making perfectly good plant protein mimic the taste and texture of haggis."

Angus turns his attention back to Allegoris. "Why would you do this?"

"That part is easy, my friend. We desperately need your help, on the bagpipes, as accompaniment to a prelude in E-minor."

"Seriously," Hudson interjects, "a quartet of cello, harpsichord, flute, and bagpipes?

Hans agrees, "I'm not sure we can achieve much harmony, for the cosmos or anywhere else."

"Certainly not with the current arrangement," Olga concurs.

Having overcome the effect of the drugs, Angus becomes increasingly indignant. "First you ruin my haggis, and then you ask for my help? You can go to hell! I absolutely refuse to participate in this nonsense."

But Allegoris remains adamant. "This, I believe, is what the celestial spheres are trying to tell us."

"The what?" Angus scowls at Allegoris.

Rhapsody of the Spheres

"Believe me," Hudson tells him. "You really don't want to know."

But Allegoris' voice rises above the cynicism. "Entropy, that's the key. The basis of the harmony of nature is the entropy that always seeks a more disordered state."

Angus scans the room. "What sort of lunacy have I fallen into here?"

Hudson nods, "Now you're beginning to get it. Allegoris here's stark raving mad."

But Allegoris refuses to acknowledge such negativity. "Visionaries are always considered mad in their own time. They called Nietzsche mad. They called Nostradamus mad."

"They even called the Marquis de Sade mad," adds Olga.

"M-hm," Angus concurs, "They were right in all three cases."

"But," Allegoris argues, "my calculations clearly show the bagpipes to be the solution, the most entropic instrument known to man."

"You have calculations?" Hans asks incredulously.

Allegoris pulls out a crumpled notebook from beneath her black robe. "Yes, I've conducted a most rigorous analysis."

Angus immediately snatches the notebook. "Let me see that."

Allegoris takes a step back and draws a deep breath. "Listen people, I cannot force you to perform the prelude. But I'm begging you, for the sake of all that's good in the world, for the sake of all that remains. You must play it as if the world is hanging in the balance, because it really, really is."

"This is ridiculous." Hudson remains dismissive. "It defies all logic, all common sense."

But, surprisingly, after studying the calculations, Angus adopts a very different tone, "The common sense

Celestial Notes

may be lacking. Aye, that's true. But the math is indisputable. And what sort of physicist would I be if I didn't accept math over common sense?"

Allegoris clutches at these words like a drowning woman clinging to a fragment of floating wreckage. "You mean?"

"Aye, count me in, Doctor," Angus announces decisively. "I'll be a part of your quartet."

Allegoris springs into action, waving her arms like a desperate conductor showing up late for the performance. "Excellent! Olga, please, for the love of all that is holy, take hold of your cello. Gently embrace it. Prepare to make it sing."

"Fine, but I'd still rather be propagating." Olga positions herself over her cello.

"Hans, gather your flute. Hudson, prepare to tickle that harpsichord."

"Alright then." Hans picks up his flute.

And even Hudson reluctantly agrees to participate, "Oh, why the hell not?"

With another encouraging wave of Allegoris' hands, Olga begins to play softly. Hans and Hudson smoothly ease into the piece. And then, several bars later, Angus fires up the bagpipes, eradicating all the rest.

They pause at the end of the movement. Angus grins appreciatively. "A truly majestic sound."

"This can't be happening," Hudson exclaims. "According to the Climatic Fitbit, there's been a noticeable reduction in the percentage of carbon-based molecules in the troposphere. The base elements are being washed away. And for some reason, they're sinking like stones into the ocean and being absorbed through the ocean floor at an astounding rate. The atmosphere, the seas, the entire world, it's all being cleansed."

Hans observes, "We must've finally hit the right notes."

Rhapsody of the Spheres

Hudson taps at his Fitbit, shaking his head in disbelief. "This is all happening way faster than it should."

Outside, the winds have died down, and the rain has diminished, tailing off into a gentle drizzle. Sunlight streams through a break in the clouds, and a rainbow begins to form in the sky above the lighthouse.

"I knew it!" Allegoris shouts enthusiastically, "I knew it! Ancient Sanskrit texts are never wrong." She waves her hands wildly at the assembled musical ensemble. "Play, my friends, for the love of all humanity, keep communing with those celestial spheres!"

Olga, Hans, and Hudson recommence the prelude, now more enthusiastically than before, knowing that their music will not go unheeded. Their notes will not be lost in time or distance but will find their way up to the very heavens. And Angus, standing proudly erect, once again overrides them in a cacophonous crescendo, a climatic climax.

About the Author

Robin Pond is a Canadian writer of plays and prose fiction. His plays, mainly comedies, have received hundreds of performances and publication with Eldridge and YouthPLAYS and in numerous anthologies. Robin's mystery novel, *Last Voyage*, was published as an e-book in 2018. Since then he has had sixteen short stories (almost all sci fi or fantasy) and one poem parody published in various magazines and anthologies.

*****~~~~~*****

Peer-Reviewed Spellcasting
by M.A. Dosser

Dear Sorceress Minnora Elastria,
    I wish to submit an original spell entitled, "Volantem Lux" for consideration by the *Quarterly Compendium of Arcana*.
    With this spell, a person will be able to create an enclosed source of light and heat, enabling a sorcerer to freely move through the darkness without having to carry an open flame in their palm. My hopes are that this spell can contribute to the *Quarterly Compendium of Arcana*'s strong tradition of producing charms that appeal not only to tenured sorcerers but also have applicable uses outside the academy, such as eliminating the need for candles in many homes and providing sources of heat for minimal-to-no cost.
    Thank you for your consideration. I look forward to your response.
    Best,
    Adik Kut, W.A.
    . . .

Rhapsody of the Spheres

Dear Adik Kut,

Your spell, "Volantem Lux," has been received and is presently being given full consideration for publication in the *Quarterly Compendium of Arcana*. Presently, it will be sent to two anonymous peer reviewers, who will provide recommendations on whether to accept it for publication. The process can take up to three months, so please wait to query until that time period has elapsed.

If you have any questions or concerns before then, please let me know.

Sincerely,
Minnora Elastria, Soc.S.
Editor of *Quarterly Compendium of Arcana*

. . .

Dear Adik Kut,

Thank you for submitting your spell, "Volantem Lux," to the *Quarterly Compendium of Arcana*. Based on my reading of the spellcraft and the reviewer feedback, I invite you to *Revise and Resubmit* "Volantem Lux" for further consideration. The *Quarterly Compendium of Arcana* only invites resubmissions from sorcerers we believe can produce an effective revision in a reasonable amount of time, so I hope you take this as an encouraging response.

I have provided the reviewers' extensive but very useful comments below. It should be noted that although Reviewer Two "rejects" your spell, I believe that your implementation of their recommendations will elevate your already interesting and quite valuable work. If possible, please send me your revisions before the autumnal equinox.

As always, if you have any questions or concerns, please let me know.

Sincerely,
Minnora Elastria, Soc.S.
Editor of *Quarterly Compendium of Arcana*

Peer-Reviewed Spellcasting

Reviewer One

Thank you for your spell, "Volantem Lux." The creation of a contained light source is an intriguing innovation for our discipline and could be a potentially strong addition to the *Quarterly Compendium of Arcana*. In their scroll, the author expertly weaves together the expansive foundational lore, and the "Volantem Lux" charm produced the described effects and then some. A great strength of this spell is the incantation's accessibility, though I did note a few awkward lines. I left smaller suggestions regarding the prose on the enclosed scroll. You should find the comments in the margins of the incantation. I should emphasize that these recommendations are meant to be helpful rather than dictatorial.

I do, however, have two larger suggestions that may benefit the utility of the spell. First, while working with the charm, I found that the sphere is entirely stationary. While this is not a problem in and of itself, other charms such as Quinn Pylk's "Partum Lux" and Griff Thomson's "Thoghairm Ghrian" do something similar. The innovation with "Volantem Lux" is the *contained* nature of the light. With a slight alteration of the nonverbal components of the spell, you would be able to have the light follow you, which could greatly expand the charm's uses. For more on mobility movements, I recommend reading Leonie Maer's tome about the Pied Piper, *Magie des Rattenfängers*.

Second, the light sphere would continue to grow warmer as the spell wore on. Given that people may use this charm in the winter for warmth as well as during late summer nights as a source of light, the level of desired heat may vary. If there were a way to control the heat output, it could ensure the charm is useful year-round. I have no immediate suggestions on *how* to create this

Rhapsody of the Spheres

control, but perhaps shield charms could be a place to start.

I'm unsure if my comments constitute a major revision, but this might be a bit more substantial than a minor revision. Regardless, I am happy to see this piece through to publication.

Good luck with future iterations of this spell.

Reviewer Two

Although there is some interesting spellwork here, I would recommend "reject." There are large swaths of lore that need to be addressed for the author to carve out a place for this charm in the ever-swelling sea of spells. While missing some key citations is not necessarily a reason to decline a spell, in this case, the conceptual development is stunted by not engaging the vast amount of literature on charmwork and atypical incantations. Where are Fiona Rene, Ksad Illya, or János Molná? The lack of a discussion of these preeminent sorcerers makes the author appear unread and the spell built on shoddy foundation. The charm *does* function as stated and seems to have strong potential, but without a solid basis in previous spellcraft, might the author have arrived at it by luck? Might another sorcerer have a better version of this spell more firmly rooted in seminal arcana that would be denied were we to accept this charm?

Moreover, the fact that the incantation is based in Latin makes me question the credentials of the author. Have we as a field not progressed beyond the Latin charms of Quinn Pylk, who, it must be noted, the author fails to mention, despite his foundational light creation charm? Latin spellcraft overwhelmed the field for so long that if one is going to use Latin, they need to demonstrate *why* it could not be something else. By utilizing Latin, the incantation becomes, for the lack of a better word, too simple. While it is accessible, might it not be *overly* so? Latin lends itself well to incantations with a more musical

Peer-Reviewed Spellcasting

delivery, but this also enables nearly anyone to access it, regardless of their intentions. Why not try another language, such as Hungarian? János Molná has demonstrated the efficacy of the Hungarian spellcraft in several compendiums and monographs. The lack of consideration of non-Latin-based incantations has me questioning whether this charm would become outdated even before it appears in the pages of the *Quarterly Compendium of Arcana*.

With all this in mind, I cannot in good conscience recommend anything but reject. I am enclosing a scroll for the author. Within the thirty-six inches, I have provided a list of citations the author should read and contemplate before submitting this spell elsewhere.

I wish them the best.

. . .

Dear Sorceress Minnora Elastria,

Thank you for the opportunity to revise and resubmit my spell, "Volantem Lux," for potential publication in the *Quarterly Compendium of Arcana*. I am grateful to you and the two reviewers for reading and critiquing the scroll. I have revised the spell with the various recommendations in mind, and I believe it is now significantly improved. Below, I summarize the changes that have been made.

Both reviewers astutely suggested I engage with sorcerers who have worked with similar charms such as Quinn Pylk. Through discussions with Pylk, Griff Thomson, and other sorcerers that Reviewer Two suggested such as Ksad Illya, Rasa Karan, Nevik Nailo, and Poesa Masse, I have greatly clarified and strengthened the theoretical foundation upon which the spell is built.

Reviewer One's suggestion to read Leonie Maer proved extremely helpful in revising this spell. Based on Maer's exploration of the Pied Piper, I have added nonverbals to the incantation that permit the sphere to be mobile. I have also included instructions in the arcana for

Rhapsody of the Spheres

performing an incantation *without* those nonverbals if the caster wants the sphere to remain immobile. Reviewer One correctly noted that both Pylk and Thomson created charms that produce light—but without the shaping of the light into a sphere, the light is diffuse and fades with time. As such, having options for how the sphere moves greatly enhances the potential utilization of the charm.

Maer's work also proved useful in addressing Reviewer One's suggestion regarding the heat produced by the charm. I have added arcana relating to Maer's charm, "Cingo Sisto," which applies a permeable layer to the orb that allows heat and light to escape but prevents the orb from growing hotter after the moment of application. This addition will enable the caster to choose the intensity of the heat, and it can easily be worked into the initial incantation once they know how long it takes for the orb to reach their preferred temperature.

Additionally, I appreciate Reviewer Two's suggestion to engage with non-Latin incantations and have added a discussion about the benefits and limitations of French and Hungarian incantations popularized by Fiona Rene and János Molná, respectively. As Reviewer One highlighted the accessibility of "Volantem Lux" as a strength, and one of my goals with this spell being to provide a charm that could be utilized by professional sorcerers as well as those not in the academy, I found that the increased complexity of both syllabic control and nonverbal components of the incantations made the charm less accessible. Due to this, I have kept the incantation in Latin.

Further small changes can be seen throughout the revised spell, such as addressing instances of stilted language and correcting improperly cited tomes.

Once again, I would like to express my thanks to the reviewers for their helpful comments and to you for your guidance through this process. I believe the

resubmitted spell is stronger and responds to the calls for revision. I look forward to your response.
Best,
Adik Kut, W.A.

. . .

Dear Adik Kut,
I am happy to inform you that I am accepting your spell, "Volantem Lux," for publication in the *Quarterly Compendium of Arcana*. Congratulations!

While Reviewer One was satisfied with your revisions, Reviewer Two still had many suggestions. Given the tone of the review and my decision to accept, I hesitated to include the review with this scroll. I ultimately decided that there are useful suggestions within the review that you may wish to implement, but your spell will be accepted with or without these revisions.

When you are able, please send me a finalized version of the charm. I hope to publish it in the spring edition. Congratulations again, and thank you for this excellent contribution.
Sincerely,
Minnora Elastria, Soc.S.
Editor of *Quarterly Compendium of Arcana*

Reviewer One
Thank you for your careful, thoughtful revisions. This is now a much stronger, clearer charm. I will be pleased to see this spell in print and become more widely accessible.

Reviewer Two
I was concerned enough about the original submission to recommend a "reject" decision. Seeing the revised version, those original concerns remain and have somehow multiplied.

I appreciate that the author has attempted to engage with some of the literature I recommended, but

Rhapsody of the Spheres

much of it is at the surface level. The discussion of János Molná in particular neglects his most recent tome regarding charmwork for enhanced eyesight. Given the author's desire for the "public" to be able to utilize the spell to help them get around in the dark, is this not extremely relevant? And much of my suggested literature is nowhere to be found. Perhaps the author was worried about the length of the spell, which, if I'm correct, is nearly too long for the *Quarterly Compendium of Arcana*. If so, they should have withdrawn the submission and sent it elsewhere, to an outlet with a less restrictive scroll length. They also could have reduced the discussion of classic charmwork, such as that by Quinn Pylk and Ksad Illya, which only tangentially relates and is far too dated to be of much use. Instead, their arcana section moves too quickly and lacks any kind of thorough engagement. It feels as if the author was merely pandering to my request for additional citations rather than taking my recommendations to heart.

This especially applies to the complete disregard of my suggestion to move away from Latin. I understand that Reviewer One praised the accessibility, and I do not want to attempt to overrule another reviewer, but the *Quarterly Compendium of Arcana* aims for exquisite spellcraft, and this often results in spellcraft that requires specialized knowledge to utilize. I won't get into a rant about how the push for accessibility in our discipline has led to ethical quandaries. If an apprentice can pick up the latest *Quarterly Compendium of Arcana* and cast whatever they read, what happens if they do it incorrectly? Who is to blame for the damage caused? And, moreover, what is the use of having a master if they can comprehend the latest advancements in spellcraft themselves? What becomes of the academy and our roles in it? Latin not only hinders the complexity of the spell itself, it also lowers the bar for achievability of casting.

Peer-Reviewed Spellcasting

On a more positive note, I did find the author's reasoning for not utilizing Rene's French-language incantations compelling, but, in truth, French is only a step above Latin. There is much to be gained from utilizing incantations from Hungarian, or even Belarusian. The author really needs to engage—*truly* engage—with spellcraft by sorcerers such as János Molná and A.E. Chyzh before continuing with this work.

I could go on, but I fear it would be of little use. At this point, I wonder whether we have reached an impasse, as the author of this spell—a sorcerer who clearly has some promise—squanders this opportunity by refusing to make alterations that would strengthen their spell. Until they at least make a gesture toward addressing the myriad underlying issues, I cannot change my recommendation: Reject.

. . .

Dear Sorceress Minnora Elastria,

It is wonderful to hear that the *Quarterly Compendium of Arcana* is accepting my spell, "Volantem Lux," for publication. Given Reviewer Two's many concerns, I have made additional changes to the spell that I believe will satisfy them. The most notable change is altering the incantation. While I still believe the original Latin incantation works best, I have added an alternate version: "Fénygömb Feltörni." Is it possible to send the revised spell to Reviewer Two for a final round of peer review?

I appreciate all the work you have put into this spell. Let me know if you need anything else. Also, please wait to attempt the new incantation until you hear back from Reviewer Two.

All the best,
Adik Kut, W.A.

. . .

Rhapsody of the Spheres

Dear Adik Kut,

I apologize about the delay in responding. Upon attempting to follow up with Reviewer Two on your latest revisions, I learned from one of his colleagues that a ball of flames burst inside his office. Regrettably, he is no longer a reviewer for this compendium, nor a sorcerer at his institution. Nor any institution, for that matter.

As it will be impossible to receive János's notes on your latest revision, I am happy to accept the previous version of "Volantem Lux" for publication. Please send a clean manuscript when you can, and we will proceed with the production process.

Additionally, there is an upcoming a special issue of the *Quarterly Compendium of Arcana* that I encourage you to submit to. Given what happened to Reviewer Two and provided you can alter "Volantem Lux" so rather than following you, it moves in the direction of your choosing, I believe the "Fénygömb Feltörni" incantation would be perfect for our theme: Battle Magic. Do keep in touch.

Sincerely,
Minnora Elastria, Soc.S.
Editor of *Quarterly Compendium of Arcana*

About the Author

M. A. Dosser is a co-founder and editor of *Flash Point SF* and is a PhD candidate at the University of Pittsburgh. His short fiction has appeared in publications such as *Daily Science Fiction*, *Wyldblood Magazine*, and *Martian: The Magazine of Science Fiction Drabbles*. You can read more about his creative and scholarly work at maxdosser.com.

*****~~~*****

An Autograph

by Stetson Ray

Cara laid her hands on the keyboard and waited. Her father sat in a chair behind her, rasping for air. He cleared his throat, and Cara readied herself.

"Richard was only twelve years old when he died, but he decided he wasn't going to let such a trivial thing as death stop him from living."

Cara typed the words and waited for her father to continue.

"Delete that," he said.

"Oh Dad, that was a decent opening. Can't you keep going? It could be something."

"No. It's rubbish. Delete it. Quickly."

Cara held down the backspace key and erased the words from the computer screen.

She waited.

Her father said nothing.

She typed, "*Cara sits in her father's study, waiting for him to speak, waiting for her life to start, waiting for him to finally—*"

"What are you typing?" her father asked.

Rhapsody of the Spheres

"Nothing," she said, and deleted the words.

"Cara, you know the Muse eludes me unless I have total silence."

"I know. I'm sorry."

Cara waited.

A few minutes passed.

Her father said, "Thomas Evans did the same thing everyday: he went to work, he came home, and he went to bed. This pattern continued for years until one day—"

He stopped.

Cara waited, fingers primed.

She prayed for the Muse to stay in the room, for her father to continue.

"Delete it."

"Oh, Dad, can't you—"

"No. We must begin again."

Wanting to scream, Cara deleted the words.

She waited for an eternity.

Then her father began to snore.

She shut down the computer and turned around and looked at him. Her father was old, fat, and nearly dead. Still, Louis Vaughn was a literary genius—or that's what everyone said: the critics, the fans. They called him a visionary, an explorer of hidden worlds, a traveler of both time and space. He was also a stroke victim who couldn't type his own stories anymore; it was Cara's job to put them on paper. Her father trusted no one else with the task, and voice recognition technology was not up to his standards.

Cara put a blanket over him and went to the kitchen, poured herself a cup of coffee, and thumbed her phone while her father snored. Time passed. She grew tired of scrolling. Her father mumbled something incoherent, then farted.

Cara called for Martha, her father's caretaker.

"I'm going out for a while, but if he wakes up and wants me to come back, just text me."

An Autograph

Martha nodded.

Cara grabbed her things and left.

. . .

"*There wasn't much interesting about Lana Finch. She rarely left her home. She wasn't a sociable person. She wasn't married, and a suitor wasn't likely to come calling anytime soon. Lana was a great disappointment to her family, or so she thought. It had never been said, but—*"

Cara stopped typing and read the words. They seemed. . . anemic, predictable. She was sitting at her favorite table at her favorite coffee shop, but she was having trouble getting into a groove. She wondered if the Muse had stayed at home with her father.

A man who Cara had never seen before appeared beside her table.

"Excuse me, but are you a writer?"

"I am."

"Wow, that's awesome." The man stood there, grinning at her. "I'm sorry, I've bothered you. I just think that's interesting—being a writer and all."

The man was kind of goofy looking, but also kind of handsome. He was oddly dressed, like he had walked into a thrift store and grabbed the first set of clothes he had seen.

"I don't mean any offense, but you don't really look like the type," the man said.

"Excuse me?" Cara narrowed her eyes.

"You don't really look like a writer."

"Please tell me: what's a writer supposed to look like?"

"I don't know. Old. Miserable. Beady-eyed and disheveled. Not like you."

Cara wasn't sure if she was being hit on or insulted. The coffee shop was her refuge, her sanctuary, and she wasn't used to being interrupted while she wrote. The man remained where he was, grinning.

Rhapsody of the Spheres

"Are you lost?" Cara asked.

"No."

"Do you have anywhere you need to be?"

"Nope. My whole day is free. I've got all the time in the world."

He stood there, either dumb or desperate to meet her. Or both.

"Would you like to have a seat?" Cara exaggeratedly asked, hoping he would catch her sarcasm and go away.

"Thanks." The man sat down on the other side of the table. "What are you working on?"

Cara's eyes darted to the mostly blank screen in front of her.

She closed her laptop and said, "I'm not sure."

"A short story?"

"Maybe."

"What's it about?"

"A girl. I think. I don't really know."

"Sounds good," said the man.

The longer she looked at him, the more familiar he seemed.

"Have we met?" Cara asked.

"No," the man laughed, "I don't think so."

Cara didn't get the joke.

"Do you have a name?"

"I'm Roscoe Bartlett. And you are?"

"That sounds like a made-up name."

"Well, it's not."

"I'm Cara."

"Nice to meet you."

They shook hands, miming the gesture more than doing it in earnest.

"How long have you been a writer?"

"As long as I can remember. Writing kind of runs in my family."

"Have you written anything I might've heard of?"

An Autograph

Cara wasn't sure how to answer the question. Technically, she had written dozens of award-winning short stories and three bestselling novels, but in reality, all she had done was type them; her father had done all the hard work while Cara sat in a chair and moved her hands. Her original stories had always struggled to find an audience, unlike her father's. His words were printed on gold. Hers, toilet paper.

"I've published a few short stories," Cara said. "Not in any big magazines or anything. Mostly anthologies. Small presses and such."

Roscoe nodded, still grinning. He was starting to look a little crazy. There was a look in his eye, an eagerness that was off-putting.

"You ever tried writing a novel?" he asked.

Cara's stomach sank.

"No," she answered quietly.

The word spun in her head: Novel. Thousands of words. Tens of thousands. Maybe hundreds of thousands. Nowhere to hide. Black and white. Her soul laid bare for all the world to see and judge. And judge her they would. The daughter of acclaimed writer Louis Vaughn would attract critics like flies to a sun-baked moose carcass. Everyone would be keen to knock her down a few pegs, make sure she knew that just because her father was arguably the greatest science fiction writer to ever live, it didn't mean she could write worth a squat. Nobody likes a nepo-baby.

"You should try writing a novel," Roscoe said. "I bet you'd be good at it."

"What makes you say that?"

Roscoe didn't seem to hear her. His eyes kept darting to the door of the coffee shop.

"Can I ask you something?" he asked, leaning forward.

"Sure."

"Why do you do it? I mean, why do you write?"

Rhapsody of the Spheres

Sometimes Cara wondered herself. She would never be able to compete in the same league as her father, let alone surpass his literary achievements. She was trapped in his shadow. It was a cliche, but it was also true. And writing wasn't fun anymore, not like it was when she was younger. The process pained her. Cara was divorced, childless, unsuccessful, and almost forty. Staring at a blank page day after day only served to remind her of her failures.

"Because I have to, I suppose," she finally answered.

Roscoe nodded. Again, his eyes darted to the door. He wasn't smiling anymore. His movements and mannerisms were hurried, and he was sweating.

"Would you do something for me?" Roscoe asked, digging in his clothes. Out came a book which he laid upon the table. "Would you sign this for me?"

The book was old and worn. The dust jacket had been removed. There was a strip of masking tape over the spine covering the title.

Cara started to ask why he would want her signature, but then the answer came to her: one of her father's fans had found her. Roscoe knew that Louis Vaughn could no longer physically sign books, so he had resorted to the next best thing: Cara the copy-editor.

"If that is one of my father's books, then you should know I had very little to do with its creation."

Roscoe shook his head, annoyed.

"No, it's not that. This has nothing to do with your father. I like his writing, but I like yours better—*a lot better*."

"You thought I'd actually sign something for you after that whole act? Pretending like you don't know me?"

"No, I mean, I just thought—"

"I'd like for you to go away."

An Autograph

"Please," Roscoe said, a wild look in his eyes. Cara decided he wasn't handsome after all. He was weird looking. "I probably should've said this before, but—"

His eyes darted to the door once more, and his words caught in his throat and the color drained from his face. Cara looked where he was looking. Two large men wearing navy blue jumpsuits had entered the coffee shop—law enforcement from the looks of them—and everyone was staring at them. They did not fit in. They stood out worse than two uniformed football players on a baseball diamond.

Roscoe lurched over the table and grabbed Cara's hand and cried, "*Please! I'm your biggest fan!*"

He opened the book and tried to force a pen into her hand. She leaned back and yanked her hands away from him. The two men stormed over to the booth and grabbed Roscoe and dragged him out of his seat without saying a word.

"*One more minute! Please! I almost had—*"

One of the men jammed a small device into Roscoe's ribs, and he went limp; Cara assumed it was some kind of taser. The men hauled Roscoe toward the door—then one of them turned around and began walking back to Cara's table, taking big steps, his eyes fixed on her.

Her heart leapt.

Her mind failed to come up with a way to escape the huge man.

The man slammed his hand on top of the book and pulled it off the table.

"Sorry for the trouble." He turned and walked away.

The two men left the coffee shop, dragging Roscoe behind them like a ragdoll.

The cafe was silent.

Cara remained in her seat, her heart racing.

. . .

Rhapsody of the Spheres

"Where did you go?" legendary sci-fi author Louis Vaughn asked.

"Out for coffee."

"Coffee? I'm ready to write!"

"Well, it looked to me like you were sleeping, but I'm here now, and I'm ready if you are."

"No, no, the Muse has passed. I can only hope She will visit again tomorrow."

Cara's father looked every day of eighty-eight years old. One side of his face sagged and was without form. His hair was nearly gone; what remained was thin and white. His body was wasting away, but for the most part, his mind was holding out. Strokes and heart attacks and high blood pressure and diabetes couldn't stop Louis Vaughn. He still had stories to tell.

"I'm sure She will," Cara said. "She's never abandoned you before, has She?

"No, I suppose not. . . but She has been late a few times."

He looked at her and smiled half a smile. Even if he could be hateful and short-tempered and an inescapable force larger than life itself, he was everything to Cara: her only living parent, her best friend, her source of income.

An odd thing happened occasionally: while looking at her father, Cara would become starstruck. It's like she would suddenly remember who he was. So many people loved him. So many people wanted to meet him. So many wanted him to sign. . .

"Why are you looking at me like that?" Louis asked.

"I was just thinking," Cara muttered. Then Roscoe was in her mind. She could clearly remember the desperate look in his eyes. He'd been desperate for her autograph, but why?

"I don't say this often enough, but you are very important to me," Louis said, and Cara snapped out of her trance and looked at him.

An Autograph

"Because you wouldn't be able to write without me?" She was only half joking.

"No, it's more than that."

She waited for him to go on, but she knew he was finished. Her father didn't get sentimental often. But he didn't have to. He saved it for his stories. All of it. Every bit of him went onto the page. Her older siblings didn't understand. Her mother had never understood. Cara was the only person who truly knew him. No one got Louis like she did, and never would. Super-fans, eat your hearts out.

"I think I'll take my bath now," Louis said, and Cara called for Martha.

. . .

Staring down at her feet, Cara paced the floors of her father's house, lost in thought. An idea burned inside her head—forming, growing, gestating—whether she wanted it to or not. She sat down and opened her laptop and stared at the blank screen, stared through it. She was somewhere else, plumbing the depths. The house had never been so quiet. The Muse was in the room. Cara could feel the weight of Her presence.

Only vaguely aware of what she was doing, Cara started typing. Words appeared on the screen—line after line of them, page after page. The writing came easy and felt as good as it ever had. All she was and ever would be poured out of her. She forgot that no one wanted her stories. She forgot about her father, her career, the readers, the critics.

She was doing what she was born to do, and doing it well.

And all that mattered was the next sentence.

###

About the Author

Ray has had stories published by *Sans Press, Pyre Magazine*, and *Liquid Imagination.* He lives in Tennessee and spends most of his time reading and writing ghost stories.

*****~~~~~*****

Dog's Body

by Edward Barnfield

The first thing I saw on my first day in the lab was half a dog. Specifically, the hindquarters, fully-formed legs and tail, with a spine leading to where the skull should have been. The thing sat there, suspended in green fluid, tended by a swarm of buzzing machines.

"I do hope you're not going to be sick," said EJ Hemmings. "Only, we don't have time to go back and change, so you'll have to wear whatever you bring up."

Everyone in the lab was clad in full PPE, plastic suits with slits for the eyes, so people had to turn their whole heads to catch my response. Clearly, this was a company tradition.

Of course, things weren't normal leading up to that. In order to get the job, I'd sat through so many interviews about my thesis ('Bio-Fabrication: Exploring the Convergence of 3D Bioprinting and Nano-Biomaterials in Tissue Engineering') that words ceased to have meaning. They always talked to me in rooms without windows, a portrait of the Ministry's Legitimate Leader glaring down.

"So, we've made most progress with the canines to date," EJ told me as we strode across the concourse. "There's something malleable about their somatic cells, which seems rather fitting. Man's best friend and all that."

EJ—Elizabeth Jane Hemmings, to use her full name—was team leader. She was one of those classically English women, grey hair cropped like a helmet, a brisk and dismissive manner, and faint smiles you suspected held deep prejudices. She moved so fast, even in the PPE, that my visor was fogged with panting breath.

"Now, the research team's living quarters are over there. The core laboratory is out-of-bounds, I'm afraid, unless they up your security clearance. You're in the secondary area. We're restricted to the east of the island. The rest is mostly grassland and swamp, but they did use it for biological warfare testing back in the '20s, so we're being cautious."

I'd looked over the landscape on the flight in, my first-ever helicopter ride. When you hear 'island,' you think palm trees and white sands, but this place seemed far more desolate, a black rock in raging waters. There was a high seawall, and rabbit warrens of concrete in the inhabited section, and then a great expanse of nothingness beyond.

"Any questions?"

"I'm sure I'll have technical questions."

"Well, don't ask me. Not my field."

"But, why here? Why is the laboratory out so far from anything?"

She looked at me for a moment, hard blue eyes. "Well, this island is peaceful, no distractions, no predators in the undergrowth. It has clean water and a self-sustaining power system. But more importantly, it's far away from any regulatory oversight. I do hope this won't be a problem, Dr. Guha."

Dog's Body

"No. Not at all."

In truth, the immersive nature of the project was the attraction. There's a line in the 'Analects of Confucius' that I remember —'To study and at times put your learning into practice, is that not a joy?' I'd been without purpose for so long. There was no academic appetite for my kind of research, and the idea of joining a weapons company, squatting over a microscope to squeeze out a few more centimeters of kill-zone, didn't appeal.

And those first weeks were bracing. Our team was small, smart, and focused, and I was seeing things my colleagues could not. For the first time in my career, there were few restrictions, no approvals. Some of the scientists missed home, were tired of canteen food and the cold wind whipping across the concrete, but I was intoxicated.

Day by day, through our careful intervention, the dog grew more complete. Fur and paws emerged, and the ribs stretched like fingers. Mr. Takahashi, our genetics specialist, compared it to a jigsaw, although one assembled in the most inconvenient way, with the skeleto-muscular structure preceding the development of the internal organs.

It was Takahashi who took me to see Subject X27, the living model. The original animals were all located at the far side of the compound, past the maintenance team's quarters. A couple of men in blue jumpsuits eyed us suspiciously as we squidged through the mud, past a litter of pigs and the birdcages, to the last pen with its noisy inhabitant.

Subject X27 was a golden rust Smooth-Haired Vizsla, who barked exuberantly as we arrived. Takahashi was down on his haunches quickly, holding a hand out to sniff.

"We call him Hachiko," he said, fussing behind his ears.

I am better with animals than with people. At first, I mistook the laboratory for a level playing field, an

Rhapsody of the Spheres

assembly of peers, but I quickly became conscious of the rising competition. I suspected EJ Hemmings was setting us against each other, balancing every favor with some bureaucratic cruelty, some forfeiture that cut to the professional quick.

The core team, with the highest clearances, were the worst. You couldn't engage in conversation without worrying about it afterwards, as though your banal observation on the weather was destined for an official report somewhere, your file growing thick with disloyalty.

I cut myself off, focused on the work. Socially, I spoke only with Takahashi, about his life back in Japan, the convoluted path that had brought him here. People around me were forming attachments—workplace friendships, ill-judged affairs—but I kept to a tight triangle, oscillating between bed and the lab, with occasional trips to the animal pens. To put your learning into practice, is that not a joy? I was happy enough.

"What do you think they're doing in there?" I asked Takahashi during one of our dog visits. "Why the secrecy?"

He looked over his shoulder once, twice, and spoke in a tight whisper. "It's something for the Ministry," he said. "Something we shouldn't talk about."

Around that time, we started working on the brain stem. I had thought establishing and connecting the radial nerve would be the most difficult, but it was a birthday party compared to the higher systems. I was in the lab for 36 hours one time, unwilling to leave in case my absence enabled the slightest error. The machines were so finely tuned, so delicate.

"This is where it went wrong last time," said EJ Hemmings, appearing behind me at the worst moment. "That was when the Ministry started making noises about your predecessor."

"It is a highly complex operation." I tried to keep my tone neutral.

Dog's Body

"Do you think the animals gain consciousness when you plug the brain stem in? A sudden flood of muscle memory, like a light switching on? I mean, there must be some response. Maybe they see the machines and the gloop they're suspended in, and think, 'Is this it? Is this my go?' Awful swizz, if so."

I checked the electrical stimulus, nudged the voltage up an increment.

"We're developing a replica of Subject X27," I said. "When the clone comes out of the tank, it should inherit its responses from the original. That's the theory, at least."

She left, and I had that awful sense that I'd been adjudicated according to some secret criteria again. It was another three hours before I reached my bed.

On Day 43, the subject was ready for release. Helicopters had arrived through the night, and the observation booth was packed with pale men in grey suits. They'd suspended the rules on protective clothing for this special occasion.

It was left to Takahashi and me to extract the animal. We drained the sustaining fluid and carefully removed the monitors, all the while conscious of the unsmiling observers behind the screen. We snipped the holding straps and gently carried the body to the marble examining table. The beast lay there, warm but unmoving, as Takahashi listened for life signs through a stethoscope on its side.

In those situations, you can see quickly how the different scenarios will pan out. I was imagining the reaction if the experiment failed, picturing the weight of official disapproval if all we had to show was an anatomically exact cadaver. I was thinking of this when:

'Woof.'

The noise from the observation booth was deafening, cheers and hearty backslaps. You would think those men had achieved something. And they missed, in

Rhapsody of the Spheres

their self-congratulation, the true miracle. It wasn't just that the animal was alive. We had created a distinct mode of parturition, an entirely new aspect of existence. The mirror dog stirred, fought its way to its feet under its own locomotion, and went to Takahashi, tail wagging.

After that, the rest of the day was a parade, with our colleagues invited to inspect, ask questions, and take notes. Lucas from the Core Team was particularly scornful, casting doubt on the creature's long-term survival prospects, querying the cellular stability. The clone responded with a prodigious stream of urine on the laboratory floor.

When we took it to the pens, the original Subject X27 was there, staring through the bars. As we locked his progeny in a separate cage, he howled, a single note that held for a full minute. The same/other dog, the parallel, joined in, sustaining the same pitch, until his lungs gave out. I'd never seen animals do that before.

I couldn't sleep that night, excited as I was by the opportunity that extended in every direction. We could revive the dodo from DNA bone fragments or create crashes of black rhinos to adorn the African plains. The Ministry must see the potential, I thought.

"Congratulations. We're upping your security clearance, moving you to the Core. They have a brain stem issue," EJ Hemmings told me the next morning.

"But, I mean. . . " I stuttered. "There's still work to do with the canines."

Those fierce blue eyes again. Her office had the same vibe as those faraway interview rooms, windowless and festooned with military paraphernalia. She even had the same glowering portrait above her desk.

"The Core work is the foundation of this project. Everything else, included your four-legged freak, is a sideshow."

"What kind of research will I be doing?"

Dog's Body

"Lucas will brief you. But I'm sure you've worked it out by now, no? You're a clever man, after all, Dr. Guha."

I looked at her blankly.

"Well, we always test these processes on animals first, no?"

Lucas was no kind of scientist, just a middle manager of the lowest rank, a target-setter, a promise-maker. When I was finally admitted to the main laboratory, with its 15 upright tanks and next-generation bioprinter, it proved to be a showcase of failed hypotheses. One tank held a slumped half-skeleton, another a decomposing brain floating in sustaining fluid. And Lucas dealt exclusively in bureaucratic evasions.

"Who is the living model for this?" I asked.

"That's classified, Guha. Above your paygrade."

"How are you dealing with neuron response?"

"Focus on the brain stem. Other team members are dealing with neurons."

It's strange how a simple change in environment shifts everything. The work was fundamentally the same, the manipulation of living cells through digital intervention, but the atmosphere was utterly different. There was no joy of discovery here, no excitement in exploration—just dour mediocrities chasing an arbitrary deadline.

My only relief came with evening catchups with Takahashi. His team were making huge progress, creating the next dog in 21 days. The Avian Genetics team had made a breakthrough of their own, developing a full batch of bio-printed eggs. Of course, the Ministry's attention had moved on. Rather than applause in the observation booth, they were sending angry memos to the Core.

It took me a month to understand their urgency. I was working late again, trying to correct the ham-handed efforts that had scrambled the medulla oblongata, when EJ

Rhapsody of the Spheres

and Lucas came in. They moved at speed, the pitch of her reprimands rising with a doppler effect.

"It's not good enough. The amount of time and investment poured into this project, and all we have to show is a barnyard of animals. You are aware that they can purchase animals for significantly less than the cost of accelerated cloning, yes?"

"EJ, if you could just—"

"Are you aware of how bad things are getting on the mainland? The interagency struggles, the power grabs? This project was fast-tracked as a security countermeasure. Two years without progress does not feel fast-track to me."

"Yes, but—"

I watched as she punched a code into the main terminal. A photo appeared on the screen, an old man in a loincloth undergoing a CT scan. The legend on the bottom read, 'Subject 1A.'

"Are you missing information, Lucas? Is that the issue?" She ran through a series of slides, digital images of bone, organs, and blood vessels. "Only, if we can create a dog in 21 days, I'm stumped as to why human duplication takes so much longer. God only needed seven days for the whole universe, after all."

The photos settled on a facial scan. EJ paused her invective for a moment, straightened her spine. It was difficult, from the tomography, to decipher the image at first, but I had seen it so often I was conditioned to recognize the bone structure. The face from official portraits that hung on so many walls. The Ministry's Legitimate Leader.

It made sense, of course. Dictatorships always have an issue with succession and the concentration of power. Cloning provided a new pathway to ensure longevity for the Legitimate Leader, possibly even eternal control if we could iron the kinks out.

Dog's Body

I didn't tell Takahashi when I saw him next. He was too excited by the behavior patterns of his cloned pack. The animals had overcome their initial aversion to each other, and had begun moving in a kind of unison, sensing each other's presence and adapting accordingly.

"It's as though each dog is an aspect of itself," he said. "Like individual cells within the same organism."

He told me, in confidence, that now they had perfected the process, he was going to start variations. Create a female Vizsla, a new puppy.

"No one is watching us now," he explained.

Back in the Core, I managed to get the team on track through a combination of deceit and Herculean effort. Lucas was one of those corporate types whose only interest in an idea was laying claim to it, so I let him take credit, while I soldiered on. I wasn't really thinking about the ethics of the project—the damage that multiple iterations of the Legitimate Leader could inflict—only trying to get us to the end point.

We were on the path to completion, when EJ Hemmings called me to her office. We had the central nervous system in place, and the brain work was mostly done. The eyes were still an issue, as I remember, and there was some funk in the digestive tract, but we were, at most, a week away from release.

"I need you to supervise the euthanasia of the trial animals. All of them," she said. She was stuffing documents into a brown envelope as she talked.

"What? Why?"

"We don't really have time for questions. A boat is coming in"—she checked her watch—"about 13 hours. By then, we need to have smudged every trace of these operations."

"I don't. . . We're leaving?"

"You were always very clever, Dr. Guha. We're evacuating. Likely to a transit camp or a short

Rhapsody of the Spheres

conversation in a room with a sloping floor, but we're getting off this rock with rather rapid effect."

"But we've done it. Don't they understand? We've pioneered human replication."

She stopped then, stared at me. Judging from her eyes she'd been crying that morning.

"No," she said. "This project didn't succeed. In fact, it never happened. Nobody tried to create a clone of the former leader, and if they did, they certainly didn't do it with the approval and support of the Ministry."

EJ dropped the stuffed brown envelope into her metal wastepaper bin and chased it with a small incendiary device.

"The former leader was executed by the incoming regime this morning. They made a point of destroying his body on a cellular level to prevent any attempts at reconstruction. Do you see now why these experiments never happened?"

The fire cast fragmented shadows on her office wall. It was the last time I saw her.

. . .

In the event, it was easier to release the animals than it would have been to execute them. Takahashi and I just walked down and opened their pens. The maintenance team were occupied throwing possessions into plastic bags and looting whatever they could. It was equally painless to avoid evacuation. We just followed the dogs onto the west side of the island and waited.

Sitting here now, it's peaceful. You can hear the occasional bark over the scrub and see the brood of hens nesting in the grasses. We'll see if the Ministry takes an interest in this island again. Can they spare the resources to track down two missing scientists and a flock of unwanted research animals? I doubt it.

I'm not sure how comprehensive the destruction of the laboratories has been. Knowing my colleagues' level of diligence, I suspect there will be plenty to salvage. I

Dog's Body

even wonder if the last human specimen is still in his tank, eyeless and half-alive, wondering if this is his go.

For now, Takahashi and I will study the effect of released cloned animals on a wild environment. If they can survive and thrive, it gives me hope for the future. Perhaps we can create a better Eden on a biological testing site. If not, then it doesn't matter. I will find joy in the study itself.

###

About the Author

Edward Barnfield is a writer and researcher living in the Middle East. His stories have appeared in Roi Fainéant Press, Ellipsis Zine, The Molotov Cocktail, Galley Beggar Press, Third Flatiron, Strands, Janus Literary, Leicester Writes, Shooter Literary, Cranked Anvil, and Reflex Press, among others. He's on Twitter at @edbarnfield.

*****~~~*****

Dream Bones

by Neethu Krishnan

When the first tremor rippled through the night, Nila was in the dreamless, gossamer crease between light and deep sleep and thus easily roused. She opened her eyes, making no move to get out of bed, and listened intently for whatever it was that nudged her awake to repeat itself. All she could sense was an unnatural stillness, as if a hive of invisible, expectant ears hovered about her. She then remembered the mute earphones still plugged in her ears and yanked them out; the audiobook had long droned to a close, its epilogue lost to her subconscious when she dozed off. And there it was. Again. The knock at her temples. Neither sound nor touch. *The opposite of a thunderclap,* she thought, her first instinctive abstraction making absolute and no sense at once. Something fundamental had reversed, like all audible sound had recessed up and away from the ground to the skies, and the reverse tumble of it, of the vacuum left in its wake—the silvered prongs of tangible, pulsing energy, anything but of passive silence, conjured no better

Rhapsody of the Spheres

approximation in her mind than the imagined opposite of a thunderclap.

She surveyed the dark bedroom through sleep-silkened eyes, anticipating correctly she'd find nothing amiss. One half of the ancient, gnarled-wood bedroom door was ajar, just as she'd left it, the sepia yellow from the corridor illuminating the room in dancing shadows, the power that'd gone out in the evening still predictably out. She climbed off the bed and padded to the half-open door. On a wicker chair in the corridor leading to the threshold of the house, the black bud of the kerosene lamp ribboned soot from its long, yellow petal flame, unflinching even as the third thrum plucked the air. The reverse thunderclap was more beckoning than unhinging, almost mischievous, but most pressingly, affecting in its finality, like it was her last and only open invitation.

Her heart should've raced, an apprehension twinged at her spine or reason cautioned her against unlatching the front door and stepping out alone into the eavesdropping night, but, of course, none of her faculties conspired against her. The urge to answer the soundless call fizzed and crackled in her with a vigor that vaporized all rationale. So, there she was, dusted powder blue in the full moon, barefoot and dressed in mismatched pyjamas, gliding towards the left of the front yard, towards the house well that beaconed.

The old-fashioned well with its thigh-high walls and rectangular raised perimeter of cement-plastered concrete, ordinarily hair-raising in its magnetic, concentric depths, its mossy velvet scent and its crystal reverberations of the tiniest flutters from its womb, was even more unearthly tonight, for its blue-gray waters with a heart of green lay not far and mysterious in the eye of the well but at arm's reach near the rim, cradling the spectral disc of the moon on its still surface, its otherwise constantly speckling sheet of water taut as a cowhide membrane on temple drum. While she'd heard of well

Dream Bones

water rising dramatically overnight up to two or three rungs shy of the algaed, stony mouth of wells come monsoon, she'd never seen or imagined one so full, with all its splintered, green-freckled tunnel rungs devoured in a column of water so formidable, so majestic, so inviting.

She reached for the pearlescent moon at the centre of the opaque water leaning over the wide, slippery rim, one hand clutching the supporting beam to her left, the other trying to graze the still skin of water. The girth of the old well was massive, which meant its centre lay far beyond the reach of her short torso, no matter how hard she tried to lean over whilst maintaining a sensible footing, and though the water looked close enough, at a normal arm's depth from the concrete mouth, hers was too short an arm to close the distance between her fingertips and the smooth lid of water. Her urge to touch it, nonetheless, was visceral, all-consuming, dictated by a force beyond herself. She was cognizant of an inaudible countdown timing her every move, her window of opportunity on the verge of shuttering any moment now.

Even as nothing stirred in her periphery, the presence of an other was unmistakable, tangible, undeniable. The night was quiet, as it shouldn't be. No cicadas sang. No frogs choired. No leaves whispered. In the dense thicket of intertwined shrubs and creepers encircling the well, night blooms of Arabian jasmine luminesced white like stars, their heady, sweet scent suffusing the still night, and the milky pink tea roses that peeked through the brambles floated loose their gauzy petals in a shower of anticipation. The preternatural, viscous silence, cool and dove-gray, like of clouds, overlaid the stillness of water, the mirror of its interface now a window, now a door, now a fleeting portal to unfathomable depths awaiting her entrance. If only she could touch it without imperiling her life, she bemoaned. The answer shone in aluminium.

Rhapsody of the Spheres

Her eyes traced on cue the ever-wet, thick coir rope tightly wound overhead on the pulley, the metal-gray bucket tied to its one end resting on the concrete floor to her right, full to the brim with old water. She lifted the heavy aluminium vessel off the floor, rested it on the parapet, unwound a length of holding rope from the disarmingly quiet and unsqueaking pulley and dropped the bucket in. The water didn't as much as dimple. No splash or echo registered the sound of contact. The bucket, still full, merely sat upright, almost levitated, as if its weight had landed on magnetized foam instead of water. She gasped with glee.

Ever since childhood, whenever she watched men, ropes tied to their waists, descend into the well, climbing down the green-matted rungs to either retrieve an accidentally fallen-in bucket or clean the mud lodged in the water pumps or increase the depth of the well by excavating out mounds of silt and placing more concrete rings underneath, she was mesmerized, both by the well and the men brave enough to monkey down its walls. Now that the water was close enough, almost still and safe like a swimming pool, and with the mouth of the well and the rope secured on one of its beams at grasping distance, she didn't see the harm in doing what she felt the quiet, invisible presence also wanted her to do. Wasting no time to even brace herself for impact, she sat herself on the ledge, eyes shut, short legs dangling still precariously above the evasive water, and dove in.

In her impulse dive, she had very little time to formulate expectations, but the ones that bubbled in her were the obvious. Maybe she'd float, dry, not quite touching the water, like on an invisible lily pad, and stroke the lifelike moon to her fill and be satisfied with its enchanting proximity. Maybe she'd find, much to her disappointment, the water saturated with salt like the Dead Sea, thus ruining the magic, but also offering her the gift of novelty, of having backfloated inside a village well just

Dream Bones

because she wanted to and could; a tale no one would ever credit to occurrence. Or maybe she was the chosen one as in fantastical tales; the mere touch of the calling water'd transform her, bestow her with secret, transcendental knowledge, and she'd never be the same again. One of her guesses may or may not have been right, but what she'd not thought to anticipate was the possibility of the other side, which is why when she opened her eyes to an infinity of hazily illuminated water, she almost believed herself dead and in the afterlife.

She looked like a swaying black aster, with her inky hair billowing in a radiating halo around the paler centre of her face. Her brown skin where her clothes didn't cling and balloon in wavy rhythms glowed dewy in the watery light. Much to her befuddlement and relief, she could breathe convenient lungfuls of what surely seemed to be air, despite the mind-boggling expanse of opalescent waters pressing in around her. Most discombobulating of all, however, were the people. So many and so kaleidoscopic. All of them translucent. Most in pairs or groups or massive congregations, each distinctly, familiarly human, but also appearing to be slightly modified replicas of each other. She looked unnaturally solid in their midst, and yet no one noticed or even acknowledged her presence as they floated past. She dodged those on an inadvertent collision course with her, afraid they'd wisp through her like ghosts did in movies. All the more reason to confirm her sign-off from the corporeal. To think she was on a fantastical indulgence when she'd only foolishly jumped to her untimely death for no believable, valid reason made her blush crimson with embarrassment. Before she could coast to her worries about her unassuming family back home receiving the news of her, a light swoosh reverberated around her, flooding the place with sound.

She'd only sensed the place smelling like dried, pressed flowers until then and not registered the

Rhapsody of the Spheres

constellation of people communicating with moving mouths expelling no sound, or at least, none she could hear. Now, she could pick out from the rumble of the collective murmur, like of an incoming wave at sea, that each had a voice, a screech, a whoop. One of the voices directly addressed her.

"Don't worry, you're not dead," the tall voice assured from over her shoulder, their intonation friendly, calm, soothing.

"Don't turn around," the voice added hastily, just as she tried to manoeuvre herself to turn through the water that suddenly felt like jelly. She hadn't yet moved a limb to navigate the place as her body floated about with a mind of its own, but now that she tried to physically steer herself, her limbs resisted. She couldn't help but picture herself trapped inside a mammoth comb jelly, the transparent kind with its otherworldly rainbow bioluminescence strobing on and off along its squishy, clear-as-glass blob; a transparency lithely navigating another. She wasn't even sure the creature was real, her lived life, for some peculiar reason, seemed far and over and unverifiable as having ever existed, scrambled like a cud-chewed memory bordering on fiction.

"So this is a dream, maybe?" she hoped aloud to the faceless, reassuring voice behind her.

"Maybe", the voice stalled, for suspense or for personal amusement, she couldn't tell.

"It's not Your dream, though," they laughed. "You are in the collective dream," they offered by way of conclusion, as if she was supposed to know what that meant without further elaboration. It greatly relieved her to know, for one, that she wasn't technically dead if the voice was to be believed, and if she really was in the collective dream, whatever that was, there had to be an eventual waking up.

"Every dream that ever was, seeps in here," the lingering voice offered, as if intuiting she was only

Dream Bones

waiting to wake up, without any more participation in the purpose she'd leaped into by choice.

She tilted her head in bemused concentration towards the voice that continued. "This water, at first only sparsely flecked with brittle and incomplete chips of visions at the beginning of humanity, has only been fissioning and fusioning ever since sentient dreams evolved and etched themselves hopeful in the bones of humans. The ever-burgeoning population of them only adds or iterates, but never subtracts, from the pre-existing ocean of dreams. But with the mushrooming number of bodies, the need for recycling and refurbishing arises, until pristine ones are born anew in corresponding proportions, which is where dream keepers such as you and I figure in."

The water softened. She could feel her body propel up and away from the live fabric of translucent humans. Did the voice just address her as a dream keeper? Sparing no breath for her to probe or wonder, it continued uninterrupted, even as she shot higher and higher up through quickly thinning water.

"The dream-tattooed bones when returning to the earth in a pyre, a coffin, a dusting of ash; in ceremony, memory or in a lack of witnessing; in snow, in sand, in water; in forgetting, in invisibility, in the recesses of unaccounted, undocumented departure, each sheds its scroll of dreams in an exhalation of vapour. It seeps into the water below, rises to the clouds above. What sublimates rains back, and what pools wings again. In this water of dreams, the ancient and the embryonic, enmesh and entangle, the albino catch colours and the coloured bleach, the artefacts update, redact or trespass, and in the crosstalk between the infinite permutations, we dream keepers make sure to keep the circulation going, of the actualized and the infant alike, and separate one platinum strand from another when they overlap and blend too much to tell apart, for it garbles the integrity of the

Rhapsody of the Spheres

intricate, glittering web of connection, of immortality. While the human condition is a guaranteed vehicle of hope written in abstract life purposes realized even in unconscious pursuing, even if not pinnacled with fulfilment, we always keep the wheels of hope and possibility oiled, nudge it to be the reigning, unifying image of the fragile numerosity of them."

If the swarm of questions ping-ponging her chest didn't suffocate her, the fast-changing water around her would make sure of it, she panicked, as the voice grew farther away from her as she jettisoned up an expanse of ribbed water that seemed to stretch on forever above her. She rummaged through her murky, racing thoughts, unable to distinguish in her glossary of recently amassed knowledge, the life-saving from the profound, she'd have no use for anyway once dead. Did the voice mention immortality at some point? Should she ask for help to survive once the water normalized enough to plug her lungs? Was the speaker even around anymore? The voice answered instantaneously, though it sounded slightly warbled and echoey.

"Yes," the voice replied, referring to no question in particular.

"Humans are wired to crave immortality. In the dreamscape, you might've noticed none of them were alone; each had at least one companion. The inanimate surrounding them was only as high as an ordinary termite mound, puny and inconsequential in comparison to the equal or larger-than-life humans each had around them. It is the crux of sentient life itself. Once you physically occupy a perch in space, you wish to leave by instinct a signature of your existence that lives past your lifeline, for your tribe that knows to read you, unassuming, of course, of the possibility you might return over and over again to the same planes many times over before extinguishing into light, and remember only fleetingly, even on return, your own geography of memories in ephemeral, absurd

Dream Bones

flashes of déjà vu, of the exactness of being encapsulated in a replica moment somewhere in an obscure timeline. So, you leave pieces of yourself, immortalized in deeds, in ambitions, in legacies, in art, in progeny, in kindness, in discoveries, in inventions, in the silly and in the magnificent, in the ordinary and in the divine, to live on, even when you don't. But you so do, by means of your singular act of existing, in memories, in fables, in history, in anecdotes, in possibilities, in unsuspecting dreams, in prayers, in creations. Which is why in each individual's dream, the ultimate protagonist is the immortalizing other, the golden connection and recognition with another. A gaze, a touch, a laugh, a tear; a held hand, an appreciation, a gratitude, a pride; a shared joy, a shoulder, an acceptance— to be mirrored in another of our kind the best our dream bones desire of us, is the foundational web of humanity, of belonging to a species that tapestries its individual motifs together as an immortal, conscious whole."

  The gelatinous sheath around her ran thin as familiar water, and she wasn't sure of how much longer she could hold in her breath. She kept zooming up the lightening waters like an untied helium balloon whistles up before deflating to a shrivel.

  The voice whispered again. "The next time you hear me stealing soundscapes for dreams on an unassuming night, you'll know where to join me. For now, you have about thirty seconds to save your life. Hold onto the concrete as soon as you break water."

  The whisper receded with a thump, and the sounds of water and cicadas and trees and the sway of an overhead pulley squeaking to the breeze churned around her. She grabbed onto the rough, mossy rim of the well, her legs slipping and kicking on the topmost rung as the water raced to the bottom in a gasping breath, with all its gurgles and splashes. Panting for dear life, she hoisted herself out, her pruned fingers grabbing the anchoring

Rhapsody of the Spheres

mouth with a death grip. Freezing, wet and dazed, she shivered at the dimpling face of water, a floating biome of leaves and crickets and tadpoles criss-crossing the distant coin of a moon.

###

About the Author

Neethu Krishnan is a writer based in Mumbai, India. She holds an MA in English and an M.Sc. in Microbiology, and writes between genres at the moment. Her work has appeared or is forthcoming in *The Spectacle, Bacopa Literary Review, The Polaris Trilogy, Fu Review, The Saltbush Review*, and elsewhere. She is a 2022 Best of the Net poetry nominee, and recipient of the Creative Nonfiction Award in *Bacopa Literary Review*'s 2022 contest. You can find her @neethu.krishnan_ on Instagram or on facebook.com/neethu.krishnan.944

*****~~~*****

Discordia

by Liam Hogan

      The aliens had an itinerary, and I was along for the ride.

"Where to next?" I asked, leaving gawping scientists behind as we headed to cars pulling up outside the biochem institute's polished glass and steel exterior. I didn't expect an answer.

      Their itinerary ran like clockwork, utilising every minute of every day, everything perfectly orchestrated from transportation to whomever they wanted to meet, whatever they wanted to see. They didn't bother sharing the details with me. The three cars and their passengers, the usual assortment of summoned scientists and visionaries to occupy the journey, were just another spookily smooth element in the week-long hallucination.

      One of the aliens opened the central car's door. I peered inside, surprised to find no wide-eyed genius waiting. "It is a journey of two hours, Avin," the alien

Rhapsody of the Spheres

said, its intricately articulated face reflecting a picture of exhaustion, despite the golden glow. "You should sleep."

Grateful, I clambered in, the alien sitting with the driver upfront to give me space. I knew the journey would be smooth: no traffic jams or roadworks, probably not even any red lights. And I, at the heart of it, as oblivious as anyone how they managed all this. More so, probably.

Whatever my role was supposed to be, and the thought it was some vast cosmic joke was never far away, someone, somewhere, would be spitting feathers that I wasn't learning everything I could about these alien visitors, that I wasn't asking the *right* questions, that I dared to sleep. Unlike the aliens, I had to. Had to sleep, eat, had to stop to use the toilet. Though I never had to ask—they always seemed to know what I needed, and when.

Even so, my brain was fried. Running on empty after doing little more than keeping up as the aliens flitted around the world, a whistle-stop tour of universities and science experiments buried beneath mountains or running rings under the France-Switzerland border. Listening as the aliens asked scientists oddly personal questions, questions that couldn't be answered by looking at funding applications or research papers or anything else online, which they claimed to have already read. It was only ever silent when they thought *I* needed to be, like now. I was asleep before the convoy rolled smoothly onto the street.

My fever dream began when it did for everybody. The aliens didn't need to ask someone to take them to your leader, because they made first contact by gatecrashing a meeting of the United Nations in New York.

"Please do not be alarmed," the disembodied voice announced, and it was said in the earpiece of every delegate simultaneously. "We apologise for the interruption."

The overhead screens and the desk displays lit up to show Dr. Valerie Heasman, of the Jet Propulsion

Discordia

Laboratory, her identity captioned beneath her monitor-lit, frazzled face.

"Dr. Heasman, please confirm the sighting."

She'd half-shaken her head, a bank of screens glimpsed in the reflection from her glasses, before spouting a set of distances, speeds, and luminosities that meant nothing to me, nor to anyone else there.

"Please confirm your interpretation of the sighting for the UN council," the same neutral voice asked.

She narrowed her eyes. "It's not a comet, or an asteroid. It's not *natural*. Impossibly fast, and showing signs of altering its course, of acceleration."

"Extraterrestrial?" the secretary general asked, after a lengthy but far from silent pause.

"If you mean not of our solar system, then yes."

"You said *acceleration*? Not deceleration?"

"We'll have visual confirmation as soon as NASA can bring Hubble or Webb to bear. But whatever it is, it appears to be doing a gravity assist slingshot manoeuvrer around the sun. Not stopping, not even getting all that close to us."

"One more thing, please, Doctor." This time, it was the US ambassador who spoke. "In terms of distance. . . how long would a signal take to arrive here?"

"It's currently crossing the asteroid belt, approximately thirty light minutes away. If I hadn't been told exactly where to look, and it wasn't so big and bright and fast, we'd not have spotted it."

The screens went back to showing the UN logo, the blue, laurel-wreathed projection of the earth.

"Then whoever you are, this is a hoax," the US ambassador said with angry defiance. "You can't hold a conversation with an hour's round trip delay."

"That is correct, Ambassador Merrick, but we are no hoax. We now introduce our earth-side representatives, our avatar-agents."

Rhapsody of the Spheres

Three sleek, golden figures entered the prosaically named General Assembly Meeting Room, waved in by security. They were humanoid and impossibly graceful, faces angelic and genderless. Utterly, deliberately, artificial. One took to the lectern, the others flanking, doing simultaneous British Sign Language translations.

They were passing through, they explained. They intended to use the week of relative closeness before they swung around the sun and headed out of the solar system to learn more about our Earth, having already exhausted the world wide web and every connected system, including the ultra-secure ones.

"We agents will travel the globe, visiting your centres of science and learning," the avatar announced.

"We cannot permit that, not unattended!" the US ambassador protested.

"It will happen with or without your cooperation." The golden figure smiled benignly. "But we're not adverse to someone travelling with us."

. . .

It was the car pulling to a stop that woke me. I peered, blurry eyed until I wiped away the sleep, at the sign: Rutherford Appleton Laboratory Space Research Centre. No idea which city we were in, or close to. Only the language told me we were still in the UK.

The alien-avatar was watching, and, as if I had only just asked the question, smiled and replied: "We're off to see a woman about a god."

The woman turned out to be Professor Dana Benedetto. White-haired, but not ancient. Someone who, I guessed, had decided that cheating time, appearance wise, might be counterproductive in the dusty male-dominated halls of academia.

After the aliens had asked her their questions, which included which classical music she listened to while she worked, they turned their attention to technicians who were already wheeling trolleys piled high with computers and other requisitioned equipment. It seemed the aliens had something of a demonstration in mind. We—the professor and I—were momentarily superfluous.

"What do you do here?" I asked. She blinked in surprise.

"The aliens don't tell me much," I admitted.

She paused, no doubt wondering how far to dumb it down. "We study the evolution of the solar system. Running simulations, and comparing the results to what we see and to what we can predict by winding things backwards."

"Backwards?"

"Like a clock. The interplay of orbital mechanics allows us to study disturbances that lead to periodic increases in asteroid activity, spelling doom for the dinosaurs. We try and run it back further still, to a time when the earth was shiny and new, and things were even more dynamic." Her look changed again, a flicker of concern. "Are you okay?"

"Tired." I grinned weakly. "Any chance of a coffee?"

We sat in the professor's cluttered office, cradling mugs with faded science conference logos.

"Any idea why the aliens picked you, Avin?" she asked, after not very much small talk.

"None whatsoever," I laughed. "I suppose as a UN employee, rather than a delegate, I'm considered neutral, especially with my mixed-up heritage, my mother's refugee status. But that's all just a guess."

"I assume you've asked?"

"Oh, yes. The aliens say they have their reasons."

She took another sip of the coffee that was still too hot. "What did you do at the UN?"

I laughed again. "Mostly, I filled water jugs, handed out documents, did my best not to offend the sometimes prickly delegates. One of a legion of hosts and hostesses, flunkies to keep things running smoothly. A nobody."

"And now you're famous."

"Excuse me?"

She gave me that look again and I felt like a failing student. "Everywhere the aliens go, they're headline news. And you, with them."

"Oh." I shrugged. "They confiscated my mobile phone."

She took hers out, a surprisingly dated, scruffy model, and filled me in on what I'd missed. Most of it filmed by scientists and admin staff. The world's press, it seemed, never knew where the aliens were going next either. In plenty of the handheld footage, there I was, following in their golden footsteps, listening and looking bemused.

There was a section of the internet that was adamant I was a traitor to mankind. Another, overanalysing what little was known about me, coming up with wild theories on everything from my nationality to my sexuality, to what made me *special*. Lots of fake social media accounts, some satirical, some just bat-shit crazy, to make up for the lack of posts to my real ones, which had been suspended anyway. All rather frightening.

Professor Benedetto reclaimed her phone. "Of perhaps more importance is what the UN and the world's governments have been up to. They're spooked. It's not just that there are aliens and they're interested in us, but not quite enough to pay a visit. It's the avatars themselves. The where did they come from, and why all doors, physical or otherwise, open for them. I guess that's why they haven't moved against them, that and the worry about what might happen if we did. Plus, the only insight we have into the aliens is what their agents do and ask."

"Good luck learning much from that."

She eyed me for a moment. "You went to CERN, didn't you?"

Discordia

"Yes," I said. "But don't ask me when. The days blur into one."

"One of the quirky things about the sheer amount of data that CERN generates is how they share it. Mostly by sending hard drives by courier. Too much data for the internet.

"The aliens claim to have tapped into our world wide web to learn our languages and our customs, to organise this hectic tour of research centres. All from five hundred million miles away.

"My theory is that the mother ship, busy speeding out of the solar system, is only going to receive a fraction of the data these three autonomous agents collect. A 'mostly harmless' summary, at best."

I stared into the depths of my mug. "You think the avatars are here to condense all of human history and art and knowledge, into the available, limited bandwidth?"

"It is only a theory. We don't actually know how they're doing *anything*. But our own Deep Space Network would take a million years to transfer the entirety of the internet."

I had the sudden image of aliens watching cat videos as the earth vanished to a blue dot behind them, and gulped my coffee.

One of the avatars opened the door of the professor's office, smiling a golden smile. "We're ready."

I wondered if it was the one I'd been with, twenty-four seven, traversing the US, and then Europe. The trio were impossible to tell apart. Two had done their own tours of China, and Russia, and Africa. But, since reuniting at CERN, they and I had travelled together.

We followed to the auditorium. Which, unsurprisingly, was packed. The avatars hadn't batted an artificial eyelid when cameras were set up, so I guessed everyone in the world was about to see this particular demonstration. And I had a front row seat, as did the professor.

Rhapsody of the Spheres

The lights dimmed, and on the screen the solar system was projected.

"This is based on models Professor Benedetto has generated, combined with the latest images from your spacecraft." The avatars were always respectful of our scientists. Less so, of our diplomats and politicians, who they mostly ignored. "Prove it," they might say, when offered a hasty reason for the way things were. And of course, no politician was ever able to do that.

"We have enhanced the visualisation, so that all may see."

The lights dimmed further and the projection expanded to cover the whole of the hall, an impromptu planetarium despite the uneven walls and ceiling. There were low, delighted gasps as our viewpoint meandered between the planets, rendered in exquisite detail, like a fully immersive title sequence of the latest Star Trek franchise. Complete with a soundtrack: I became aware of a growing noise, a haunting melody, ethereal and otherworldly.

"Like musical scales, a solar system is built on harmonies. And like music, merely playing those scales is not particularly interesting. It is the interplay, the transitions, that create the complexity and beauty.

"Professor; we ran the starting conditions for your simulations through an AI, to grade them."

"Grade them?" Benedetto echoed.

"We wanted to know which scenarios were the most beautiful."

Sat so close, I could sense the professor's hand flutter in agitation. "But... why?"

"We have found a correlation between harmonious, *beautiful* solar systems, and civilisations that believe in a deity, even when they are on the cusp of expanding beyond their system. It is most interesting. It would seem that if there is a god behind it all, as many of you believe, then that god is an artist.

Discordia

"We believe we see evidence of that artistry in the evolution of your solar system during the relatively brief seventy-two million years immediately after coalescence." The avatar gave an all too human shrug as the screens and walls showed new-born planets scooping up dust in their path, a set of darkening bands around the sun as rubble was sorted by gravitational forces, the pattern perfectly organised, the music like an orchestra tuning up, gathering itself into a coherent whole. "Then. . . something went awry."

The simulation ran on. One planet was spun from its ordained path, hopping the bands to circle a near companion. The twin planets danced their waltz, the music bright and enchanting, almost joyful. Then, a heavy off-beat and the planets lurched as if one had missed a step, throwing them both as though drunk or out of control.

The noise was ugly, discordant, building up to a squeal that threatened to crack my skull. It abated for a moment, one final clumsy pirouette, then crashed back even louder as the two planets messily collided. It was impossible not to flinch, the sound like a sack full of cymbals being dropped, a clatter of marbles on a tin roof as molten rock was flung outwards. I made to cover my ears, but the sound had already vanished, leaving the audience so quiet I could hear the faint tick, tick of a clock somewhere above and behind.

A spotlight rested on the golden avatar. "What you call *Theia*, crashing into the proto-earth, creating the moon and resetting the earth's evolution.

"We can't be sure exactly how the solar system was meant to be. The chaos of the collision is impossible to precisely predict. But we do know it was not meant to be as it is. And our projections suggest it was *Theia* that carried the seeds of life, that was meant to be our audience, perhaps two billion years earlier than this, rather than the earth."

Rhapsody of the Spheres

My brain was stuffed with cotton wool, the words muffled and nonsensical.

"We're. . . an accident?" Professor Benedetto asked, her voice a croak.

"A *happy* accident, yes." All three avatars entered the spotlight. "We thank you for your patience, professor, Avin Khan, and everyone on Earth. We are done here."

They froze like golden statues. It took a while for someone to bring the lights up in the auditorium, and I sat for even longer as chaos erupted around me.

The anatomy of the avatars wasn't even that interesting, in the end. When we got brave enough to take them apart, after they'd stood surrounded by cameras and armed troops and the like for a week. All their parts were parts that already existed on Earth. They'd been ordered six months earlier, from all across the globe. The agents weren't even autonomous, they'd been controlled, that much was clear, by what, and from where, less so.

Their exteriors were real gold, though. There are replicas in museums from New York to Moscow. No one is willing to say where the originals are. But that was all for later. I escaped the hall and blundered up a grassy bank overlooking the car park. Dusk had fallen, and I was thousands of miles from home.

Professor Benedetto sat beside me. I wasn't sure how long she'd been there. The full moon, in all its stark, bone-white splendour, hung low in the night sky.

"I'm not sure I can look at it the same way again," I said.

She nodded. "I've spent my entire academic career looking at the moon in ways that others would find unusual."

"And now?"

"It is still as beautiful to me as it was when I was a child, and I thought faeries rode on its beams."

I turned this over in my head and came up short. "How do you like being a failed experiment?"

Discordia

"I prefer 'happy accident.'"

"But. . . you believe them?"

She shrugged. "It does feel rather unscientific. All we know for certain is what the aliens want us to hear."

"You think they're telling us a lie?"

"A fairytale. Something that lets people understand that which cannot be understood. That our solar system *is* special—sculpted by some unknowable deity. But that they lost interest, cut the strings, dropped the conductor's baton, long before the first multicellular lifeform evolved. Which means we're solely responsible for who we are now, for what we do to our planet and our solar system."

"No pressure, then," I quipped. A stupid thing to say, but it's like being a little drunk when you were as tired as I was.

We sat as something—bats?—fluttered through the darkening sky. "Do you worry? That they might come back?" I asked.

"Who?" she said, and I heard the smile I couldn't see. "The golden aliens? Or the gods?"

I wondered if we'd be able to tell the difference.

###

About the Author

Liam Hogan is an award-winning short story writer, with stories in Best of British Science Fiction and in Best of British Fantasy (NewCon Press). He's been published by *Analog, Daily Science Fiction,* and Flame Tree Press. He helps host live literary event Liars' League, volunteers at the creative writing charity Ministry of Stories, and lives and avoids work in London. More details at http://happyendingnotguaranteed.blogspot.co.uk

*****~~~*****

Matryoshka
by Douglas Gwilym

Lois Francine Fung went by "Francine." She'd always been Francine, in fact.

She'd never thought about it, but "Lois" made her think of her mother's generation, the carefully obeisant and immaculately coiffed thirty-somethings of the fifties. Francine was very careful to be neither coiffed nor agreeable.

(Eleven. There were eleven hanging signs in the aisle. It was a comfort.)

Besides, she was a scientist, and scientists—it was conveniently common knowledge—have neither time nor patience for hairstyles. She pulled all the hair back or up or over, depending on her mood and where her carefully cultivated appearance of *abandon* took her.

Francine was certain she was no *Lois*. She was an empiricist, and as an empiricist, she knew that all knowledge follows from experience, and that the word for what she was only made sense because knowledge is an *empire*, a place to build a castle on, to take pride in, and to make a little bigger every day.

Rhapsody of the Spheres

She was a chemist. A self-sufficient woman. She worked hard, in an unmarked laboratory in an unmarked suburb. She took the train on trolley tracks to work for a pharmaceutical company that had been, among other things, a major player in the development of RU486, the infamous sweep-it-under-the-rug drug. And she was herself—she found the irony oddly intoxicating—*pregnant*.

(Eleven. There was a man standing in front of her, and a sentence was coming out of his mouth. The sentence was ridiculous but, wait for it, it had eleven words.)

She was only *four months* pregnant, mind. That quasi-intellectual Marilyn Monroe wannabe from the second circle of pop hell kept singing "Ahm... keepin' mah baby" in her head at inopportune moments. When she was trying to balance a four-pound chemical equation, for example. Or when she was trying to push complex ideas about simple social graces through the thick, introverted skulls of her colleagues.

She reflected that the emergence of that song from the depths of her subconscious had actually been the most inconvenient side-effect of her new state-of-being so far. That was unlikely to remain true, of course.

The little OCD hiccups predated her state of incubation. A counselor had once told her they were harmless so long as they didn't cause her or anyone else any harm.

"Thanks," Francine had said dryly, "I appreciate your clearing up what *harmless* means."

She had not parted ways with her parents over politics the way her sister said. What was really at issue was a difference of opinion over the *importance* of politics, and she still had little patience for nonsense. Nonsense, at least, that didn't have solid reasoning behind it.

(Eleven hams huddled in the cooler. *Bliss.*)

Matryoshka

It was the grocery hour. Every other Tuesday from 9 to 10. A time settled upon after some experimentation as the optimal one for minimizing unnecessary and time-consuming human interaction. She'd chosen the store for its strategic position in the city's socioeconomic landscape, of course.

Pring!

There was a certain sound Francine liked to hear, a certain *just right* quality that could be achieved if a grocery item hit the metal basket at just the right speed and angle. It was necessary to improvise, to calculate for size, shape, and shifts in package contents on the fly, in order to get just the right sound. She was hitting her stride today. Holding at about 85 percent success.

A woman stood gawking at her. It was a woman she knew. She smiled, because she knew it would be more of a hassle not to. *Mrs. Norris.* Just as soon as it was socially acceptable to do so, she looked away. Woman was a talker. . . and a trunk-wearing politicali.

Pling! Nailed it again. Holding at a cool 90 percent. Feeling confident, she sent a bag of lima beans in after the block of spinach.

The bag produced a disappointing *krangle* sound. Nothing right about it. It was a hit to the percentages.

Francine frowned and muttered "eleven." If Mrs. Norris heard her, she didn't make any indication. She was walking off at a right angle, grandson trailing behind her and manipulating a wooden toy with his hands.

Sometimes Francine felt suddenly tired. This was threatening to become one of those times. All of the moments were just so unmercifully *complicated.* The possibilities for any given instant too infinite.

Sometimes she felt like she was perched, hovering, at the apex of the universe, looking out across every variable at once. At the best of times, she could see all the moving parts at her feet and knew—sensed—what they were doing and where they were going.

Rhapsody of the Spheres

The boy, Norris's grandson, was standing close by now. Looking up at her with colorless eyes, through washed-out brown hair that looked almost gray under the fluorescents. The toy in his hand was a sort of doll, but shaped sort of like a bowling pin. The boy smiled shyly and held it up for her, first popping the outermost figure apart—then the next smaller, and a smaller one inside.

The baby. This baby I'm carrying. It could be a boy or girl. It doesn't matter, Francine thought. *But dark hair and green eyes would be nice.*

Norris was back. She collected the boy without meeting Francine's eye. The semi-hunchback septuagenarian and the boy—he had a bowl cut—disappeared behind a mountainous advertisement for hearing aids.

Francine had enough incontinence garments at her elbow for a bingo-playing army, but she suddenly went from feeling tired to feeling grand. *Matryoshka*, that was the word. Such a beautiful one. Russian nesting dolls. Boy or girl, the baby would have the perfect name: *Matryoshka.*

She saw clearly then, and the vision made her teeter over the smoked salmon.

She was *matryoshka* herself. Baby Francine inside toddling Francine inside tattling Francine inside all-sass-all-the-time teen Francine inside grad student Francine inside divorcee Francine inside respectable chemist Francine. She could see them all in there, one hiding behind another, and not a single one of them was a *Lois.* That added a sense of security to the clarity.

(Eleven hairs broke free and hung close to her right eye.)

The salmon she tossed made a beautiful *pring!* sound and her mind came into even greater focus. Those so-called "OCD" moments were not just "harmless". . . they were potentially un-harm-ful. They brought some

Matryoshka

simple sense—contrived or not—to the ceaseless complexity of the world all around her.

Her heart welled. She wanted that for Matryoshka. *Mattie?*

Francine looked away from the wall of competing breakfast cereals and abruptly stopped the wheel of the cart from spinning with her left foot. She closed her eyes and took a deep breath. She dared to say it a little louder now: "Eleven." She drank in a breath.

She knew what she wanted for her Mattie. And in an instant, she could see that she would get what she wanted, that it was in fact already a beautiful thing of truth.

"Eleven," she mouthed like a mantra. Was there anything more beautiful? It was a *prime* number. A practical number.

It was a symbol of all that she hoped for for her girl. Or boy. It could be a boy. She would be perfect—they would be perfect. The cashier was smiling too big, looking troubled for her, showing too many teeth. But what did it matter? She felt the smile coming to her own face, this time more naturally.

Everything was right now, and she didn't need the lima beans or spinach to know it. Her girl, her boy, her *Matryoshka*. In her mind's eye, she could see their perfection, wiggling and flexing even now. Plump and pink and glorious.

It would be eleven, and it had always been eleven.

Five on one hand, six on the other.

###

About the Author

Bram Stoker Award finalist Douglas Gwilym has been known to compose a weird-fiction rock opera or two. His short story, "Year Six" is on Ellen Datlow's

Rhapsody of the Spheres

recommended reading list for *Best Horror 14*. He edited *Triangulation* for four years and now co-edits The Midnight Zone—forthcoming edition, *Novus Monstrum,* a collection of never-before-seen monsters, featuring original stories by greats, and new voices, in strange, dark fiction. He reads classics of the proto-Weird on YouTube and has been guest staff at Alpha Young Writers workshop. His short fiction appears in *LampLight, Lucent Dreaming, Novel Noctule, Shelter of Daylight, Tales from the Moonlit Path, Penumbric Speculative Fiction Magazine,* and *Tales to Terrify.*

*****~~~*****

A Touch of the Grape

by Sharon Diane King

    Norma Lamoureaux straightened up from the banker's box, wincing at the pain in her lower back. She pushed back a lock of graying hair, sneezed, sighed deeply, sneezed again. Even before her Aunt Louise had left her doublewide for hospice care, her house had been mired in the dust of decades. Even a sturdy K95 mask, worn religiously, did not go far.
    But the "Friends and Neighbors Grab-Bag," Norma's invitation for coffee and cookies and the chance to leave with sundry mementos from her aunt's house, had been an undeniable success. To wit: Norma no longer had to find a home for her aunt's zebra collection, once occupying nearly all of the spare room. The widower down the block had secured the tinkly goat-bell on its embroidered ribbon, destined for his truck. Isobel, a tiny woman with twinkling hazel eyes and thick white hair, had nabbed half a dozen framed prints of mountain climes: the Alps, the Himalayas, Mount Fuji. Louise's perennially-becurlered next-door neighbor would now cherish her friend's memory via a pearly porcelain egg

Rhapsody of the Spheres

bearing the dewy-eyed face of Jesus, set on a gilt stand. Her aunt's antique brass candle snuffer? Out the door. Her assortment of amulets and talismans? Disappeared. One by one, friends had walked off with treasures: appliances, tools, linens. A book they might never finish, a record they would never play. A few had even carried away an album or two of Louise's exploits to Guam, Lapland, Sri Lanka, Ghana, Bali. Though Norma had selfishly squirreled away for herself the notebook of her aunt's trip to the Galapagos. There, in snapshot after fading snapshot, was her auntie in a gray swimsuit with bold red flowers, flattened on the rocks amidst a colony of salt-sprayed marine iguanas. All were basking in the cloud-minded sun, sharing the same Mona Lisa smile.

One item that had not, alas, departed the premises: the still-dusty-in-places cluster of large acrylic grapes, set among pale green plastic leaves on a thick stem of twisted driftwood. Most of the Lucite globes were of a clear amber color—heaven knows why—but a few, heightening the surreal abnormality of the piece, were shot through with white, giving them a milky tinge. Norma struggled to recall where she might have seen the knickknack in its heyday, during one of her visits to her aunt at her old home. Atop the china cabinet, perhaps? Or on the hi-fi, next to the silver coffee service that always needed polishing, and never got it? No matter. Once its era had passed, the cluster had been shunted into a box, tucked away in a closet, and forgotten.

Until Norma rediscovered it, dusted it off with a rag, and set it prominently on a small inlaid wood table that had belonged to Louise's mother.

"Look at this," Norma had said smiling, as trinket-laden guests headed for the door. "A 70's classic. Now it's retro. We've lived that long."

Some of her visitors had nodded, passing a finger gently over the smooth spheres, chuckling at the thought of how bizarrely ubiquitous they had been, decades ago.

A Touch of the Grape

Others had picked up the cluster, marveling at the heft, the unabashed artifice of the object.

But nobody took it with them.

Ah well, Norma shrugged as she locked up after the last neighbor, clutching an opaque Tupperware full of oatmeal crispies, had left. *To the goodwill tomorrow.* And she fell into bed.

. . .

The blaring of car horns trailing back half a mile had reached an outraged crescendo when the uniformed man strode up to the battered pickup.

"Sir? Is there a problem?"

The wizened, balding man with two days' growth of stubble shook his head, his face fixed on the road ahead of him.

"Sir, I'm afraid you can't stop your car here."

The man nodded, his eyes still focused straight ahead. He smiled.

The car did not budge.

The officer took a breath. "Sir? Just start your truck and move on. I won't cite—"

"Woo-hoo! Take a look at that one!" The man interrupted, bouncing on the padded seat, making the goat-bell hanging from the rear-view mirror give a merry tinkle. He turned grinning to the policeman. "Can't move till they've all gone past, can I?"

The officer stared.

"They?"

"The parade! Never seen anything like it, man!" The grizzled man let out a whoop. "That float with the troll dolls shooting out of the giant Jiffy Pop pan? Far out!" He tossed his head as if shaking back long-lost locks. "But who knew cowbelles could ride polka-dot steers AND do macramé? And that buck-naked band that just passed, playing 'The Streaker?'" He pounded on the steering wheel. "*Don't look, Ethel!*"

Rhapsody of the Spheres

The policeman gazed at the man's euphoric grin, his blown-out pupils, then at the utterly unremarkable intersection in front of them. He took a step towards the pickup's open window, sniffed deeply, pondered for a moment. He shrugged.

"Sir, could I ask you to please step out of the cab?"

The man gazed over the man's shoulder, pursed his lips.

"No problemo, officer. But could you tell that big ol' honeybee buzzing behind you to fly off first? I'm really allergic."

The policeman passed his hand over his eyes, sighed, and called for backup.

. . .

"I'm so sorry, young man," a voice quavered softly. The freckle-faced bank teller looked up from his till and met two wine-dark eyes becalmed in a sea of wrinkles. He nodded, trying to hide his confusion.

"I don't want you to be afraid, or upset," the tiny woman with thick white hair went on, glancing down at her handbag, a capacious brown number in peeling faux leather. Her mouth curved upward, showing small but powerful teeth. "But I have something in here you won't like, and I will use it, if you don't give me 1,400 dollars cash."

The teller's face paled, even to the freckles.

"Larger bills, please. Time's of the essence. It's for Godzilla."

Her hazel eyes peered past the teller as if seeing far into the distance. She waved, smiling toothily once more. The teller glanced over his shoulder at the blank wall. He gulped.

The woman shifted from one foot to the other as the teller counted frantically. She hummed to herself, giving occasional giggles interspersed with gasps, as if all of her dreams were coming true. The wide-eyed youth, trembling, waited until the frail hands with their

A Touch of the Grape

prominent veins had grasped the money before he pressed the panic button.

Which of course was out of order again.

The woman smiled once more as she snap-closed the hasp of her purse.

"Poor Godzilla. Can't fight that nasty Smog Monster without our help. Thank you, young man."

. . .

"Hey, Mom," Colleen Chepstow's voice rang out from the den. "Come see what I just whipped up for Dad's birthday!"

Her mother rounded the corner from her home office, stopped short in the doorway.

"I found this old sewing machine at your friend Louise's estate sale," Colleen said, her long silky hair tumbling around her shoulders. "Giveaway, I mean. So much free stuff—there was this old bunch of grapes, it was so cool—but the machine I knew I could use right away. And I did. See?" She held up the outfit with a flourish.

"It's a leisure suit," she said, oblivious to her mother's openmouthed stare. "Just his size. Material's just too groovy, right?"

"Your father will be. . . overcome." *That much is true,* Mrs. Chepstow thought frantically. The suit's fabric, evidently once a bedspread, was of a paisley chintz in which placid greens and browns alternated with petulant crimsons and irate ochres. Her daughter had paired it with a rainbow peace-sign print shirt she had dug out of the far reaches of her father's closet. The ensemble's eye-watering smell gave assurance that no moth larvae would come near her parent for many generations. If ever.

Mrs. Chepstow gazed at the cacophony on a hanger dangling in wait for her unsuspecting mate, then at her daughter's starry eyes, her smile of joyous pride. She swallowed.

"It's lovely, sweetheart. Lovely."

Rhapsody of the Spheres

. . .

Norma awoke to the buzzing of her cell. She blinked, wincing: the sun was streaming in the bedroom window much too energetically. She groped for her phone.

"Hello?"

"Norma, this is Don Raymond. Ellen won't be able to pick up that clay pot of Louise's she wanted today," the elderly voice rasped. "Can she come by maybe tomorrow?"

"Sure, Don," Norma said, gazing around her in confusion. The room seemed to grow and shrink every time she turned her head, like a sped-up version of *Alice Through the Looking Glass*. "Is she ill?"

"Nope. In jail. Have to go bail her out," the soft voice said matter-of-factly. "Gotta get the funds together. Dunno how long it'll take."

"In jail?" Norma sat up and immediately wished she hadn't. She clutched her forehead. *Were things with wings lurking in the corners of the ceiling?* "What happened?"

"Don't know what got into her, but this morning she got up onto the roof of City Hall and belted out a rendition of 'I'd Like to Teach the World to Sing.' He let out a sigh. "That might not have landed her in jail, but the bra-burning part did." He chuckled. "She did look good up there, have to say."

"Okay, well. . . " Norma took a swallow from the water bottle on the nightstand and swatted at the fairies in iridescent tutus that had descended and were now circling above her. "Shoo!"

"What was that, Norma?"

"Nothing, Don. You take care of Ellen, the pottery will keep."

"Thanks."

She fell open-eyed back onto her pillows. The fairies circling her head linked arms and began a

A Touch of the Grape

rhapsodic chorus of Three Dog Night's "Joy to the World."

Norma's taut face rearranged itself into a smile.

. . .

Norma's head was spinning.

Not merely because she had been seeing horseracing candy bars, singing Wiener Wagons, and tangoing cats every time she opened her eyes, for three days straight. Not because she saw them even when she *didn't* open her eyes.

No, it was the nonstop contacts from her Aunt Louise's friends and neighbors that had been upending Norma's world.

"We just *loved* Louise. And you look so much like her," Dolores Chepstow murmured as she stepped into the living room. "Here's a coffeecake I just baked. You know, I could put on a pot of Yuban, and we could visit, if you have the time? Before I forget, my daughter Colleen knitted this pair of potholders for you. Oh, and she mentioned a funky bunch of grapes you had put out somewhere, and I just had to see?"

Norma now counted half a dozen crocheted afghans draped over her aunt's loveseat. A plethora of copies of *Jonathan Livingston Seagull* and *I'm OK, You're OK* cluttered the coffee table. Around the room there was an explosion of Avon collectibles, sand candles, down-to-the-dregs bottles of Enjoli and Love's Lemon Fresh perfume. Mood rings, pet rocks, ornamental gewgaws displaying LOVE? Too many to count.

But Norma's visitors came to her bearing other gifts: their stories, most of which were, truth be told, implausible in the extreme. The becurlered neighbor swore a phalanx of Scrubbing Bubbles had been duking it out with Mr. Clean in the cleaning supplies aisle in the supermarket. The widower claimed to have seen a giant Alka Selzer tablet plopping into the municipal pool, causing it to fizz up all over the swimmers and prompting

Rhapsody of the Spheres

a near-riot. Who would challenge them? Norma herself had witnessed the Fruit of the Loom Underwear Guys crooning "Rocky Mountain High" to her in her kitchen that very morning. And the neighbors' follow-up tales of traffic citations and lockup details seemed to bear out their accounts.

But the constant irruptions, the cornucopia of curios, did not bother Norma. Quite the opposite: she was filled to bursting with joy at the bounty of visits, the unending stream of new friends that had emerged, unbidden, from the chore of dealing with her aunt's estate. She had never before had neighbors drop by and stay chatting for hours, in all her solitary, quiet, workaday world. Moreover, the universe her new companions brought with them was infinitely comforting, a kind of déjà vu on steroids. Norma's nostrils were filled with the scents of patchouli and sandalwood from reanimated potpourris brought over in ornamental jars. On her aunt's improbably still-functional hi-fi, ""I Can see Clearly Now" vied with "Black and White" for prominence, and guests dancing rhapsodically—albeit equally spasmodically—around the living room was *de rigueur*. Norma's refrigerator-freezer now teemed with retro familiar foods: meatless tamale pie, tuna casserole, jello molds of both sweet and savory persuasions, Watergate cake, endless variations on seven-layer dip. The mini-pizzas that had once been all the rage were flawlessly re-created one evening by Louise's friend Ellen—once she was sprung from jail—split, toasted English muffins covered with tinned marinara and shredded mozzarella, and set under the broiler. After far too many of these—accompanied by Don's endless pours from a gallon bottle of Mateus—Norma had slumped over the table in a carb overload, and slept there all night.

  She awoke the next morning groggy but invigorated, and with a problem.

  She didn't want to leave.

A Touch of the Grape

. . .

"I'm sorry," the mobile home's administrator said, tapping his finger on the red-bordered contract on the table. "Ms. Lamoureaux, your aunt left you her estate, but the mobile home space is a lease. She can't have left that to you, she didn't own it. And we have already leased the space. That home, I'm sorry to say, is going to be demolished at the beginning of next month."

Norma gazed at him levelly. "I'm a senior now, I qualify for admission to this park, correct?"

"Correct. We can put you on the list, you'd be at the top right now. But you are not entitled to *that* space. That's already been rented."

Norma's face clouded. "By whom?"

"I can't tell you that. Just. . . well, someone close who wants to turn it into his garden. I mean, their garden. We allow that, if they pay the full rental price every month."

Norma gazed at the floor, chilled. The one neighbor who had not responded to her invitation, on the other side of her aunt's home, was a man with a withering glare. There was little doubt who her adversary was.

"He—I mean *they*—already paid, you say? But the month isn't over yet."

"Well—" the administrator's voice trailed off. "Sometimes they get a little eager, and we, well, we let them have dibs. Long-term tenants. If you know what I mean."

Norma stared out the window. All the shared good will of the past several days had drained out of her, and she felt hollow.

"Thank you for your time. I guess—put me on your list."

"I'll drop off the papers tomorrow."

. . .

Rhapsody of the Spheres

Norma sat at the dining room table with her fifth cup of coffee. She was clear-eyed in a way she had not been for days. It didn't feel good.

Before her was a note with the numbers of moving vans and storage sheds. She picked up her cell phone, put it down again.

Her glance fell on the inlaid table on which sat the cluster of grapes. She gazed at it for a moment, stood and picked up the arrangement, scrutinizing it from all angles. She turned it over, stared at the label on the bottom.

Her eyes widened.

Made of pure (Hal)Luci(Ni)te by Psychedelics Anonymous, the twisting, curving font read. *For your hippy trippy friends! Fun for all aged!*

Norma sat back down and poured herself the rest of the pot.

. . .

"I'm sorry, but she absolutely insisted," Norma chirped at the sour-faced man standing well back from his screen door. "It was in her will. She gave away things to a lot of different folks, and that one was to go to you." She lowered her voice. "I have to tell you, I think there's something valuable hidden inside. Maybe in the wood stem piece, or in the spheres. She kind of hinted at that."

The glaring eyes lit up. The screen door swung open.

"I'll take it. Thanks."

. . .

Bon Voyage! and *We'll Miss You!* read the signs in front of the mobile home. There were clusters of colorful balloons outside, some twisted into the shapes of tortoises and lizards. Inside the house, bedecked with flowers and seashells, Norma presided over great dishes of lobster rice, plantains, and grilled octopus, while Don Raymond kept popping open more than a few bottles of fine vintages for the partygoers.

A Touch of the Grape

"Well, the place won't be the same without you," his wife said, shaking her head. "Three weeks in the Galapagos!"

Norma's face lit up. "Can you believe it? Longest trip I've ever taken. Pretty much the only one I've been on in decades." She smiled. "I can't wait to swim with the iguanas."

"Just like your aunt," chimed in Isobel, raising her glass. "She waxed rhapsodic every time she talked about it."

"But the best part will be the homecoming," Colleen Chepstow enthused. "We'll make sure to have this place all cleaned up, ready for your welcome-to-your-new-home party."

Her mother chuckled. "From one rapturous moment to the next!"

"Have to say, I don't know what got into Garvey Hilds, changing his mind about this space so quick," Don observed in his soft rasp. "He never struck me as very flexible."

"Well, he said he's coming to this party." Norma smiled. "I wouldn't trouble him much about it, really. He said he's been having trouble sleeping, something about demons and hellhounds chasing him all night long. He'll be ready for a nice touch of the grape, don't you think?"

###

About the Author

Sharon Diane King is an Associate at UCLA's Center for Medieval and Renaissance Studies and director of the troupe Les Enfans Sans Abri, which has performed short medieval and early modern plays in her original translations or adaptations for over thirty years. Her fiction has appeared in numerous publications, including *Dark Recesses Press Magazine*, *Galaxy's Edge Magazine*,

Rhapsody of the Spheres

Kaleidotrope, *On the Premises*, *All Due Respect,* and several anthologies by both Dragon's Roost Press and Third Flatiron Press.

*****~~~~*****

Lost and Hound

by M. R. Abbink-Gallagher

Beyond the cracked sidewalk and the telephone pole with layers of flyers in a rainbow of colors, beyond the patch of dry brown grass, there stood a ten-foot-high concrete block wall caked with dozens of coats of paint. A small shrine was at the foot of it, with burnt out candles, dead flowers, and a few soggy teddy bears. One word of graffito filled the entire wall—red letters on a gold background: Rejoice!

Immediately, Anna flashed on Anthony Burgess's *Re Joyce*, his erudite explication of James Joyce's *Finnegans Wake*, two books she would never read but whose titles always intrigued.

"There's a cock-eyed optimist, huh, Dimes?"

Since he had a dime in each ear, Dimes didn't really hear her murmur, so she repeated it a little louder. But not too much: the morning was too gorgeously translucent to shatter with pointless chatter.

Dimes turned his head from the shrine and gave her his ghostly grin. Still dapper in a suit that was probably older than Anna. And cleaner!

Rhapsody of the Spheres

Anna shrugged, not caring. She'd cared about—*everything!*—for as long as she could stand it. For so long that it wasn't days or years or decades anymore but a *Lifetime*.

And somehow she'd been resurrected. Exhumed herself, so to speak, like a corpse opening and sitting up in the casket as it's being lowered away. No, that was the wrong metaphor. What she had done was way more prosaic, even a bit cliched, something countless others had done, were doing, and would do, what Jack Nicholson did at the end of *Five Easy Pieces*: she just walked away...

Just stepped out of one Life and into another...

In tennis shoes, old Levi's, her husband's gray work shirt.

Didn't say a word to anyone: just left her "wallet" behind at the bus station, in this case her Smartphone (her whole identity was on it—*that* identity—Mrs. Konda—*Please steal it someone!* she'd half-jokingly pleaded then). But instead of hitchhiking a ride on a big rig and disappearing into the misty forests of the Northwest, she had simply disappeared and reappeared on the opposite side of the country, on the stark streets of Bakersfield, California, as far West as that bus ticket she'd bought with her last money could take her.

And at the terminal Anna hadn't stepped out, she'd floated off... was still almost levitating here next to Dimes. 'Course she was a lot lighter now, all that "civilized' fat quickly gone, because eating to survive is a lot different from eating to live. She was a lean, mean thinking animate machine now—as devised by Nature to be one of a multitude of "one-of-a-kinds," like stars.

Dimes set a fresh teddy bear down and then patted her head, and she remembered she was a dog now, had been since getting off the bus, somehow unknowingly transformed during that long ride so long ago. Dimes then had been standing just outside the terminal, rummaging through an overflowing City Of Bakersfield trash can.

Lost and Hound

She'd trotted up, he'd given her a crust of pizza, patted her head, and they'd been inseparable since.

They walked everywhere together, but were a particular fixture in some place called "Oildale," where his deceased older sisters had lived. Their ancestral abode was a big old two-story Victorian-style monstrosity (quaint it ain't!), with ledges of hedges of roses that encircled it like a rosary, that always seemed to be blooming as if rubescently shouting, "Rejoice!" Anna loved it when they'd return here, though it was more than infrequently and only occasioned by some obscure whim only Dimes could decipher. They had a front or back yard or porch and plenty to eat just about anywhere they went in Oildale, yet here was "home," at least to Anna.

"Vamanos, Rainbow," Dimes commanded, as she slurped from a tiny puddle provided by a rare recent summer storm. Realized with a start—*I'm Rainbow now*, and trotted alongside him as he slowly ambled down the sidewalk—the Anna she was forever forgotten.

In the early morning emptiness they started across Chester Avenue. Then she heard it, and Dimes couldn't. A fast moving vehicle, faster then they. It was on them, and all she could do was leap at Dimes and knock him back out of the way. The small car tried to swerve, but its rear bumper clipped her haunch, throwing her in a neck-snapping spin.

She woke up as Dimes and a young man were lifting her into the front seat of a car. "Her name is Rainbow," Dimes was obviously replying to the young man's query. She was surprised she was so lucid. And not racked with agony. The distraught young man ran around and climbed in on the driver's side of—obviously—his car and waited impatiently for Dimes to climb into the back. Dimes leaned in, patted her on the head, gave him a smile either beatific or maniacal, and lurched off into the misty morn.

Rhapsody of the Spheres

She watched the old man creak away, not really surprised. *I love you, Dimes!* She psychically shouted.

After a moment, shaking his head in wonderment, the young man leaned over to pull the car door closed, murmuring to himself, "Why'd that guy have dimes in his ears?"

"Because quarters don't fit," she replied, and that cracked her up. . . and there was the agony. . . along with an aroma of. . . pizza? "Why's it smell like pizza in here?" she asked, raising up a bit to look at him, the pain subsiding. "And yes, I can talk—to you—telepathically. We're somehow linked. 'Kay? Now, why's it—' inhaling doggedly '—why does it smell so *good* in here?"

For a breath catching, unblinking spell, the young man just sat there, poised with his fingers on the ignition key.

Luckily (as usual) he was stoned out of his gourd, so this was easier to take than it might be elsewise. So, after a breathing, blinking few moments, he just said, almost conversationally, "I deliver pizzas, for the local *Parcheesi's*. My name's Gene Emerson. And I'm taking you home with me." Not a request, she noticed; he swiftly adding, "As quickly as possible," and no apology either; but she heard the earnest concern in his voice, saw it on his face—along with that almost comical awestruck disbelief. Believe it he would, she Yoda'd, the rippling pain stifling the ripples of mirth as she settled in for the trip.

When the ride ended, she was lifted again. As tenderly as Gene could, he slid her body onto a soft pile of clothing among the boxes in the garage. He pulled an old coat over the top, creating a cave that emanated the sweetness of old ladies who frequently powdered themselves—a light rose motif that ached with atavistic irony deep in the ancestral interior of her canine brain. Then gently the pizza kid lifted her head to help her lap water from a hubcap. He broke bits of pepperoni and crust

Lost and Hound

into bite-sized pieces and left them where her tongue could reach them. Much later, she heard him practicing within the house what he called his "Orations," that were like songs of rejoicing, as if a jubilantly stoned monk was slamming out poetry of innocence and redemption and universal love. They lulled her to sleep.

Soon she was twitching, lost in canine dreams, her wounds healing even as that (now giant!) vehicle bore down on them, she and Dimes, as they, almost comically, slipped and slid on the slipperiest of streets trying to dodge it.

In the kitchen, dipping his Oreo into a glass of milk, Gene heard Rainbow's little yelps of distress and hurried into the garage. Gave a *Whew*ing smile when he saw she was just dreaming, and looking radiantly healthy, he also noted, a grudging acceptance of the miraculous replacing the stoner astonishment which superseded that rational disbelief.

"She's a *magic* dog," he whispered, which still awakened her, her senses attuned to the subtlest emanations of the streets' zeitgeist.

"Hi," she said to his again wide, astonished eyes. She gave him a moment, knowing Gene's reaction way more appropriate and logical than Dimes's, who'd just treated her as if every dog he met had telepathic powers of human speech. And from their peregrinations she'd found that just wasn't true. She would say something to every kind of canine they met, and all she ever got was indifference or a growl in return. Though, in return, she had no idea what their barks and howls were about, though she certainly felt great doing them herself. As she did now, barking Gene out of his slack-jawed stupor.

After a wan smile, he sank down to the cement floor, almost in a faint, absently nibbled the moist Oreo. There were words floating around in his head, but he couldn't direct them to his tongue. Finally got out: "It's just, you know, just a lot, uh, a lot to get ahold of. . ."; her

Rhapsody of the Spheres

own meant-to-be-comforting smile not helping to dispel the surrealistic unreality.

"I know, Gene, 'cause I'd be freakin' out myself... and—" changing the subject, taking a different tack "—you're not stoned." Her more accusing than questioning tone kind of shaking him aware, hemming and hawing.

"Uh, I, uh, I gave it up. I promised I would if, uh, you know..."

Rainbow couldn't find the right words herself, so she just gave a sharp bark as she climbed out of the clothes pile and sat in front of him, her tail thumping the floor. And now Gene was grinning back.

She stood up on all fours, stretching, and let him tousle her head for a moment, then stepped away, sitting, saying, "Okay, enough. I think we need to address that 'greedish' glint in your eyes."

Indeed, his pupils were like dancing dollar signs as he watched that pile of gold rising. *A dog that—!*

"And only for you, Gene—*Oreo-gone* that you are—wow, that's like a verbal turd, huh? But just like the other kind, once they're out, they're out, right?"

"Right!" Gene chuckled, though still obviously gazing upon her as if beholding the Golden... well, not *Calf*, she thought, but (*What am I?* giving herself a quick glance: *Right:* a mutt)... *The Gilded Mongrel*?

Patiently, she elucidated: "Gene, remember that cartoon with the Vaudeville frog that sings and dances, but only...?"

She couldn't help smiling a little at his falling face. 'Cause she was also picturing in her canine mind that singing and dancing frog doing just that, as obviously a brightening Gene was also thinking the same thing as he began to sing, "Hello, my baby, hello, my honey," she joining him as they each mimicked in their own way that miraculously talented amphibian doing his shtick:

"... Send me a kiss by wire, baby my heart's on fire..."

Lost and Hound

With his arm around her narrow shoulders, and their heads together, they belted out the finale—"Hello, my ragtime *gaaal!*"

Rainbow finished it with a "Ribbet." Drooped to the floor, curled up as if to doze. With that keen dog eye she spied him busting up, and then joined him, his mirth infectious. And then the decider, the divider between friendship and acquaintance—seeing the same worth of a bar of gold in the gold of *silence*. Knowing without crowing that loyalty and love only bloom on a silent flower. If you can hang like the hung, suspended between epiphanies, mutely dangling in a vast emptiness crammed into a finite profusion, then you can befriend. And if it's repeated regularly, be beloved and beloving.

Then, as dogs are wont to do, Rainbow really did doze off. Was with Dimes again, had been with him now for—how long? doggedly calculating. . . how many suns moons summers and winters?. . . and soon realized how hopeless it was, how pointless really, to try to kowtow to the arrogant assumption humans have that Time can be *measured*. It must be *treasured*, certainly, yet Time was truly more an ever-flowing river, immeasurably deep and vastly wide, and Gene's life and her life and all lives merely flotsam and jetsam bobbing along on its current.

"That's trite," Dimes observed. Not a loquacious man but certainly astute.

"Hey! wha'd'ya want, I'm a dang *dog*, dagnabbit."

"No excuse for silly solipsism. And Time *can* be quantified. It is *Life* that eludes any quantifying, any explication. It is truly a mystery—"

"*That we'll never crack*, yeah yeah," Rainbow finished for him, this being an oft-repeated trope, its pat aptness for some reason always annoying her.

"Smarty pants," Dimes said, tousling her head as they stood before that simple shrine again, both admiring this one bold and bright word so brightly and boldly

Rhapsody of the Spheres

rendered in the blood of the Soul and the treasure that is Life there on that stout wall.
 REJOICE!
 And now no longer even a word. Just uh. . . *b'duh.*
. . .
 She smiled up at Dimes smiling down at her. Said, "Whoever graffitoed that is a genius."
 Dimes nodded absently, saying, "Your new friend did it. Gene. When he is stoned—immaculate, as Jim sayeth—'enraptured,' as *he* calls it—then he may possibly be the only Artist extant who can both unravel the skein of the zeitgeists of this era and transcend them with the only durable Truth there is."
 A little stunned by that first revelation, Rainbow hung there suspended, waiting for that second one to be revealed. Her hackles were bristling—even in reality, as she twitched and yipped on the garage's floor while Gene stroked her flanks, almost reverentially, his touch instantly calming her, reassuring her, as in Rainbow's dreams she now ran joyously under a golden sun, almost gliding over a glittering landscape that was almost too heartrendingly beautiful. Touching her, Gene became the dream he'd dreamed dreaming of becoming, of creating. . . something, something so elusive it could only be captured in rapture. *Pursued*, rather, like existence, the dreamers comprehended now, transcending.
 That night she rode with him while he delivered pizzas. And in-between listened raptly as he honed his Orations. Back at the house after work she convinced him that The Wasted Life was the only life for *them*. "You just need a sober co-pilot!"—he agreed.
 So he fired it up, and into the wee morning hours, where the magic was its wildest, Rainbow and Gene howled and Orated, barked and bonged, jubilantly.

###

Lost and Hound

About the Author

M. R. Abbink-Gallagher was born on the bayou and raised in the barrio, with Sister Sledge and brothers Mario—a hue of Man whose # is the &.

*****~~~*****

Museum of the Multiverse

by Anne Gruner

He was ensconced in the *Homo sapiens* exhibit, listening to music, as he often had over the past millennium. He'd fallen in love with humans when he first studied them in his "Sentient Species of the Natural Universe" class. He was impressed that their physiology, though smaller, was so similar to that of his own race, minus the wings, of course. He was young then, still in his birth body, about 40,000 years ago. It seemed like yesterday, a sign he would soon depart for the Ethereal Universe. Back in those days, he'd spent countless hours with the probe tetracubes of Earth, experiencing some 2,000 generations of *Homo sapiens* collected over time. He wrote his school thesis on human cerebral evolution as manifest in cultural and technological advancement.

It haunted him that a sentient creature could live so briefly. In his thesis, he had metaphorically compared humans to a species on their own planet Earth—the butterfly— a flying insect with beauty and purpose that

Rhapsody of the Spheres

lived less than a thousandth of a human lifespan. Though the insect's life was stunningly short, the humans admired them anyway and even collected and displayed their dead bodies. Humans too were interesting and purposeful, but so short-lived their advancement was phlegmatic. It made it easy to dismiss them for not being a serious species. When he was in school, he had argued with his father, who was a Council elder, that they should have given the humans some biosynthetic assistance to allow them to live longer and thereby progress further and faster.

    His father disagreed. "Life is fleeting, Solarik," he would say. "It's also relative. Look at our own race. We have the Extenders who think 50,000 years isn't long enough and want the Council to approve a sixth SimBod so we can live another 10,000 years. But law and tradition have held that five SimBods provide more than sufficient time for our existence in the Natural Universe. It's the nature and quality of the species that matters. It wasn't their short lifespan that caused the downfall of *Homo sapiens*."

    What his father said made sense to him at the time, at least with respect to their own species. One got his or her first SimBod at around five millennia, and if maintained properly, and used with selective regeneration, it lasted another ten to fifteen millennia. The Council had decided eons ago, after disease had been eradicated and artificial intelligence perfected, that they should limit their physical lifespan in the Natural Universe to around 50 millennia. One could depart for the Ethereal Universe sooner, of course, if that were desired, but most did not depart early and found that 50,000 years was adequate time. As Solarik approached the end of his own fiftieth, he wondered what the transition would be like. Would he still be able to hear music? Most other things of a physical nature he was prepared to totally leave behind in the Natural Universe. But music, especially human music, was another matter. He knew it would always be in his

Museum of the Multiverse

mind, but would his being be able to access it? Indeed, would his being desire to do so?

As for the humans, he still believed they merited a longer existence than they ended up with. The probe tetracubes had captured these fascinating creatures in all of their gore and glory. The tetracubes literally absorbed, recorded, and transmitted everything back from distant planets, enabling them to study other sentient species, many of which were now extinct, including the humans. The cubes "did everything but read minds," their scientists would say. Experiencing the tetracubes was like walking among the humans.

Solarik also read all the ancient transcripts from their own early intergalactic explorers who had journeyed through space and time to the planets themselves. The explorers had done this using hypersleep and a large quantity of SimBods—they were the only ones exempted from the SimBod limit. It was almost always a one-way mission due to the distances, and by the time the cube transmissions were received back home, they were so dated that most students were not interested. But not Solarik, who loved ancient intergalactic history. The tetracubes, and the probes and spaceships that transported them, had been a major technological breakthrough of their ancient forefathers. The development of these amazing devices had proceeded virtually without living input once artificial intelligence surpassed their own cognitive capabilities. Many of their citizens doubted that the propulsion and tetracubes could be invented today, like other things that enabled them to live and thrive in comfort that they could not now reinvent. Some thought that meant the final end was near, though most just shrugged off any such concerns as they spent their days traveling for pleasure to near-distant planets.

One of the early explorers who particularly influenced Solarik to study the humans was his 25th great grandfather, who had traveled to Earth during his middle

Rhapsody of the Spheres

millennia years, a period which included humankind's final generations. Solarik studied Grandfather 25's meticulously recorded observations and thoughts. His grandfather had marveled at Earth's staggering biodiversity, which the explorer attributed to the abundance of water, which was what had attracted the probes to the planet in the first place. As far as Solarik knew, the bonding of the hydrogen and oxygen atoms in such immense quantity remained relatively rare in the Natural Universe. Grandfather 25 believed that Earth must have been one of the most beautiful and special planets to exist and thought that the human species was incredibly fortunate. To those given so much, much can be expected he had predicted.

But it didn't turn out that way. The *Homo sapiens* survived a mere cosmic nano-second, succumbing to the carbon trap, which heated up their planet and destroyed its atmosphere. "Carbon-dated," was the phrase used by the Council elders to describe those species unable to master the carbon buildup. The problem was ubiquitous in the Natural Universe, the basic chemical elements and physical forces being the same throughout. Their scientists estimated that fewer than 25% of known civilizations conquered it, though many subsisted much longer than the humans. Solarik knew in the ancient times multi-generational bets were placed on which species would make it. At first the odds on the *Homo sapiens* were very good. They had many redeeming qualities, and the initiative and intelligence to solve the problem.

As it became increasingly clear the human race might not endure, however, some on the Council argued fervently in favor of providing the carbon key. But that violated the Golden Commandment and was forbidden. Minor assistance—technological and medical—could be provided during a species' development, but not the carbon key. The carbon trap required both indigenous ingenuity and cooperation to overcome, and without the

Museum of the Multiverse

latter, it had been shown that a civilization would not advance for long, even if it were given the key. So, in almost all cases, it was denied. The elders judged that humans had the technological potential, but their will was a matter of debate. Some elders pointed to the humans' attempt to colonize a desiccated neighboring planet rather than working together to save their own verdant one. In the end, the Council voted against assistance. It turned out the humans did not manage to rescue their planet, and probe transmissions eventually reflected their extinction.

It made Solarik sad to think about it. Should they have helped the humans? He wondered if *Homo sapiens* still existed in the Multiverse. Their own species had not mastered how to concretely communicate with those who had transitioned to parallel universes once leaving the Natural Universe. So it was still unknown which species they might encounter later. Solarik knew he would no longer exist in the Natural Universe if and when sentient life reemerged on Earth and doubted his descendants would either. Whatever sentient life that might reappear in tens of millions of years wouldn't be human anyway. Well, not very likely. So he was glad he'd mastered *Homo sapiens* studies and knew its history so well, as short as it was. And he was always the invited guest lecturer when *Homo sapiens* was on the agenda.

What still continued to bring him pleasure after all these millennia was listening to music in the *Homo sapiens* exhibit. In these hallowed museum halls, the elders, with the accumulated knowledge from the beginning of time, had preserved for eternity one item, one aspect, of each civilization. So eons after the extinction of a sentient race, there would be a remnant representing the species, constituting its eternal contribution to the Natural Universe. At the time, it was said that with respect to humans, the Council's decision what to archive in the museum was quick and unanimous—their music. Solarik regularly borrowed large

Rhapsody of the Spheres

chunks of it to enjoy in his residence. His favorites list of music was extensive, and by far, the human species was the most represented.

It was rare for a species to possess such a depth and breadth of spirit so pleasurably communicable to other species that one could spend tens of thousands of hours listening to it and never tire. He was not alone in feeling this way. The music exhibit was a favorite with most museum members. He would listen for hours to the richness and variety, and when there were words, he heard the original sounds and sensed their meaning through intuitive translations. He could dial into any period or style and Control would match his mood and subconscious needs. Having actually studied *Homo sapiens*, the words meant more to him than to non-specialists. Sometimes the sounds made him cry, sometimes rejoice. Sometimes the rhythm made him want to shake every part of his SimBod. It was better than ingestion, drugs, or mental stimulation. They were really good at music, even if they couldn't save their planet. He shook his head—considerably larger than his human counterpart's—and shrugged his wings. What a magnificent race the humans could have become.

As he listened, his attention was caught by one tune, similar to others, but not quite the same. He queried Control. Twentieth century. Sixth decade. Ah, yes— rock and roll, his memory reported from its pre-modern sentient species stack. The piece integrated beguiling instrumentals from their eastern world, so different from the resplendent seventeenth and eighteenth century concertos and symphonies that he adored. His great grandfather actually had warned of the danger of addiction to human music. It must be hereditary, he thought, as he planned to spend the preponderance of his final days plugged into his *Homo sapiens* music collection.

###

Museum of the Multiverse

About the Author

Anne Gruner's work includes a Pushcart-nominated short story in "Constellations: Journal of Poetry and Fiction," and other fiction, creative non-fiction, essays, and book reviews in Hippocampus Magazine, Avalon Literary Review, Silver Blade Magazine, Chicken Soup for the Soul, Stories from Langley anthology, The Intelligencer: Journal of U.S. Intelligence Studies, The Cipher Brief, and War on the Rocks. Her poetry has appeared in Beltway Poetry Quarterly, Plum Tree Tavern, Jalmurra, Humans of the World, Written Tales, Spillwords, Superpresent Magazine, Topical Poetry, Old Mountain Press anthologies, and is forthcoming in Amsterdam Quarterly and Take 5ive Journal.

*****~~~*****

Physics for Witches

by Monica Joyce Evans

"He paints faster."

I set my glass down, carefully, and counted to four. "That shouldn't matter. Why does that even matter?"

My agent shrugged. She was drinking something pink and bubbly, like she'd been celebrating. I was drinking Scotch I couldn't afford, talking to her on the video wall that I definitely couldn't afford, that she'd talked me into buying because she thought maybe video art would sell. And I hadn't sold a piece in months. "Tantrums won't help," she said.

This time I did throw my drink, which shattered on her oversized face, right above her temple. Then I took a breath. "Helps a little," I said.

"I raise my glass to your continued bad temper," my agent said, and waved it at the empty studio behind me, devoid of canvases. "Shouldn't you be working?"

"David Marks," I said, like it was a swear word. The wall flickered badly, and I was still sane enough to know how much its loss would hurt. And the Scotch. "Hell with him."

Rhapsody of the Spheres

"Oh, he's friends with everyone there," my agent said. "And half the angels. You look a little like him, you know."

I pulled a cheap beer from cold storage and considered throwing it too. David Marks was a tall, rangy, soulful man with dark eyes and the charisma of an incubus. I was a tall, rangy woman with the same dark eyes and angled cheekbones, which made me look like an angry vulture. "I think he looks like me."

David Marks and I lived seven miles apart. We'd gone to the same school, had the same teachers, the same tastes and influences. And yet, I'd had two shows. He'd had seven. I had a minor profile in *Forum Aesthetica*, he'd had a major one. Another show in the works, a big one.

And every piece of his I'd seen lately, everything getting attention, was near identical to work of mine. Work I'd started but hadn't finished.

"And he's very good looking," my agent said, musing on her glass. A little too long and thoughtful.

"You've signed him," I said.

"No," my agent said, but she drew the word out and wouldn't look me in the eye.

I waited.

"Not formally," she said. "Nothing official."

I sat down, the beer between my hands turning my fingers cold. She'd been a good agent. I really thought she'd be the one to turn things around for me. Once David Marks signed—and he would—she'd drop me faster than I could throw the beer.

"He's just so productive," she said, and looked reproachful for a moment. "Your last show, the pieces on the wall were barely dry."

"They were up, though," I said.

"Not that many," she said. "It might be a good thing, you know, a little healthy competition. You and David could be very good for each other."

Physics for Witches

I turned to look at my half-finished canvases and sketches, piled up out of the video wall's camera range. Good ideas that I just wasn't ready to stop thinking about. And now I was afraid to work on them, wondering how many of them I'd see at David Marks' next show.

How the hell was he doing it?"

"He can be very charming," my agent said.

"Yes, he can," I said, and fired her. Fifteen minutes later the video wall was decoupled, the canvases were draped in protective film, and I was leaving the city to break a promise to myself.

It was time to visit Nonna.

. . .

She had what she called a "hut in the deep dark woods," which was a nice house that she'd dressed up to look as dilapidated as possible. There were bird's feet hanging from the porch rails when I got there—mostly sparrows, but one might have been a hawk—and flat clusters of hanging crystals, and something wet and red hissing over a brazier.

"Entrails?" I called. "Really?"

"I'm trying a look," Nonna yelled back, and stuck her head out the window. She grinned at me, face fat and squashy as a wizened apple. "Not sure it fits."

"It really doesn't," I said, stepping onto the porch, past two dead rosemary plants and a metal thing hung with strips of gold-edged paper. The porch brazier was lit by an old Bunsen burner, hooked up to a solar battery. No video walls here. Nonna only ever saw people in person.

"If I had the time," Nonna said, waving me around to the kitchen, "I'd raise the whole thing on stilts and dress 'em up like chicken legs."

"It would certainly leave an impression." Inside, there was gumbo on the stove, close to burning, and four flat-faced cats glaring down at me from the cabinets. One was wearing a little pointed hat. "Had a lot of visitors lately?"

Rhapsody of the Spheres

"About the same," Nonna said, and stuck a spoon in the gumbo. The cross-eyed head of a snake surfaced, hissed in my direction, and sank back into the gloop. A digital overlay, I thought. It was definitely a look. Nonna wrinkled her nose and pushed the pot to a backburner. "Bit of a failure," she said, and made two swipes on an off-kilter datapad she'd stuck to the wall. The word "gumbo" was crossed off, under "fesenjun," "bibimbap," and "risotto."

I rolled my eyes. Nonna was a retired physicist, the sort that had been Department Head here, Dean of the School there. Federal granting agencies knew her by first name. Insufficiently productive professors had quailed at the sight of her, hustling down the hallways and poking her head uninvited into labs, like she was somebody's nosy grandmother. Which, technically, she was.

"Fanesca," Nonna said, making notes. "Haven't tried fanesca. Have a seat there," and she waved without looking at the kitchen table. I obliged. The witchery was a new hobby, one that had apparently been going well. I'd promised myself I would never take advantage of it. Better to succeed on my own merits.

Of course, that was before my merits were succeeding without me.

I let Nonna hand me a bowl of simple brown rice and a beer, and sat under the little abstract painting I'd given her, the first one that had been worth anything, and poured out my troubles. "I just don't understand it," I said at the end. "He's never been to my studio, there's no cameras, my work's under lockdown. My brain is on lockdown. How is he doing it?"

Nonna smiled and leaned back in her chair. "I've always liked that one," she said, gesturing to my painting with a thick-stemmed pipe before lighting the bowl.

I looked again. It was close, very close, but. . . "This isn't mine," I said. And then, "He's been here. David Marks."

Physics for Witches

"Well, then," Nonna said, and blew a smoke ring. I slapped the smoke ring away, and it dissipated into fluff. "But it's my work. My shows, my career. Even my agent. Nonna, he's stealing me!" I stood up, spilling rice across Nonna's white and yellow tiled floor, and the cats scattered. "Everything. Even you. How does he even know about you?"

"I introduced myself," Nonna said. "At your last opening. Which was a while ago, you know. Sit down, honey, you'll give yourself an aneurysm." She waggled the pipe at me, and calm washed over me like a tide.

I sat down.

"Now," she said. "Let's talk about physics."

"Nonna, I'm here for witchcraft," I said.

"Physics first," she said. "What do you know about quantum entanglement?"

"It's spooky business. Nonna, I'm not a graduate student."

"Einstein said, in fact, that it was spooky action at a distance. Not far wrong," Nonna said. She pushed herself up out of the chair, pipe in hand, and opened the pantry. Two of the cats trotted back into the kitchen, hopeful. "Do you remember how it works?"

I sighed. "It's when two particles are completely separate, but their states are correlated in ways that don't make sense with normal physics."

"Classical mechanics," Nonna said. "All physics is normal, even the bits we argue about. Close enough!" She pulled a small canvas from the pantry and brought it to the table. My original painting, near identical to the one on the kitchen wall. "Now. Subatomic particles, yes. Could two people become entangled? In a quantum way?"

I stared. "Nonna, that's the stupidest thing I've ever heard."

"Isn't it, though." Her smile was brighter than the knives on the wall. "Never let it be said that you and David Marks are that alike."

Rhapsody of the Spheres

"Does he think. . . " I looked at his painting, then back at mine. "Nonna, are David and I entangled?"

"Of course not. Even the undergrads know better. You're upset, so we'll let it pass," Nonna said, and sat back down. "But David Marks thinks you are. And he's remarkably eager to take advantage of it." The gumbo burbled, and Nonna smacked the pot with a spoon until it died down. "You were always the more talented artist. Even I could see that."

I touched the canvas I'd painted and snatched my fingers back. The paint was so hot it burned. "Nonna, what did you do?"

"An experiment," she said. "That's the nice thing about witchery. No forms, no grant proposals, no institutional review board worrying about how you treat your human subjects. . . . It's refreshing, really."

"You connected us," I said, looking from David's painting back to mine. "That's how he's stealing my work. He's pulling directly from me."

"I'll admit he gave me the idea," Nonna said. "It was just coincidence at first. You do have similar influences, similar styles." She snorted. "David Marks doesn't know a thing about physics, but five minutes of looking up a definition, and he thinks he's got the keys to the universe." She sat back, smug as the cats on the cabinets. "How fortunate, that he met a sweet old lady who just happened to be an expert in spooky quantum weirdness. I thought I'd overplayed my hand, getting him to repaint something of yours."

My hands were shaking. I put them flat on the table. "So, he thought he was stealing my ideas. . . And you fixed it so he actually was? Why would you do that to me?"

"Sweetie," Nonna said, and smiled bright as a moon with teeth. "Because I love you. And because your former agent is right. He paints faster."

Physics for Witches

I thought about it. Nonna brought me another bowl of rice. By the end of my second beer, we were laughing like a pair of super villains, and I was planning my return to the city.

. . .

When I got back to my studio, I painted fast. It felt good, I realized, not to feel like everything had to be perfect, or even passable. I slapped paint on canvases like a bomb would go off if I didn't finish in time. I finished a whole series in seven days, then a second series in another five.

Then I waited.

Two months later, I covered the finished canvases, dressed myself like an adult, and left my studio for David Marks' big new show. There were rumors that he'd made some last-minute changes, very exciting—that was my former agent at work. But she was savvier than David. "Bold new direction" was often code for "lower your expectations."

There were more people than I expected, but nobody was mingling. The gallery hummed with low, concerned voices, some very intense. Some of them quietly angry. Hesitant congratulations, demurring comments to the artist, who stood in the center of the crowd, tall and charming and very much alone.

I moved closer to where he was standing.

"Dana!" he crowed when he saw me, and there was desperation in it. "And how's your work going? You've been quiet lately."

"I've been busy," I said. His eyes flickered back and forth, searching my face for answers. Did I know what he'd been doing to me? Had I figured it out?

Had I done something back?

"This is striking," I said, nodding towards my work on the walls. "Brave choices."

His smile was a rictus. "I've had some very positive reactions this evening. Lots of interested parties."

Rhapsody of the Spheres

He waved at the array of paintings behind him. Among them, slapdash copies of a Lassnig, a Pica, a McKenzie. Two by El-Salahi. Another by Marden. Not their most famous works, not by far, but brazenly obvious to a critic.

I'd worried, briefly, that it would backfire. How bold, they might say. What fresh commentary on art as branding, or art as commerce, or art as ego. Turns out I hadn't given the critics enough credit.

They eviscerated him.

I kept my favorite review, the one that called the works "defanged. . . A witless waste of blatant self-aggrandizement." My own show opened a few months later, to little fanfare but modest reviews, three sales, and a happily busy new agent. Nonna didn't come, but she sent me David's copy of my little red painting: cool to the touch, and crisped at the edges.

I hang it next to the video wall, which I'm refusing to fix. There's only room for one painter like Dana Marx in this world, and—thanks to my Nonna—that's me.

About the Author

Short fiction by Monica Joyce Evans has appeared in multiple professional markets, including *Analog, Escape Pod,* and *Nature: Futures*.

*****~~~~~*****

Grand-Père's Last Transmission

by Bev Vincent

Everyone in town gathered at the meeting hall whenever a new message from the man they called Grand-Père was announced. They could have watched from home—the transmission was available worldwide—but the locals held Grand-Père in high esteem. He had come from here, after all, and look how far he had gone.

His messages were coming less frequently, though, and after each one people wondered if this might be the last. The most recent, nearly two years ago, had been interrupted by galactic interference. Grand-Père's image had been faint and jerky, and then he was gone altogether, after only a dozen minutes or so.

The stage where Grand-Père was expected to appear was currently occupied by a roaring artificial bonfire that made the fermium-powered radiator warming the room seem homier, even though it had been generations since anyone had burned wood or anything else for heat.

More than half of those present claimed to be direct descendants of Grand-Père. For many this claim was true, and there were some in the hall who didn't make

Rhapsody of the Spheres

the claim who were also descended from the town's most famous resident, unbeknownst to them. A century is a long time in the life of a tightly knit community, and not every liaison becomes common knowledge, the active rumor mill notwithstanding.

Some of the men were playing cards—a version of Auction 45 that would have been more or less familiar to Grand-Père—and a number of the women were knitting, but most of those in attendance simply chose to catch up with their neighbors while enjoying snacks and beverages. There was plenty of steeped tea and coffee, plus sandwiches and sweets made by the women of the community, just as they'd done since time beyond memory. The world may have moved on elsewhere, but here the old traditions were still observed. This was a special place, after all, a *chosen* place, and the town clung to its glory with a ferocity reserved for those who knew they lived in a location that would forever be part of the world's history. Though the town was remote and the climate often unwelcoming, people still came—all these decades later—to visit the place selected by The Visitors.

A few minutes before the appointed hour, the bonfire flickered out and was replaced by a man perched on the edge of a tall stool. He looked to be about sixty, with a wild mop of curly blond hair tending toward grey. His face was long and narrow, and he wore glasses, an affectation of a long-ago era that made him seem quaint and paternal. He had the mien of someone about to launch into a tall tale—and that was exactly what those in attendance were hoping for. Although Grand-Père was too young to remember the days when storytellers wandered from community to community, exchanging the promise of a lively story for a hot meal and a place to sleep, he fashioned himself after those long-ago wanderers. For what was he if not one of their kind translated into the modern era?

Grand-Père's Last Transmission

The children—and there were many, for the nights here were long and dark and cold—stopped their playing and gathered in a semicircle on the floor in front of Grand-Père. For the moment he was stationary, a placeholder for the celebrated man himself. Then the image flickered and came to life, becoming Grand-Père, projected from some far reaches of the galaxy. Maybe even from a different galaxy. Who knew? The locals understood little about the universe outside of this small, isolated town, no matter how much they pretended otherwise.

The room fell quiet. Cards were laid on tabletops, face up or face down, it didn't matter. Sandwiches were lowered to plates, half-eaten. Tea, so recently sipped with eager affection, was allowed to grow cold. Even the eldest present sat up straighter in their chairs.

"Greetings, my friends," Grand-Père began, as always. He spoke in a heavily accented form of the language, a relic of his upbringing many, many years ago. "I hope you are all doing well, and I send you my fondest greetings from. . . " Here, the sound went strange, as if something had interfered with the transmission. Or it may have been that the words Grand-Père uttered were so odd, so *alien*, that they sounded like static to human ears.

His image was clear—better than during his previous transmission—but even so he flickered alarmingly from time to time. "I'm pleased to see so many of you gathered here tonight," he said, and the people of the small town knew he was talking specifically to them and not to the billions scattered around the planet who were also watching and listening.

"I know it's been a while since I last spoke to you, although I must confess that my concept of time has changed during my wonderful travels." Indeed, he looked almost exactly the same as in images captured on the day he departed. Generations had blossomed, withered and died, but he hadn't changed much.

Rhapsody of the Spheres

"I am feeling particularly nostalgic at the moment," Grand-Père said. "I've been remembering with fondness the days when I lived among your ancestors. So, if there aren't any objections, I thought I'd tell you about what happened when The Visitors came. I'm sure you all know the story, although it may have changed with the telling over the years. This is how I remember it, anyway, like it was yesterday. Which, for me, it almost was. Time runs oddly out here. Sometimes I wonder if it passes at all.

"They simply appeared overnight," Grand-Père began, and just like that, everyone was swept away. They forgot where they were, captivated by a tale that was integral to their cultural identity. This town continued to exist in its present form because of that day.

They simply appeared overnight, materializing much as Grand-Père did before his audience, except they were *really there*. They didn't come in rockets or flying saucers. The residents of the town went to bed one night, and woke up the next morning to discover they had been invaded. The *planet* had been invaded, in fact, but only here.

At first, of course, there was panic and confusion. The townspeople were ill-equipped to fend off an invasion, but they weren't defenseless. Polar bears were a constant threat, so everyone owned a rifle. However, the aliens—for they were clearly not from 'round here, as one old timer so succinctly phrased it—didn't seem threatening. They appeared to be unarmed, and no one was harmed in the aftermath of the invasion, although a few warning shots were fired by men who would later deny they had been afraid.

The Visitors looked unusual, but their overall shape and features were vaguely humanoid. They were short and stocky, like sumo wrestlers. Their bodies were covered with thick white fur, which made them resemble movie renditions of the abominable snowman, so they were called yetis at first. They molted whenever the

Grand-Père's Last Transmission

temperature rose above 25°, which made them unpopular house guests during the summer months.

Their heads contained the same sensory apparatus as the people of Earth, plus a couple of extras. On their foreheads they had recessed cavities that allowed them to perceive emotions, a feature that greatly enhanced their ability to communicate long before a mutual language was established. They also bore dark panels on their necks, behind the unusual flaps that served as ears. These, the townspeople came to understand, allowed The Visitors to perceive time in much the same way that their eyes allowed them to comprehend distance.

As The Visitors explained, once people learned how to communicate with them, they had never bothered attempting to master space flight because they had realized its limitations early on. No one would ever reach a distant planet through jet propulsion. Rather than spending valuable resources and time on a method of travel that had obvious, severe limitations, their smartest and brightest had contemplated the nature of reality, deduced its most sophisticated secrets and figured out how to make great strides across space and time. Their trip to Earth had been instantaneous, although enormous amounts of energy had been expended, using technology they couldn't begin to explain.

The Visitors brought their own accommodations and supplies with them, so the locals were not inconvenienced. It took a while for a measure of trust to be established between the species. This town was a place, after all, where people from nearby communities were regarded with suspicion. They could be warm people, but they could equally be cold. Now, though, they had a secret that became a point of pride. The Visitors reassured the townspeople that this was the only place on the planet they had chosen to visit. For months, their presence remained unknown to the rest of the world. The townspeople knew that as soon as the news got out, they

Rhapsody of the Spheres

would be invaded once more, by citizens of Planet Earth. Everything they treasured about this little place in the frozen north would be trampled and ruined.

Eventually, of course, word of The Visitors' presence did get out to the world at large. The Visitors wanted it that way, and so it was. But they were aware of the implications and took precautions. No one was allowed to come to the town without the express permission of the residents. This was generally only granted to people who had moved away and wanted to come back to visit family and friends, not to curiosity seekers or foreign dignitaries, which were much the same to their way of thinking.

The Prime Minister and a small entourage were offered a private audience during a low-key visit to the town that was primarily ceremonial. The Visitors then sent delegations around the planet to pay their respects to—and to share intelligence with—the various world leaders. This was back in the days when the globe was divided into numerous, arbitrary political entities. Such travel for them was as simple as a trip next door.

The Visitors arrived at a time when there was relative peace on the planet, but there had been, in recent years, an alarming trend toward nationalism that had the potential to boil over into ugly conflicts. It didn't take long for the political and social climate to change in response to the news of their arrival. It was such a subtle invasion that few felt threatened, and even the most paranoid nations soon realized they were dealing with entities with vastly advanced technologies. No sabers were rattled, no threats issued against them. For a wonder, most of the minor skirmishes between nations died down, too. It was almost like The Visitors had brought a peace serum with them. However, it was simply their presence, according to Grand-Père, that had that effect. Their timing couldn't have been better.

Grand-Père's Last Transmission

The Visitors learned everything they could about the Earth, its inhabitants and their technologies. They always discovered something new in their travels, they said, no matter how primitive the civilization. *And how primitive are we?* the people inquired, afraid of the answer but needing to know all the same. *Advanced enough for us to visit*, came the response, and that was enough to satisfy most.

They stayed in their northern enclave for three years. They couldn't explain to anyone's satisfaction exactly where they came from—they had been traveling for so long that they came from myriad places or from nowhere at all—or why they had chosen this remote town for their base, so myths arose about what made the place so special. No outsider had the nerve to debunk these fables, and Grand-Père was always happy to reinforce them during his transmissions. He was from here, after all.

Eventually, the time came for The Visitors to depart. They offered to take two people from Earth with them, something they did everywhere they went. Ideally the two would be a mated pair from this town. No one would be forced to go, though, and if no one on the planet wanted to join The Visitors on their travels, so be it.

Grand-Père and his wife, Eloise, talked through a long cold night. They had several grown children, old enough to have spouses and children of their own. How could they leave their family behind? How could they give up seeing their grandchildren turn into little people and, eventually, big people? How could they miss out on meeting the others who would come after? The Visitors reassured potential volunteers that they didn't have to miss anything. They would be able to see their family and friends whenever they wanted.

So, they debated back and forth all night long, and by the next morning they had arrived at a decision. They didn't share it with their children or anyone else, because

Rhapsody of the Spheres

they were afraid someone would talk them out of it. That's how fragile their resolve was.

After breakfast, during which they ate hardly anything at all, they made their way to the compound where The Visitors lived, afraid they would see a long queue of people—other volunteers vying for the opportunity of a lifetime. The chance of a thousand lifetimes.

But, no, they were the only ones there, and it seemed like The Visitors had been expecting them. They were welcomed with open arms, and The Visitors immediately sent out word that the positions were filled.

So, Grand-Père and Eloise joined The Visitors and, the very next day, vanished from the planet as mysteriously as The Visitors had arrived, traveling to the next place on their itinerary. They reported back often on their adventures, and a message from The New Visitors was guaranteed to bring the planet to a halt, as everyone clamored for details about places so exotic that language could scarcely contain it.

Not all of their "return visits" were global. The New Visitors sometimes appeared to just their family, or to the people of the town. They never returned in their natural forms, but it was almost as good as being there, and if they had any regrets about their decision to leave, they didn't let on. Grand-Père and Eloise were the surrogates of everyone on Planet Earth, their emissaries to the stars. If no one else could hope to travel to such far-flung places—for The Visitors had not seen fit to share the secrets of interplanetary travel—they were gratified to know that two of their kind were having the most amazing experience anyone could ever hope for.

There came a day, many years after The Visitors departed, when the man who had come to be known around the world as Grand-Père—in part because of the passage of time and in part due to the generations that he had spawned who continued to live in the town—appeared

196

Grand-Père's Last Transmission

to them alone. Grand-Mère, he said, had taken a different journey. These things happened, even to The Visitors, he said, who were more like us than they were different.

After that, Grand-Père travelled with The Visitors by himself. He continued his occasional transmissions, and always seemed enthusiastic and excited when recounting the things he'd seen and experienced, but there was a tinge of sadness about him, too. In a transmission to the town, he confided that he had lost some of the thrill of adventure now that he didn't have Grand-Mère to share it with him. He enjoyed the company of The Visitors, and meeting creatures on so many different planets, but it wasn't quite the same.

Still, he ventured on, and the years and the decades passed. Grand-Père was always interested to hear news about his descendants and about world events. The Visitors' arrival hadn't been a panacea, but things improved greatly over subsequent generations. Borders fell, peace between peoples was established, and few were hungry, thirsty, or otherwise disadvantaged. The planet faced an ecologically uncertain future, but measures had been taken to forestall a crisis, in part using technology supplied by The Visitors. People were still human, though, and they occasionally did horrific things to each other—both on a small scale and large—but on the whole things were vastly better than before The Visitors arrived.

Grand-Père pulled himself upright, his story drawing to an end. The children gathered at his feet were the first to notice something happening. The transmission suddenly grew clearer than ever and there was a sense of a presence in the room that hadn't been there before. The room went completely quiet—no one dared breathe for several seconds—and then a huge grin broke out on Grand-Père's face. He stepped down from the dais and opened his arms to be embraced by the townspeople. His long journey had come to an end.

###

About the Author

Bev Vincent's most recent book is *Stephen King: A Complete Exploration of his Work, Life, and Influences.* She is also the author of over 120 short stories, including appearances in *Ellery Queen, Alfred Hitchcock,* and *Black Cat Mystery* magazines, two MWA anthologies, and a few of the Level Best anthologies. Her work has been published in over 20 languages and nominated for the Stoker (twice), Edgar, Ignotus, and ITW Thriller awards. In 2018, she co-edited the anthology, *Flight or Fright* with Stephen King.

*****~~~~~*****

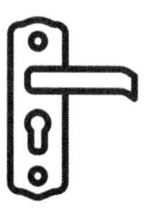

Changing of the Guard
by Taylor Dye

Two kids.

Seemingly no older than thirteen, they stroll down a cobblestone, residential sidewalk in the in-between hours of sunset and darkness. The street that runs alongside them is devoid of traffic, and as such, the neighborhood children stake their claim to the road amidst their own activities—hopscotch, jump rope, an improvised baseball game with a chalked out *X*, a spare glove, a trashcan lid, and a storm drain standing in as the bases. The children are all busy with their diversions—they hardly pay any mind to the two unfamiliar amblers.

The two of them are dressed in similar fashion, as long-lasting pairs often are. For this occasion, they take on the appearance of the dispossessed: down-at-heel boots and scruffy pants, slightly torn; plain, unbranded shirts under dirtied overcoats; worn scarves and faded winter caps. Though the children playing in the street sport clothing of a slightly higher quality, the pair on the sidewalk draw no attention to themselves.

It would be of little consequence to them, however. They prefer their unaffected style.

Rhapsody of the Spheres

"So what's the problem?" Case asks, perplexed.
"There is no problem," Beat answers.
"Then what are we talking about?"
"I don't know. You tell me."
"Oh, here we go again," Case exhales, rolling his eyes.
"I'm sorry?"
"You always do this, Beat."
"I know. Isn't it fun?"
"Hilarious, Beat."

Thunder grumbles in the distance. The other kids are too involved in their games to hear it. It isn't directed at them anyway.

Beat giggles, her laugh almost musical. Case glances up to the sky.

"Looks like rain," he mutters.

Beat looks over to him and grins. It's mischievous.

"More like, 'Dearie me! It sounds as though the Boss is displeased with the unnecessarily flippant remark that was directed at my very bestest friend in the whole, wide world. My sincerest apologies, Beat.'"

Case smiles and pulls Beat's knitted cap over her eyes.

"My sincerest apologies, Beat."
"Why, I appreciate it, kind Sir."

They continue on, and the sky grows dark enough for the streetlights to flicker on. Directly in their path, however, one lamp has long since burned out, now providing only a darkened circle in an otherwise glowing urban playground. A single child stares up at the lamp while sucking her thumb and clutching her scruffy doll by the leg, its head resting on the pavement.

Nearing the unlit area, Case gazes up at the lamp and nods, as if acknowledging its presence.

The streetlight blinks on.

The small child is bathed in an orange-tinged, fluorescent glow and pulls her thumb out of her mouth,

Changing of the Guard

spreading her arms wide, seemingly attempting to grasp as much of the light as her tiny arms could carry. Why the light suddenly decided to shine is of no importance to the girl—only that before it wasn't, and now it is. Her doll waves in the air as the girl twirls in the lightened circle.

Beat, seeing—and even more than that, sensing—the small girl's innocent and newfound delight, hops off the sidewalk and begins spinning with the child. Beat's hair, flowing out from underneath her cap, dances around her face as she twirls, emulating the wavy movements of the child's doll.

Case, still on the sidewalk, smiles.

. . .

Later, after the kids on the street have been ushered into their homes by their caregivers, Beat and Case arrive at their destination, an unassuming brownstone not unlike the others that line both sides of the street. The clear sky is showing the final remnants of twilight, and a plethora of stars and galaxies sparkle overhead, clearly visible despite the well-lit neighborhood. A porch light burns bright beside the entrance to the brownstone, welcoming any evening visitors. Beat tries to catch a glimpse through a ground-floor window, while Case surveys the multi-level residence.

"Thoughts?" Beat asks as she peeks through the glass and the virtually transparent curtains on the other side.

Case slips off his toboggan—nearly identical to Beat's—and weaves his fingers through his silvery-blond hair as he continues to look up, as though contemplating a climbing expedition.

"I wish that chimney was wider," he says. "Then, we could go down like Nick."

"Technically, we still could," Beat glances over to Case.

Rhapsody of the Spheres

"Yeah, but with a chimney that small, who knows how big the fireplace will be?"

"I can't tell," Beat said, looking inside again.

Case fits his cap back onto his head.

"Let's leave the theatrics to *Hoteiosho* then and just go inside like normal people. She'll invite us in anyway, even if she hasn't already."

"Fine by me," Beat replies. "And I see your Japanese is coming along nicely."

Case smiles in response.

"Madam," he bows and steps aside, waving Beat to the door.

Beat rubs her hands together, miming the actions of someone chilled to the bone, although she feels none of the cool November conditions. Case smirks beside her.

"Couldn't resist, could you?" he questions, chuckling. He knows she isn't cold. He isn't either.

Beat sticks her tongue out at him.

"I like to give off the impression that I am actually doing some work," she says as her fingerless glove reaches for the doorknob.

On the other side of the door, the various locks and jams release with no resistance, as though an invisible entity was unlocking the door from the inside. Even the chain-lock frees with seemingly no effort at all, everything happening before Beat's hand meets the doorknob, a movement that can take no longer than a few seconds. . . although the moment is dramatically drawn out by the girl's slow advance.

Someone standing inside watching the door *could* notice the locks tumbling. Someone standing inside *should* notice the door opening for a few moments, and then closing again in silence, the locks shifting back into place simultaneously with scarcely a rattle. Someone *could*, someone *should*, but no one does.

No one is watching the door.

No one is downstairs.

Changing of the Guard

No one notices anything out of the ordinary.

Beat and Case move through the front foyer into a short hallway that leads to a kitchen on one side and a staircase on the other. Case progresses to the kitchen, while Beat waits patiently at the bottom of the steps, attempting to detect movement from upstairs. Case assesses the kitchen with a smooth gaze, hesitating just slightly on the dials on top of the gas stove. One dial points to a notch between medium and high, indicating it had been used to make dinner and then forgotten. Case looks away as the dial snaps back to the OFF position without him touching it. Finishing his inspection, he steps back into the hallway beside Beat.

"She left the stove on," Case comments softly, not disturbing the overriding quiet of the residence.

"She has a lot on her mind," Beat replies.

Case nods, and the two of them begin their ascension of the stairs. Case's moves are lithe, bringing to mind a jungle cat roving among the sturdy treetop branches of a rainforest. In contrast, Beat dances up the steps, evoking images of a ballerina moving freely and deftly in a dance studio. As they reach the top, they make a sharp left turn and move toward an open door at the end of the hall, their movements without sound, stopping just short of crossing the threshold into the child's room. They stand at the door and look inside.

A woman and child lie on a small, simple bed, curled together. The woman—the child's mother—upon hearing the even breaths of slumber coming from the little boy, begins to carefully extricate herself from the limbs of the smaller body. The boy, still asleep, grabs for the stuffed animal lying in front of him and pulls it closer.

He sneezes, forehead wrinkling, but doesn't awaken.

The pair at the door gaze upon the scene in silence as the mother watches the steady inhalations of her young one. They also watch as she then tilts her head up toward

Rhapsody of the Spheres

the ceiling, her eyes drawing closed, her face showing signs of exhaustion.

"God help me," she breathes.

Beat can't help but glance down to the floor, her lips curving into a smile.

This is their invitation.

A nightlight illuminates the room just enough for the woman to read the face of her wristwatch. She takes a deep breath. . . and exhales slowly, as though gathering herself, before moving to exit the bedroom. Beat and Case separate to either side of the doorway as the mother nears. In respect, the two of them have taken off their hats and are holding them in front of their chests. They know the act will go unacknowledged, yet they follow through just the same.

"We'll take it from here," Case whispers as the mother passes.

Her strides slow and her brow furrows. Her steps are softer now as she listens for any sound out of place. The house is quiet, making only those barely perceptible noises that houses tend to do. She then shakes her head, the movement barely there, and continues on. Her steps are more determined.

Case smiles as he and Beat observe the woman's retreating form, making the sharp right to begin descending the stairs. As soon as she is lost around the corner, the two turn back to the child's room.

Now, they step inside.

The bedroom is far from dirty, but there are enough toys and ornamentations to present the area as the space for a young boy. Beat and Case hang their outerwear on a kid-sized coat-rack standing near the door; another coat and scarf already occupy one rung. Beat also removes her flannel-patterned, long-sleeved shirt, leaving her in a sleeveless grey tank top. Her tattoo, a pair of wings inked on the inside of her left wrist, is now visible. Case keeps on his white Henley. It covers an identical

Changing of the Guard

tattoo to Beat's, although his is much larger, spanning the entire portion of his back.

The sleeping boy sneezes again, the heat emanating from his body.

Beat takes up a position near the headboard of the child's bed and stands, head tilted down toward her boots, her eyes closed. Out of nowhere, magnificent wings unfurl from behind her back and extend wide, as though stretching after a deep sleep. Given the small size of the room, they take up nearly the full length from one wall to the opposite. Eyes still shut, she tilts her head from side to side and rolls her shoulders. Slowly, her wings retract into a more comfortable, folded posture behind her back, although they remain splendidly visible. At the same time, her tattoo fades into her skin.

Facing the doorway, his back framed by the lone window overlooking the street, Case has undergone a similar transformation. He lifts his head after swaying his wings back and forth before retracting them behind his shoulder blades. He then takes his place at the foot of the bed, near the doorway. On the two of them, their wings, framing their now statuesque bodies, radiate an ethereal glow, enhanced by the subdued incandescence given off by the nightlight.

"I can do all things," Case chuckles softly, looking straight ahead.

Beat smiles as well.

They stand ready.

And moreover, the child sleeps soundly.

###

About the Author

Taylor Dye is the author of four novels, including the most recent in The Intermediaries series, *The Intermediaries: Saint Nicholas*, and the first novel in the

Rhapsody of the Spheres Trustice Jeffries superhero series, *Fear Into Darkness*. His latest short story, "Don't Run On Riley Wolff," is available online on *Mangoprism*: https://mangoprism.com/don't-run-on-riley-wolf/

*****~~~~~*****

Sunrise on Eris

by Mike Adamson

The universe, like life, is filled with surprises, and to feel so alive, so fulfilled, was the last thing I could have expected when journeying to the outermost rim of the solar system.

At 68 astronomical units from the sun, Eris is nine light hours from the homeworld of the human species. Such a vault—an abyss of utter desolation, with the crushing knowledge that no other human beings draw breath for billions kilometers—should breed an inconsolable melancholy. But in the cold stasis where the solar system melds insensibly into the unrelieved vacuum of interstellar space, we had found many things we neither expected nor understood.

Finding that one's love is not misplaced was, for me, high among them, and though it has long been mission policy to field stable couples for long-duration missions, for a while Carol and I had wondered if we stayed together for the sake of the mission rather than each other.

It is madness to plunge into the void without every possible safeguard, and to do so with a partner about

Rhapsody of the Spheres

whom you have doubts makes no sense. Yet for either of us to waver publicly would have cost us the mission, so we patched up our uncertainties. We *wanted* this flight, *wanted* to be the first and perhaps only human beings to ever set foot upon distant Eris. Against the enormity of what lay before us, and our years of commitment to the goal, our differences had come to seem trivial.

Two years' transit, even with several stages of crushing acceleration from the nuclear drive, saw us rendezvous with the icy worldlet, slightly smaller than the Moon yet with its own tiny satellite. Two more would take us home to the space cities where so much of the human race shelters from the challenges of the ruined Earth.

Yet for all the problems the human race faces as a new spacefaring people, spreading slowly through the solar system, out here we were as remote from their concerns as any human being could be. It was as if all humanity were reduced to compressed burst transmissions through the big ship's high-gain dish—voices, faces on a screen—and had taken on a lesser importance than the vista of space before us.

Deep Space Vessel *Armstrong* swung in orbit over Eris's equator, low enough for us to see her running lights against the stars. She had seeded a dozen satellites into high orbits and as many more landers all over this frigid globe. The program of planetary exploration culminated with the descent of the Landing Module *Falcon* to a plain of methane ice and pitted rock we had named the Mordor Planitia.

Four human beings, ten billion kilometers from home—Raj and Meiling up in the *Armstrong*, Carol and myself down here. We had a week's reserves for the surface stay. The lander draws power from the Radioisotope Thermoelectric Generators, which will run the science systems left behind. In that time, we will enjoy gravity around equal to the Moon's and a day two hours

Sunrise on Eris

longer than Earth's, as the planet turns slowly under the starscape.

And just as on Earth, the sun rises every day, crosses the sky and sets, pursued by Dysnomia, Eris's single moon. How is a human meant to feel, to see a jagged worldlet racing across the star map, lit dimly by an unseen sun? Or to see the zodiacal light stretched across the sky, the cumulative reflection from every particle of matter in the entire solar system? And how should a heart beat, to see the sun, which first nourished all life on Earth, rise over the close Erisian horizon, a brighter star among countless others?

Carol and I had come to time our extravehicular activity sessions to coincide with dawn, for the magic of the moment would never be lost on us. Each day we went outside, our suits protecting us from a daytime temperature of -221° C, we would take up a viewing position east of the ship, feel the methane ice crunch under our soles, and hear the soft feed from the *Armstrong's* AI and onboard systems. We would hold hands, stare into the coming day, and let the moment fill us completely.

The zodiacal light would flash out to our wide-open pupils, rising in a straight shaft at an angle to the horizon—the very plane of the solar system, counterpointing the majesty of the Milky Way, the river of stars which circles the sky. Then, little by little, the light would grow until the brilliant point of Sol crossed the skyline. We would sigh with a joy all but inexpressible—the simple connection to all other worlds and all other life, which that spark represents. A thrill would go through us, a shared moment in which our hands closed tightly and no words were needed.

Ah, however will we recapture such a time? Perhaps, once the *Falcon* rises from Eris, we will never again feel as we did in those moments, but we will remember them and all they meant to us. We will carry that shared feeling with us to the end of our days, and

Rhapsody of the Spheres

speak of it to others who will inevitably brave the Transneptunian void of the Kuyper Belt to see the farthest shoals, where systemic matter reaches its end and only the stars beckon.

I stood in this moment of transcendence, eyes locked to the sun, breathing the cool suit air and feeling Carol's hand in mine, and could have shed tears of joy, had I known why I wept. But perhaps it was simple homesickness, for though we had today's messages in the coms buffer, waiting to be played, in this rare moment we were actually looking *at* our unseen home, which is only ever a few degrees from the sun, from this distance. To see one is to know the other is close, even though no instrument we had could actually resolve Earth.

And, in a moment we could never define, the magic faded and we once more stood on a plain of frozen primordial gases, on a dwarf planet at the edge of all that is known. Work waited, and we turned to each other to see the smile we alone shared, hug as close as the suits allowed, and resume our work with a check of activity schedules and a murmured contact with the ship above.

We would leave Eris tomorrow and prepare for the long flight home, but we had seen that home from a perspective no others knew, and, just for a while, we four mission crew had the privilege of a god's eye view on the whole human endeavor.

At such a point, one cannot help feeling rather small—yet blessed beyond all measure.

###

About the Author

Mike Adamson holds a Doctoral degree from Flinders University of South Australia. After early aspirations in art and writing, Mike returned to study and secured qualifications in marine biology and archaeology.

Sunrise on Eris

Mike has been a university educator since 2006, is a passionate photographer, master-level hobbyist, and journalist for international magazines.

Recent publications include *Strand Magazine, Metastellar* and *Abyss & Apex*. He was long-listed in the Hugo Awards in 2018 and 2020, and was a finalist in the 2019 Aurealis Awards, the 2021 Gravity Awards, and the 2022 Jim Baen Memorial Award. In the mystery vein, Mike was a finalist in the 2023 Derringer Awards. He's also a Pushcart nominee.

*****~~~~~*****

The Stellar Instrument

by Brandon Case

Aaron Lopez sat at the mahogany dining table in his parent's Manhattan brownstone, quietly loathing his idyllic life. He'd recently turned nineteen, and his childhood home had tightened into a claustrophobic box (with poor acoustics).

Tonight's family dinner was a medley of artificial meat, fingerling potatoes, and brussels sprouts. The smell of saffron and rosemary added a charming harmony—but green beans were a dissonant note that ruined his experience with their rubbery mouthfeel. He ate them anyway, refusing to waste food. But it bothered Aaron that his mom insisted on serving green beans whenever it was her turn to cook; she knew he hated them, but cared more about how parallel green lines added 'artistic flair' to the plate.

Such quibbles sounded insignificant. Aaron had access to everything prior generations dreamed of: a post-scarcity world of personal expression, AI-matched parents who still loved each other after decades of marriage, and the freedom to study, make music, and design

Rhapsody of the Spheres

instruments. Yet for him, society was a complex morass of personal insignificance and social failure.

When discussing utopia, people often left out human nature. Sure, with AI automating industry, no one had to work... *everyone* could be an artist and still afford to eat. But saturating the world with personal expression only increased the number of failing artists. There were ten billion pairs of eyes consuming media, but they still only wanted the *best*.

Finding an audience for your work was harder than ever. Aaron's IndieBeats profile only had two hundred and eighty-seven followers, and most were spam bots. But the system worked well for some people.

Across from him, his parents sat side by side in stylish evening wear, like they were attending a gala instead of this simple dinner with their son. Not that the fancy attire was for his benefit. They ignored Aaron, focused on painting little hearts on each other's arms (at the table!) and sharing besotted glances like teenagers. Their professional paintings covered every wall in the townhouse, depicting nocturnal cityscapes with surreal buildings that extended into a cosmos of stars. Critics likened their collaborative works to "Van Gogh's Starry Night, had he been graced with a third dimension of Augmented Reality."

Amidst the perfusion of visual art, there was no trace of Aaron. To be fair, his crayon drawings from childhood were displayed proudly between masterwork paintings. But his music, which he'd fallen in love with at eleven years old, was nowhere to be found. Whenever he gave his parents a setlist or t-shirt from his shows, they smiled patiently and tucked it in a box probably labeled "Aaron's Silly Music Phase."

It was amazing how consistently they made him doubt himself.

He flicked his eyes right-left-right, activating the augmented reality display implanted in his optic lenses.

The Stellar Instrument

The AR interface immediately recognized his parents and pulled up translucent contact sheets that hovered next to their faces:

Contact: Dad	Contact: Mom
X	X
Name: Dominic Lopez	Name: Jane Lopez
Handle: @TwistedVistas	Handle: @JanePaintsSky
Followers: 17.3 million	Followers: 22.7 million
Latest Video: The Domestic Artist—Can Body Painting Rekindle Your Relationship?	Latest Video: How to Inspire Your Non-Artistic Son Through the Power of Painting

Aaron concentrated on the "X" in each profile; the AR followed his gaze and dismissed their contact windows. His eyes flicked down to the right, pulling up the IndieBeats app.

MetaDestroyer, his favorite artist, was in the middle of a live stream. The video showed a man in his mid-thirties who was Aaron's opposite in every way: a frenetic blur of beard, tattoos, and muscled arms, hammering a drum kit while screaming lyrics into the mic. Over fifty million people were watching the performance—more than the total followers of Mom and Dad put together.

"Aaron?" Mom said.

He blinked twice, minimizing the AR display.

"We made some inquiries," Dad said.

"And pulled some strings," Mom said.

"You're going to the New York Institute of Integrated Arts!" they said together.

It was the visual arts school Aaron's parents had met at, graduated from, and pushed him toward since he was a child. "They don't have a music program."

His parents exchanged a significant look, and his mom said, "I know you've enjoyed making music, hon. But isn't it time to move on? You're a great visual artist."

"The t-shirts you design are a great start!" his dad said.

Rhapsody of the Spheres

"I know you'll love painting," his mom said, sliding a NYIIA pamphlet across the dark wood table. "You can join the family business. We'll get you new social accounts. Millions of our followers will flock to you."

Millions of followers. Doubt thrummed in Aaron; a low minor chord filled with anxiety. If he had any skill or future with music, wouldn't it have shown by now? He performed online every night, often with only one or two viewers. Wouldn't it be wiser to go to NYIIA, apprentice with his parents, and let that guaranteed future unfold?

No. Not yet. He hadn't gotten to play his newly completed instrument.

Aaron pushed himself away from the table and stood. "I've been making some stellar music. You should listen tonight."

His parents smiled—Dad with pity, Mom with conviction.

Despite his attempted bravado, Aaron took the NYIIA pamphlet upstairs with him.

. . .

Aaron's room rose to a high, vaulted ceiling. No paintings adorned the walls. Instead, band posters covered every square inch with riotous color. MetaDestroyer was prominent amongst them, his drum kit set against a background of skulls and flowers. The paper poster gained depth when viewed with augmented reality, making the drummer grin wolfishly and twirl his drumsticks. The room's furniture was pushed into the corners, leaving the center wide open for Aaron's performances.

It was the only place in the townhouse he felt free.

He sat at the room's heart and started some light stretching to limber up; tonight's performance would require extra dexterity. He'd finished his stellar instrument, the culmination of a year spent programing and refining the AR interface. It was ready.

The Stellar Instrument

The translucent clock at the corner of Aaron's vision read 7:45 pm. He still had a little time before the show, but he decided to log onto the stream early while warming up.

He glanced at the black computer tower beneath his desk. It lit up, remotely activated by his AR. The tiny processors in his implant were sufficient for browsing online, but his music relied on advanced graphics cards for power. Not that his old computer was particularly 'advanced.' But hopefully it'd be good enough to carry him through the performance without melting or crashing his AR.

His HD camera sat on a tripod. Another focused gaze brought it online and opened a little window in his AR display. A skinny man looked back at him, wearing an ancient Queen t-shirt commemorating their A Night at the Opera tour, when they'd first played Bohemian Rhapsody.

It always took Aaron a heartbeat to recognize himself on camera. He didn't feel his appearance suited him. He looked nothing like MetaDestroyer, nor any of the popular musicians. However, he could easily be mistaken for a weedy art student who spent too much time indoors.

A chime rang in his ears. The note sounded perfectly real, but came from another augmented reality implant that stimulated his cochlear nerves.

Moonbaby, one of his only reoccurring viewers, entered the stream. She appeared as another translucent video feed, showing a woman in a baggy gray sweatshirt and a digital masquerade mask that covered the top of her face.

"Cool shirt." She took an enormous bite of green food.

"Are you eating. . . green beans?" Aaron had discussed his distaste for them on the stream a few nights previous.

Rhapsody of the Spheres

She grinned, showing green strings lodged in her teeth.

Trolls were entirely too common online. But harassment or not, she was here, listening. The difference between zero audience and one viewer was enough to forgive considerable heckling.

"Is that a brochure for NYIIA?" Moonbaby asked.

Aaron stiffened and said nothing.

"You should go," she continued. "Your setlist graphics are vital. I could see you being a graphic designer. But your music's too ordinary. Typical synth instruments. . . although the sphere hologram is weird."

Aaron ground his teeth. Zero was such an underappreciated number. So smooth. No sharp edges.

He concentrated on her face, accessing her contact card:

```
| X    Contact: Moonbaby

      Name: (Not Telllling)
      Handle: @Moonbabyzz
      Followers: 5
      Latest Video: Reaction to
      MetaDestroyer Squeeee Vital Click
```

Holding his concentration on the "X" gave Aaron an option to ban her from his stream. It was tempting. . . to play his new set for quiet, uncritical emptiness. But it felt like backing down and hiding behind obscurity. He wanted to belong here, to make and perform music for people. Warts and all.

Besides, she'd only ever seen him tuning one piece of his stellar instrument at a time. If someone watched a guitarist inspect a single metal string, they'd hardly be able to imagine what chords and rhapsodic harmonies the guitar was capable of.

Aaron resumed his setup, ignoring the wet sounds as Moonbaby chewed green beans with her lips pressed against her mic.

The Stellar Instrument

He flicked through his sound controller and brought out his first sphere. The AR hologram was the size of a baseball and glowed blue and green. It floated at waist height.

"Booooring," Moonbaby said. "I've seen that one."

An anxious vibrato echoed in Aaron's stomach. He brought out a red sphere the size of a golf ball and placed it next to the first.

"Two?" Moonbaby asked. "I guess that's new."

Aaron added a third sphere, gold and the size of a tennis ball; a fourth, marbled and the size of a basketball; two more, tan and aqua, each surrounded by delicate rings; a tiny gray orb; a large sapphire; and a ninth sphere, huge and yellow like a radiant beachball.

The AR tracked his fingers, allowing him to "touch" the holograms. He arranged them in order, but not by size.

"They're. . . the planets," Moonbaby said in an unusually quiet voice. "And if you're using each as its own synth..." Her eyes flicked around, manipulating her AR interface.

Another chime sounded as someone popped onto the stream. Then another.

Three simultaneous viewers! That almost never happened.

The newcomers ignored Aaron and peppered Moonbaby with questions about why she'd demanded they join.

But it'd just turned 8:00 pm. Time for the show to begin. Aaron muted and minimized the audience so he could concentrate.

He started with the blue and green Earth, spinning the hologram like a turntable. The planet played a sample of orchestral strings, which changed in pitch and tone depending on how he tilted its axis. When he was satisfied with the sound, he gave the Earth a shove, sending it into orbit around the sun and looping the audio track.

Rhapsody of the Spheres

More chimes sounded as people joined his channel. Fifteen now! A new record. His parents weren't among the watchers. . . but it was still early, and they'd promised to set up notifications for when he went live. They'd join soon.

Aaron set Mars, Venus, Jupiter, and Neptune in motion, each representing an instrument family: woodwinds, brass, percussion, and keyboard. When he wanted to emphasize a particular instrument, he added its solo as a moon around the larger planet.

With five layers playing in concert, the sound was really coming together. Harmonies and counterpoints flowed between the various instruments like in a true orchestra, but the planets tugging on each other with simulated gravity added a twist of unpredictable jazz.

There were over five hundred people watching him now! Sweat glazed Aaron's palms, and he briefly expanded the augmented reality HUD to display its chat log:

@AaronLopezMusic 315 Followers	Live: 527 Watching	Chat Log: X Mesoup: damn that's vital Moonbaby: told you LoloPunk:
Recording in Progress	Midi Channel Quick Select Sun | Mercury | Venus | Earth | Mars | Jupiter | Saturn | Neptune | Uranus	DoeToes: Who the hell is this guy? Damiankill: I never seen a setup like that

Aaron grinned. People were responding! And he was just getting started.

With a flourish, he set Mercury, Saturn, and Uranus into motion. Each played synth fills, their contemporary sound harmonizing with the traditional orchestral instruments and tying them to the Sun. Through the star he ran samples of popular music, remixing each track on the fly.

The Stellar Instrument

Twelve thousand watchers!

Aaron slipped into a performance trance. He danced around the holographic solar system, nudging planets to adjust their speed and planes of rotation, controlling the music's tempo. Each alteration rippled through the system with the simulated gravity, which he'd programmed to keep the changes smooth and harmonious.

One hundred and fifty thousand watchers!

Aaron's concerns dissolved into rhythm and rhapsody. His parents' disapproval vanished in the whirl of colorful spheres. Thoughts of NYIIA burned to ash in the holographic sun. Waves of exaltation flowed through him as the number of watchers rose.

One million watchers!

Two million watchers!

It was finally happening for him. This was one of those vital moments that could launch an entire career.

Aaron bumped Earth, adding vibrato to the strings. He shot a quick glance at the chat, which was scrolling too fast for him to make out anything besides Moonbaby yelling at someone in all caps, saying she'd met him first so they'd better not post a reaction video before her.

He smelled acrid burning, like how astronauts described the scent of space after an EVA.

Five million watchers—

The music cut off.

The spheres disappeared.

A thin stream of smoke rose from his computer tower and dissipated. The graphics cards had fried. His entire AR system was offline. It would reboot, but slowly.

The stream was gone. Aaron was left standing alone in his hollow room, sweating, his arms extended awkwardly to tap where Jupiter had been.

His room looked exactly as it had before. The NYIIA pamphlet sat on his bookshelf. It was almost like nothing had happened.

. . .

Rhapsody of the Spheres

Aaron ran downstairs and burst into the living room. "Tell me you saw that!"

"Saw what, dear?" Mom said, curled up with his dad on the couch.

"My stream! My music! It went viral!"

His parents shared a long look, and his mom said, "That's great. . . and right after our talk about NYIIA. What a charming coincidence."

They didn't believe him. Not only had they not watched him perform, they thought he was *making it up.* "It was a scheduled performance. My first with the full solar instrument. It had nothing to do with NYIIA!"

"Aaron," his dad said, "That's not an appropriate tone. We worked hard to get you accepted into that school. Don't let the pressure play tricks on your mind."

Aaron's head spun. It felt like he was going crazy. Fading like an echo in this claustrophobic house.

Living half-submerged in augmented reality strained people's sense of what was real. . . but he couldn't have hallucinated having a successful stream just to avoid NYIIA and having to take up the family mantle. Right?

He flicked his eyes right-left-right. The AR interface opened without issue. Had it really crashed? Or had it just been minimized?

A message notification popped up. Aaron's breath caught in his throat as he concentrated, expanding the translucent window:

To:	@AaronLopezMusic
From:	@MetaDestroyer
Subject:	Goddamn Vital

Caught your stream.
Wild instrument. Stellar performance. We should collab.
I noticed the NYIIA brochure. Guess you're the Lopez Painters' son. New York's a small place above 10 million followers.
They're good people, but my parents pushed me toward law school and...have you considered attending Juilliard? I'm an alumnus of their AR music program and could get you an interview.
    -Meta

222

The Stellar Instrument

Aaron couldn't breathe. *Juilliard?* And he'd signed it 'Meta' like they were peers!

He turned to his parents. "You never told me you know MetaDestroyer."

"Jamal?" Dad said. "Nice man. Hates green beans almost as much as you do. Refused to eat your mother's cooking at the last potluck."

"You have a poster of him, right?" Mom's eyes narrowed shrewdly. "Meeting him might be too distracting for you at the moment. . . but we could arrange something as a celebration once you enroll at NYIIA."

Aaron scrolled through the hundreds of fan messages cascading into his AR inbox. He really *had* broken through and found his audience. And even if his parents didn't appreciate his music, hopefully they'd come to respect it.

As for dangling a meeting with Meta over his head. . . well, they were falling behind the times. With a grin, he said, "That won't be necessary," and began drafting a reply to his fellow musician.

###

About the Author

Brandon Case is an erstwhile government cog who fled the doldrums into unsettling worlds of science and magic. He has recent work in *Escape Pod, Third Flatiron,* and *Air and Nothingness* presses, among others. You can catch his alpine adventures on Twitter and Instagram @BrandonCase101.

*****~~~*****

Opal World Frolic

by Jendia Gammon

Sej Snowe twitched back a clear, green pellet under his tongue, where it dissolved and sent little tingles throughout his body, even to his phantom left arm, where now resided a polytriliad colloidal matrix, aka a cyborg arm. Due to a genetic condition (he called it a defect, but that term no longer held favor despite his morose insistence), his body would not support a generated or grafted bio-limb. The problem with the "new" arm, which by now was twelve years old, like the jumbled and unpleasant memories of the war that wounded him, was that it could not be tattooed like his flesh. The polytriliad refused to allow any substance to seep into it, whether it be ink or metal or organic grafts or paint. This disappointed Sej, who bore tattoos all over his body symbolizing battle and honor and valor, as well as favorite gemstones. His born arm had held an exquisite tattoo of a shimmering, spherical opal with a dragon curled inside it. His latest attempt at a tattoo led to a fight with the ship, who now sulked and refused to debark from its dock.

Rhapsody of the Spheres

"Why don't you get off your hulking mass and fly us outta here, *Rad*?" Sej barked at *Radiant Spinglass* once again. *Rad* refused at first to answer, powering down all functions one by one, like shutting off all the lights in a house. It left one final perfunctory device aside from minimal life support (minimal by which meant *just barely*; Sej smelled a nasty reek from what he suspected were untilled bits of compost in *Rad*'s gullet). He groaned.

"Fine. Just get us to the next pulsation."

Rad didn't answer with words, but Sej felt the pseudo-grav vanish, and he bobbed upward, smacking into the overhead tubes of the cockpit. Spitting ever-increasingly poetic swear words, he pulled himself down into his worn, fuzzily covered captain's chair and strapped himself in.

"*Rad*," his voice held a warning tone, "no more pitstops at the Golden Vials if you don't get us going again."

A snorting sort of "Harrumph!" echoed through the ship, which was devoid of most of its usual sounds now.

"Why you gotta be like this, *Rad*? What did I do this time?"

Rad's tinny voice reverberated through the quiet halls of the medium-sized ship as she said, "Where to begin? Sej Snowe, veteran of the Lessenworlds' Tactical Forces, consumer of Pellet-verts, drinker of questionable exotic spirits, caster of profane insults. . . and, oh, what's this?"

An alarm sounded, and Sej sat stiff in interest.

"Oh, good," hissed Rad, "now you've got a bounty on your head."

Sej felt a cold spike shoot through his body.

"A what?"

"A bounty. To the tune of five hundred thousand and forty-seven quidrox, payable to one Daring Waycraft Guild by. . . oh, great, next week!"

Sej yowled.

"Impossible! *Rad*, fire up the controls. Let me see."

"Nope. No way," *Rad* snapped. "Apologize first."

Sej's mouth went round.

"For?"

"For the insults. For the garbage. For taking me for granted. You know, I could turn you in myself, but unfortunately, the bounty includes *me,* as I'm an 'accomplice to crimes against the Guild.'"

"Oh, come on, that's really stupid," Sej scoffed.

"What's really stupid is that I let you talk me into being your ship."

"Well, we aren't going to solve anything by just sitting here like easy targets! The Guild will be after us by now, and we need to put some distance between us and the next system."

"I think we'd better set a course for someplace a bit more hospitable. Don't you?"

"Like what? We're out in the in-between. . . it's kind of dead. We need a pulsation course to someplace private." Sej put his drifting legs up on the console, and *Rad* growled in disapproval.

"Wrong. I say we hide in plain sight."

"What is there out here?" Sej sat upright again and moved his hands over the controls. "Show me. I'm more used to passing through, and I don't like stopping for long."

Rad let out a metallic sigh and turned on the ship consoles, so that soft turquoise and red lights illuminated Sej's careworn face. "You never did like stopping. Not for anything."

"A rolling stone gathers no moss," Sej reminded her.

"Sej, moss doesn't even *exist* in this quadrant, need I remind you."

"Never mind. Show me what *does*."

Rhapsody of the Spheres

"Well, there's a five-planet system, some of them vice worlds, another one with some sort of competition. . . Opal World Frolic?"

Sej snorted. "Okay, so it sounds like there's a lot of wheeling and dealing going on. Might be perfect for slipping in unnoticed."

"The Opal World thing isn't really our speed, though. Touristy. It's called Gladressine. We could try the next planet over, Faheldrake."

"Let's do it," Sej snapped his fingers. "Now, about the gravity. . ."

"Fine," *Rad* grumbled.

Sej felt his weight return, and he sighed. "Well, you wore me out, so let me sleep through the pulsation, please."

Rad powered all the ship's systems back online, and Sej ambled his way toward his sleeping pod, feeling disgruntled and tired, but with a little tingle of excitement. He did love new worlds; they were new prospects for business, after all.

He slept mostly without dreams, but occasionally a little shard of memory shot through his deeper consciousness. He dreamed momentarily of having a fully flesh arm, with the opal sphere and the dragon tattoo. In the dream, he rubbed the opal sphere, and then it rose from his skin and floated like a little planet, revolving. *Opal World. Gladressine.*

He woke in a jolt, drooling, and hit his head on the ceiling of his sleep pod. He gasped; the ship swerved around, throwing him back and forth.

"What are you doing?" he screamed.

"We're under attack, Sej!" cried *Rad*. "I'm trying to outrun them."

"You should've awoken me!" Sej bellowed.

"I tried. You were deep in dreamland! What was I supposed to do?"

Opal World Frolic

With some difficulty, Sej strapped in and assessed the situation. "Who's on our tail? The Guild?" He pivoted *Rad*'s guns, now in lock with his own body, and fired on one of the ships in pursuit. A blossom of bright orange and yellow flared on his viewscreen. Then another blast, and *Rad* shrieked.

"You okay, *Rad*?" cried Sej.

"Get the other one!" wailed the ship. "My guidance is knocked offline by that blast. I'm going to have to dock or crash-land. Take your pick!"

Sej whistled and pivoted his viewpoint. The other ship skimmed in and out of range. His skin crawled with dread. He got a glimpse of a symbol on one side, and his suspicions were confirmed. "Our bogey *is* from the Guild."

"Gonna have to set down, Sej," moaned *Rad*.

Sweating and tense, Sej pivoted the weapons and waited. *Rad* shuddered, shaking Sej's whole body. He went cold. She was definitely hurt.

"Hang in there, my friend," he muttered.

Finally, the attacking ship came in range again, just in time to fire right at them. Sej pivoted the ship's thrusters, and she listed badly; she was losing control of herself and relying on his symbiotic piloting with her now. He charged weapons and shot at the bogey. Its main engines exploded, sending it spinning in space. Sej took manual control of *Rad* and shot through the debris field, and on the other side of that, he grimaced at the sight of Faheldrake, dark grey green, but glistening with huge city-continents.

"Too much action down there," he muttered. "*Rad*, can we make it to the Opal World?"

"I. . . don't. . . know," murmured the ship.

Sej's jaw clenched from worry.

"Let's try. I see a whole nest of security around this ball. Hiding in plain sight won't work here, not with two ships down behind us. Head for Gladressine."

Rhapsody of the Spheres

"I... try..."

Sej bit his lip. *Please come through, my old friend.* Gladressine shone in brilliant white-blue-pink-lavender-gold sparkles in the light of the system's white star.

"Now I know why it's called Opal World," Sej remarked. His arm itched in a phantom reaction, and a little sliver of his hibernation dream sliced through to his waking thoughts. "Just like the old tattoo."

Rad rallied enough to let out a pithy moan at that.

"I know you're tired, pal," Sej said to her. "This place can't be that bad, can it?"

With a growling whine, *Rad* suddenly said, "I don't know, but there's a lot of traffic ahead, and there's a little skimmer ship headed straight for us!"

"No way," breathed Sej, but *Rad* was right. A small podlike ship, teardrop in shape and cerulean blue, hurtled straight for them. "Hail them!"

"Make it snappy, Sej," hissed *Rad*.

"You're on a collision course! I repeat, you're on a collision course! Engage your thrusters, or we'll open fire!"

"Whaaaaat?" came the crackle of a high voice. "We've lost control of our ship. Please don't shoot at us! Can you help us?"

Sej swore like his tongue was on fire. "Learn to *steer*!"

"Can't!" another voice chimed in. "Won't you please help us? We can't stop it!"

Sej turned off the comms.

"What do we do?" he asked. "Tell me quick, before I blow them up or they hit us!"

Drowsily, *Rad* muttered, "I'll set a tow on them."

"You'll *what*? We can't tow these folks! We have a bounty!"

"You want to die today, Sej Snowe?" hollered *Rad*.

"No, but I—"

"Oh, do shut up, Sej!" and a sling beam erupted from *Rad*'s belly, shooting out and over the little, tumbling craft. A sharp tug sent vibrations all through her, and as a result, through Sej as well.

It made him nauseous.

"I officially do not like this," Sej said through gritted teeth.

Rad didn't respond.

"Oh, dammit, *Rad*. Don't fail me now."

A melodious voice said, "The *Radiant Spinglass* has entered torpor mode and asks that you bring aboard the crew of the ship in tow."

"Oh, ho-lee hells!" shouted Sej. "No. No! I'm not babysit—"

The voice continued, "Drawing the ship within the docking bay in five, four, three—"

Sej attempted to blister his console with profanity but failed. He ran his hands through his hair and raged for a good five minutes, until the little ship was firmly sealed in *Rad*'s bay.

"*Rad*, we're gonna have words over this."

The ship emitted a sort of sashaying hum, and Sej scowled. With this expression he faced the little pod within the bay.

The pod, he noted, was vibrantly painted with a twisting dragon. He blinked. He thought back to his dream again, and his old tattoo of the dragon on the opal sphere. Before he had much time to dwell on this, the pod hissed open. Out popped two beings, maybe four feet tall, all clad in iridescent, shimmering suits from head to toe, with little helmets sporting what looked like antennae. They saw him. And they *laughed*.

All his heat and color returned then, and he opened his mouth to let out an opinionated stream of epithets, but *Rad* called out in an echoing voice, "Welcome aboard, kids!"

Rhapsody of the Spheres

One of them laughed again, and its face turned from mint green to dark teal.

"We're not *kids*!"

The other one laughed. "But thanks for saving us from that... whatever that was back there!"

"I'm Kra'nel," said the first one, and the other one chirped, "I'm Tra'neen."

"Sej Snowe," came the blunt introduction. "And you're aboard only thanks to *Radiant Spinglass* here."

"Hullo again!" piped the ship.

Sej prickled in irritation. He put his hands on his hips and looked down his nose at the pair.

"What are you two kids doing out here?"

Kra'nel and Tra'neen glanced furtively at each other, and they reminded Sej of his grandmother's cats from his youth, who liked to walk around pressed alongside each other, tails intertwined, just before they would get up to mischief.

Tra'neen cooed and answered, "We're going to the Frolic of course."

"Wouldn't miss it," agreed Kra'nel. They both beamed, their antennae swaying in tandem as they danced around each other.

"What's the 'Frolic'?" He didn't want to admit how curious he was, but it wasn't the first time he'd heard a reference to it. And since he had the two youths on board, he might as well get some answers, he reasoned.

"You don't know the Opal World Frolic!" cried Tra'neen, eyes bulging, antennae ramrod straight.

"Only the best scavenger hunt in the sector!" exclaimed Kra'nel.

"More like the whole galaxy!" Tra'neen emphasized. The two of them hip-bumped.

"Hmmph," snorted Sej. "Never heard of it."

Rad chimed in, "I've accessed files on it, would you like—"

Opal World Frolic

Sej held up his hands. "No thank you. Tell you what: I'll get you into low orbit and you can go from there."

"Will our ship be repaired by then?" Tra'neen asked, and the huge eyes of the two of them made Sej squirm.

"Ask *Rad* here," came his gruff reply. "She's pretty worn out from pursuit. I'll take us in."

"I can handle it," *Rad* soothed. "Gives me something other than our own predicaments to focus on!"

Sej shook his head and sauntered toward his cockpit, hands in pockets, twisting an old ten-sided die. Luck hadn't done him many favors lately: a bounty on his head and now a couple of teens—in his view—wanting to party.

"Sej," the ship said slowly, "I really think you ought to consider the hunt."

He sniffed. "I'm too old for this crap, *Rad*. Let the kids do their thing."

A few hoots of indignant disagreement echoed in the ship as he sidled up to his captain's chair and strapped in.

"Seriously, Sej. There's a prize. And you'll never guess what: it's enough to cover that bounty!"

Sej leaned in over his console, his face glowing, the lines deep, the cynicism deeper still, and he sighed.

"You know what, I'm not feeling it, *Rad*. That's not a hard-earned wage. And besides which, we blew a couple of their bogeys!"

"Those were drone ships. A write-off for the Guild!"

"*Now* you tell me!" howled Sej, but his shoulders sagged in relief. He didn't need a body count *and* a bounty. "I'm not interested."

"I don't believe you! Listen to yourself. This is easy money. You're the only one making it hard. Get these kids on board, and you'll all win."

Sej's laugh came like a chop into a sapling. "Like they'd want an old pirate like me on board their shenanigans."

"We would!" cried a harmonious pair of voices. Sej jumped in his seat, and swore, swiveling to see the two.

"Hey!" he barked. "Get strapped in, both o' you. We're about to hit that atmosphere and I don't want you smeared on the ceiling of my ship. I don't think she'd like that either. Messy cleanup."

"Can we, though?" asked Kra'nel, and to Sej's irritation they made no move to return to their own ship, but rather strapped into the two additional chairs on the cockpit.

"Yes, can we?" Tra'neen implored, and the pair stretched as far as their belts would let them toward Sej.

It took all his restraint not to bellow at them like an old, baying hound, and the feat exhausted him.

"Look," he said, squinting at their fresh faces, all agog and exciting, wriggling in their seats. "I'm taking you down there, but I don't plan on playing any games. That goes for the Opal Frolic thingy."

"But it'll help you!" Kra'nel cried, and they reached across to interweave their fingerlike digits with Tra'neen's. Their antennae vibrated so quickly; they looked like little blurs above their heads to Sej.

"I don't know the first thing about this game," protested Sej.

"But *we* do," Tra'neen told him.

"We've got the whole world mapped out," Kra'nel chimed in.

Sej glanced back and forth between the two of them. He looked over his shoulder at the hologram of his bounty, rotating slowly above his console, and he rubbed his chin. His phantom arm itched. He was tired. His distaste for associating with young people gave him a tiny,

Opal World Frolic

irritating pain in his right temple. But these two were clearly gung-ho.

"You've got the perfect ship," Tra'neen pointed out. "Reliable and wise. We've got the maps and the clues. It's perfect!"

"And you don't mind sharing the prize?" Sej looked sternly between the two of them. Their little mouths went round and opened and closed and they made the equivalent of a shared shrug.

"We'd be honored," they answered together.

The *Radiant Spinglass* crowed, "Hear that, Sej? The perfect ship. That's me."

Sej twitched and bit back a thousand insults before saying, "Fine. But let's get through this atmosphere first."

Squeals of glee erupted from Tra'neen and Kra'nel, and soft laughter shivered through the ship while she set to work both on repairing the smaller vessel and setting the course through the atmosphere of Gladressine. The system's sun set the surface dancing with the fire-flickered, crystalline colors of opal all across it as the planet whirled. Sej had never seen its like, and as the ship buffeted through the thinnest barrier separating that glistening planet from the empty black of space, he sat back and admired what spread beneath them as *Rad* sailed gracefully through sparse clouds.

Something blossomed within Sej's chest as they coasted toward their first destination, an outpost called Opulence, and he beheld other ships dancing in and out of the place and watched visitors full of excitement and joy.

When was the last time I had fun? he wondered. *I forgot what it was like.*

His new partners were savvy; indeed, they found their first clues within minutes, and bounced back aboard *Rad* before Sej had much time to dwell on things. Sej then steered the ship, with the two youths chattering over the bubble-like orb they shared between them, on to the next destination, and the one after that, and so on.

Rhapsody of the Spheres

They reached the final one as the sun set over Phyrethon, a levitating town over a deep canyon splintered with rainbow hues set dancing by the low sun. Several other ships hovered close by.

"Your ship is ready," *Rad* told them, and Kra'nel and Tra'neen sprinted to their tiny vessel.

"Your ship won't make it where we need to go," Tra'neen told Sej. "Wait for us. We'll dip into the canyon. Only after the sun's rays vanish will the final clue appear."

"We have a *lot* of competition," Kra'nel said breathlessly.

Sej felt a thrill of excitement for them and opened the bay doors. The little ship shot out and down and out of sight, so he ordered *Radiant Spinglass* to hover. Other small craft dashed into the darkening canyon, and they looked like little winking fireflies zipping to and fro.

"Do you think they'll get it?" *Rad* asked.

"You sound nervous!" Sej noted.

"So do you!"

"Pssshh," Sej hissed. "Never." But he had begun to sweat. Darkness enveloped the canyon and the ships hovering. By and by, though, a little bright streak raced upwards from the serpentine, dark walls of the canyon.

"I see them!" cried *Rad*.

"They're being pursued!" shouted Sej. "Get that bay open."

Rad obliged, and in burst the little craft, and Sej hollered, "Get us out of here quick!"

He unbuckled and pelted back as the little pod opened.

Out spilled Tra'neen and Kra'nel, holding between them a great, crystalline egg. Their eyes looked almost as big as their prize.

"We did it! We found it!" they cried.

Sej stared at the object in awe.

"That's. . . that's pure opaltrescent, or I'll eat my pants!"

Opal World Frolic

The two stared at him and then at each other, and then they hooted, "It's real! We got it."

"Um," called *Rad*, "we've got a lot of ships in pursuit, like a flock of angry—what do you call them, bees?"

"Well," Sej replied, grinning, "tell them to buzz off. Get us to the nearest station. Looks like we've got a reward to divvy up!"

And so it was that the whopping opaltrescent egg brought in an astonishing number of credits, the bulk of which Sej insisted Kra'nel and Tra'neen keep for themselves. He and *Radiant Spinglass* took their winnings and opened a channel to Daring Waycraft Guild.

"I believe you're owed five hundred thousand and forty-seven quidrox," he said, his lips curled in wry grin.

The tentacle-faced agent on the screen turned several shades of purple and green, signifying disbelief.

"We don't accept stolen goods," they grumbled. "You also owe us for the two drone skimmers you obliterated!"

"We didn't steal them," Sej responded, hands behind his head. "And anyway, aren't those things a tax write-off for you? Kind of strange you'd authorized them in this sector, by the way."

"Then how'd you get the credits?" the agent demanded, looking unsettled.

Sej grinned and shot a look at the two youths, who waved at them and boarded their little craft.

"By having fun," he answered.

Radiant Spinglass hooted and sang about it for weeks on end, which Sej would never admit to liking. But he did find himself whistling the same tune long after Kra'nel and Tra'neen had left. As they left the system, and he glanced back at the shimmering world behind them, Sej patted the spot of his former tattoo. Then he promptly signed up for the next year's Opal World Frolic.

###

About the Author

Jendia Gammon is the author of fantasy, science fiction, and horror novels and short stories. Jendia writes compelling characters within rich world-building. She is represented by Laura Bennett of Liverpool Literary Agency.

Jendia holds a degree in Ecology and Evolutionary Biology and is a science writer and an artist. She conducts workshops and participates in panels on creative writing for international conventions. She has also written under the pen name J. Dianne Dotson.

Born in Southern Appalachia, Jendia now lives in Los Angeles with her family. She is married to British author Gareth L. Powell. Visit her website at jendiagammon.com.

*****~~~~~*****

Grins and Gurgles

The Art of Music Surfing
by Lisa Timpf

If you're a science fiction fan, you've likely been exposed to not one, but many, books, movies, or TV series revolving around the notion of time travel. To go to the past, would-be travelers often step into some kind of highly technical contraption, either stationary or mobile, and are flown, scrambled and reassembled, or otherwise sliced-and-diced back in time.

But a time jump doesn't need to be that complicated. In fact, time travel is easily accessible for those who have mastered the art of Music Surfing.

What, you might ask, is Music Surfing? This emerging and exciting pastime involves riding a piece of music to the past. All you need to do is concentrate on a song that has emotional resonance for you. Closing your eyes helps, but isn't essential. Relax—this part is important!—and enjoy the show.

While en route to their Destination, many experienced Surfers claim to be surrounded by musical notes manifesting as shimmering points of light. If this doesn't happen to you, no need to worry. Just bask in the

Rhapsody of the Spheres

feeling. The sense of floating, of drifting. Of riding the irresistible Time Wave.

Precisely *where* your surfing excursion takes you is a function of your memories. In my case, the song "Horse With No Name" spirits me back to the two-storey house our family once owned, where I'm listening to music playing on my brother Doug's radio, down the hall. "Tin Man" whisks me off to the common room of a residence at McMaster University, where a friend plays his acoustic guitar for a small gathering. Your mileage can, and will, vary, depending on personal experience. Suffice it to say that each of us has our own time travel trips waiting to be triggered by music.

I can see the wheels turning. *Right*, you think. *Time travel. That means...*

Stop right there. If you're thinking about hopping back a couple of decades—or even a few weeks—so you can rig things to win some money—that's been tried.

And it has failed, every time.

For one thing, you can't choose the hit song from a particular week in 2001 and try to Surf to a specific destination; say, to the corner store to buy a winning lottery ticket, or to a race track to bet on the triumphant horse. Destination for the Jumps are programmed into your subconscious, and can't be subverted. And even if you did find yourself at the counter with the numbers from the lottery jackpot dancing in your head, it wouldn't help. Music Surfing is like Death. You can't take it with you. And by "it" I mean money, credit cards, or anything physically tangible. In fact, you aren't even tangible, as it were. To paraphrase the admonition parents have offered their children since the first pottery shops were established centuries ago, "you can look, but you can't touch."

But if you can't execute the transaction, what about your past self? Good idea, but that, too, is a no-go. Try to whisper the winning numbers to the you that you used to be, and you're more likely to provide a good scare than to

The Art of Music Surfing

profit from it. Remember that ghost you thought you saw in your old bedroom? Or maybe that was just me. . .

OK, I can hear you say. *So what good is this whole Music Surfing deal, if you can't profit from it?*

Ah, such a cynic! Not everything worthwhile has a price tag. Surfing can, in fact, remind us of who we used to be. It can put us back in touch with memories we had forgotten (okay, some of them were perhaps best left forgotten, but still. . .). Surfing can give us a glimpse of old friends or family members with whom we've lost touch, or who have parted for a different dimension.

Besides, when it comes right down to it, the urge to Surf can be hard to resist. Just *try* staying in the present when certain triggering pieces of music come into your consciousness. Am I right?

But isn't it expensive? I'm glad you asked. Like everything else in life, there are those who have stepped forward to commoditize the Music Surfing experience. Since the first articles confirming the Music Surfing phenomenon appeared in scholarly journals starting in 2027, franchised outfits have popped up on Main Street of every town from Corner Brook to Comox, offering the opportunity to Surf for a price. Eyeshades, padded sensory deprivation pods that shut out external noise, a personal playlist—but you don't need all of these bells and whistles in order to Surf. Whether played on a top-notch sound system, strummed on a guitar, or even sung off-key in the shower, the song itself is all that's required.

So what's the catch? It should be noted that Music Surfing, like most other fun activities, comes with some caveats. Indulging in the full Music Surfing experience is not recommended while driving a motor vehicle, crossing a busy street, or operating heavy equipment. Side effects of Music Surfing may include bouts of nostalgia, an exaggerated sense that things were better way back when, and an irrepressible urge to dig out your high school yearbooks.

Rhapsody of the Spheres

Still, Music Surfing is well worth the effort. So, what are you waiting for? Just queue up a favorite tune from the past, and you're good to go.

Speaking of which, I'd love to stay and chat, but I hear the intro to "Tin Man" on the radio. Surf's up!

###

About the Author

Lisa Timpf is a retired HR and communications professional who lives in Simcoe, Ontario. Her poetry, fiction, creative non-fiction, and book reviews have appeared in *New Myths, Star*Line, The Future Fire,* and other venues. Lisa's speculative haibun collection, *In Days to Come*, is available from Hiraeth Publishing. You can find out more about Lisa's writing at http://lisatimpf.blogspot.com/

*****~~~~*****

The Last Viceroy

by Julie Biegner

  The viceroy didn't realize it, but she had a rather lovely last day on earth in the hours before she fluttered into a crumpled ball behind the rhododendron bush along the freeway, thus ending the lineage of a butterfly species that had fluttered its wings for a millennium.
  She began her morning among the humans. Bill Bradley came out onto his porch in his usual orange robe, unknowingly matching with the last viceroy's sunrise-tipped wings as she tended her business in the bushes of the old man's yard.
  Bill had a piping-hot mug of coffee in one hand and the newspaper in the other. The old man hummed to himself quietly, enjoying the solitude of the early morning and balancing his mug on one knee just as the last viceroy perched elegantly on a petal nearby.
  Bill began flipping through the paper, eyes skimming over a brief article on page 22. . . "Scientists struggle to explain the rapid disappearance of prehistoric butterfly. The best guess is fast-moving fungi, the deadly killer all the more likely amid a rapidly warming. . . " But

Rhapsody of the Spheres

Bill didn't make it any further as the front door slammed, sending the mug from its precarious place on his knee to crash to the ground. The hot coffee splattered onto Bill's feet.

"GODDAMMIT MARTHA HOW MANY TIMES HAVE I TOLD YOU—"

What a ruckus; that was certainly enough racket for the viceroy at the early hour; She took off, the sun her guide.

. . .

It was mid-morning when she spotted meadowsweet in the distance. The last viceroy fluttered over to its eggshell petals and gently began feeding. She did not notice the big building behind the bushes, a large hotel chain with people marching in and out like ants, where just that day a stately meeting of top brass were gathering to discuss advances in a new technology able to suck man-made poison out of the skies.

She was suckling quietly at the meadowsweet's center, when a black Mercedes pulled up and the car door opened. Michael Grant, President of Fossils, stepped out and inhaled deeply—the breath of an unhurried man. He spotted her there in the bushes and, a nature enthusiast himself, watched poetically for a moment. He seemed to have a thought, smiled to himself, and called to his assistant for a notepad on which he began scribbling furiously.

A short while later, Grant stood under the fluorescents at the head of the conference room and looked out at the decent-sized crowd who peered up at him, respect plastered on their drab pale faces. He smiled broadly, cleared his throat, and began to address the room with his fists planted firmly on the podium.

"We face, here in this room today, a crossroads in our great nation's future. And the decisions you and I make will dictate what happens for decades to come."

The Last Viceroy

Applause broke out, led by a bespectacled younger man in the back before rippling its way through the entire room.

"Ahem," Grant cleared his throat, irritated with the interruption but continuing on, now loosening his tie and gesturing familiarly.

"You know, when I arrived here at this fine establishment, in the best state in the best country in the world, I paused for a moment. Because right there in front of my eyes was a monarch butterfly." (That was not true, of course. The last viceroy was simply a viceroy.)

"And the monarch was perched there, sucking at the tit of a flower it had claimed. It sipped its water and fed on the nectar, preparing to fulfill its life purpose: that wonderful thing which is reproduction."

Grant could feel the eyes on him, fueling his fervor. He heightened the tenor of his voice.

"By claiming the flower as its birthright, the butterfly continues on, each generation stronger than the last. And I realized—" Grant now lifted his hand and opened his palm to his captive audience, the way only a great orator can—"I realized we are the butterfly, and the butterfly is us. Those of us gathered here today have a solemn duty: to squeeze every last droplet of the earth's decadent, life-giving fossils."

He seemed to grow bigger, fingers now pointed to his chest.

"Like the monarch, we must now burst from our cocoons and look to the future. For the sake of our next generation."

At this, the conference room broke out into a standing ovation. Grant saw beaming faces every which way. He had delivered. This time he wasn't annoyed by the interruption, for it had come at just the right moment.

. . .

The last viceroy didn't last long at the meadowsweet. Just as Grant stepped out under the

Rhapsody of the Spheres

conference room fluorescents, she had caught wind of a new scent, pungent and seductive. She flitted this way and that until spotting its source: saturated into the land were the rotting corpses of countless nectarines decomposing below the lush citrus tree.

The mud-puddling viceroy took a joyous dive, one of her last, before landing on the scavenged fruit and sucking up its tender juices happily. Oblivious and entranced, these were the last viceroy's final moments.

About the Author

Julie Biegner is an emerging writer from Los Angeles, California. She now lives in Asheville, North Carolina, where she enjoys speculative fiction and exploring the stories of her Asheville writing group.

*****~~~*****

The Arbitration of Beauty
by Emily Martha Sorensen

Golden and gleaming, the apple was glistening. It was a beauty, and
Beauty was something I cherished immensely. I reached out my hand for it.
Harshly, a slap came from nowhere and halted me from my intention.

"Let it remain," said an ireful voice, and I looked up and saw a young
Woman whose eyes burned with fury and hatred. Her clothing was grandiose.
"Slaves have no right to be picking up anything they are not ordered to."

She was mistaken, for I did not live here, but I wore the garments of
One locked in servitude. Skill at disguise was my favorite pastime, so
With no correction, I simply said, "Maybe then you should collect it, and

Rhapsody of the Spheres

Make it an offering. Prettiness like this would draw in the goddess of
Beauty, so see if she'll favor you."

"Favor from gods!" With vitriol
Written in lines of her face, the young woman hissed, "Nothing good
Comes from Olympians! Pleasing Apollo meant he tried to rape me, and
When I refused him, he cursed me with knowledge that no one believes, so my
Family mocks me and says I am mad. Let them die with the others from
Slaughter in warfare! Their selfishness will be their doom, and I'm glad of it.
You won't believe me, and so I will tell you. My brother will locate this,
Take it, and judge several forcible goddesses who want its bounty to
Claim they're the fairest. Behold what it says on it? It says Kallisti there.
Hera, Athena, and foul Aphrodite will come to demand it, and
Paris my brother will choose Aphrodite, accepting her boon of the
Love of a woman he wants, be she married or sworn to another.
War will result, with destruction of nations and heroes and lovers, and
All that is left will be ashes of those who despised me and mocked me, so
Let it remain."

I listened in terror. I'd thought that the apple was
Merely a bauble, a toy that belonged to the prettiest guest at the

The Arbitration of Beauty

Wedding I'd come from. As I was the fairest, it simply seemed obvious
    I should collect it and store it with treasures above on the mountain where
    I made my home, with my sisters and others who played with these mortals for
    Fun and for pleasure. I liked them and frequently granted them boons, and I
    Could not imagine enjoying a battle. It's true that a battle has
    Tactics and skill, but the ugliness in the destruction of mortals was
    Vile and repulsive. I could not stand by and allow it to start if a
    Way could be found to prevent it, but no, I was not the most powerful,
    Merely the prettiest. Hera especially hated my sisters and
    Me for our parentage, given that Zeus's affairs were the reason we
    Even existed, but that was not something we could have prevented, so
    Bearing a grudge for her husband's betrayal was nasty to us and to
    Others he'd fathered. Oh, Zeus was an idiot; Hera was lovely, and
    Would have been passionate, loyal, and loving to one who adored her, yet
    Jealous instead, she was wrathful and vengeful, and everyone hated her.

    Bowing submissively, watching Cassandra smirk down at the apple and
    Walk off without it, I quickly ran back to obtain it and hide it, but
    Tyche was still at the wedding and not at my side, and so

Rhapsody of the Spheres

Luck could be bad, and it was. At that moment, a thundering lightning bolt

Tore through the sky and emblazoned a figure before me: a lady who

Surely would kill me if given excuse, and most likely enjoy it, so

Quickly, I chose to feign mortal and hope I could mask my identity.

"Give me the apple," demanded the lady. She held out her hand with a

Lavishly intricate emerald wristlet adorned with a cow on it.

Loath as I was to relinquish the bauble, I wasn't an idiot.

Moving to execute Hera's command, I was suddenly halted by

Radiant petals of roses that bloomed from the ground and exploded in

Masses of showers of grandeur, revealing a minx who wore nothing, not

Even a necklace. I'd tried to convince her that sensuous clothing could

Add to her glamor, but she had rejected it. There was no subtlety.

"Give me the apple," the purring minx said with a sly little giggle that

Promised enjoyment, or else the destruction of all that held happiness.

"Give me the apple," commanded an alto voice. Slicing a hole in the

Air with a spear, a cool maiden of war with a feathery bird on her

The Arbitration of Beauty

Shoulder stepped forward and lifted the spear to my throat, where it
    Tickled my voicebox. Expecting surrender. Assuming authority.

Swallowing, seeing the doom now before me, I recognized there was much
    Worse than a war between mortals. Olympus at war would be absolute
    Chaos for everyone. Skilled I was not at placating the powerful,
    But I would do what I could to remediate any disasters that
    Promised to happen if I did not try what I could to negotiate.

"How could I choose?" I whined, just like a mortal. "I can't comprehend all the
    Glory before me! If I must choose one of you, I must choose all of you.
    Could you not share it, and bask in the knowledge that you're all magnificent?"

Bristling fury appeared in their eyes at the prospect of sharing. I'd
    Known that they'd hate it. The world would be better if they were less arrogant.
    Still, since I knew how they'd try to convince me, some good might come out of this.

"Give me the apple, and you will have wisdom," Athena said loftily,
    Pounding her spear at the ground by her feet. "With wisdom, you'll have any
    Gift you could ever desire, because you can gain it by studying."

Rhapsody of the Spheres

"Give me the apple, and you will have power," said Hera, who looked at me

With a cold smile. "I see you're a slave. I can make you a master of

All you behold, with the right to destroy any mortal who angers you."

"Give me the apple, and you'll have Adonis," the sly Aphrodite purred,

Winking at me. "I'm sick of him anyway, and that Persephone

Won't hold his interest once taken for winter. Expect his affection, and

Also his passion. Or if there's another you covet devotion from,

Just say the word, and that one will adore you with absolute tenderness."

That was the boon I'd been waiting to hear. "May I ask for that gift for some

Other besides me?"

"If that's what you want, I suppose," she said flatly, "but

What about you?"

"I'll be fine," I replied. "What I want is that gift for a

Lady who lacks it, and long has deserved it."

"Then say it who it is, and I'll
Capture his heart."

"It is Zeus. It is Hera. Please give her fidelity."

Horror appeared in the face of the minx. "That is not what I meant! They are

The Arbitration of Beauty
    Married, and I have no interest in marriage! Rescind it, or —"

"Do it!" commanded the
    Queen of the gods with a triumph that dazzled, a threat that was menacing.

"Wise that is not," said Athena, adjusting her spear with a frown. "If she
    Has his devotion, her rule will be total. Would mortals be served well by
    Zeus who does all things that Hera desires? I think if you ponder it —"

    Stubbornness crept up my back and my spine, for I cared about mortals, but
    This was a matter I'd wanted corrected since I was a child, because
    Zeus's behavior encouraged all gods to treat goddesses with the same
    Faithlessness. Someday I hoped to get married, and I would not
    Do that with any man following Zeus's example. My sisters both
    Felt the same way, yet we hadn't dared say it and risk rousing wrath from the
    Gods who took pleasure in making commitments and breaking them carelessly.

    Holding the apple towards Aphrodite, I made sure Kallisti was
    Easy to notice. "The fairest of all will be lauded forever, with
    Stories and poetry, love and desire."

    "I'll take it!" she shouted, and

Rhapsody of the Spheres

Annexed the apple. She kissed it and smirked at the other two goddesses.

"Do what you want with the mortal. I'll grant no protection to someone who

Asked for a boon that annoys me." She slurped through the ground, leaving

Thorns in her wake, like the damaging shards of a shattered relationship.

Hera's mouth thinned as she eyed me with coldness. "Whatever your motives, you

Chose Aphrodite. I'll make sure she grants you the boon that you asked for, but

You will be punished."

"Well, leave her to me," said Athena composedly. "Spiders are fun."

With a laugh and a raise of the arm, Hera vanished, the

Lightning that boosted her traveling upwards.

With eyebrows raised high as she

Scrutinized each of the folds of my costume, Athena said only, "Now

Answer me honestly, or it won't go well for you. Who are you truthfully?"

Silent I stayed as I tried to look baffled. I had no desire for

Vicious reprisals from she who commanded the goddess of victory.

"Mortal, my foot," she continued, and fondled the very sharp point of the

Spear at her side. "You'll tell me, or else I will learn on my own, and my

The Arbitration of Beauty

Patience is higher when I'm not required to torture words out of you."

"Let me explain why I did it!" I shouted, with knots in my stomach to
Think of her umbrage. "If Zeus reveres Hera, the rest of Olympus will
Start to respect all the goddesses better. They'll love you the most because
You are the greatest. You cannot be beaten, and vanquish their foes for them."

"That is unlikely." She chuckled. "But it's an excuse that I like, so I'll
Let you pretend that's your reason. Your name is —?"

"Aglaia."

"The goddess of Beauty?" Her eyes were incredulous.

"Yes."

"But you're clever!"

"That's
Not incompatible."

"Huh."

Peering at me, she let go of her spear, and it vanished. "Well,
Cleverness really does please me. All right. We'll see if you've made things much
Better or worse." She vanished, and breathing returned to my personage.

Only a Grace, and I'd done the impossible. It was a victory
I had achieved. A rapture of hope and elation suffused me,
Considering all that I someday might be.

###

About the Author

Emily Martha Sorensen has 53 published books and even more short stories and poetry published in various anthologies and magazines. Her short story, "Tabula Rasa," was published in Third Flatiron's *Gotta Wear Eclipse Glasses* anthology.

*****~~~~~*****

Credits and Acknowledgments

Editor and Publisher – Juliana Rew, Third Flatiron Publishing

Cover image and design – Keely Rew

Readers – Andrew Cairns, Tom Parker, Inken Purvis, Keely Rew, Russ Rew, Leonard Sitongia, Genevieve L. Mattern

Illustrations:

"The Solution to Everything Is Disco"– Keely Rew
Paddle steamer Waverley photo – commons.wikimedia.org, provided by Robert Mason (ebook only)
"A Touch of the Grape" Lucite grapes photo – courtesy of Sharon Diane King (ebook only)
Icons for stories courtesy of commons.wikimedia.org, provided by users Andre Costa (computer speaker) and Meul (vinyl disk)
All other images – royalty-free stock art

*****~~~~~*****

Discover other titles by Third Flatiron:

(1) Over the Brink: Tales of Environmental Disaster
(2) A High Shrill Thump: War Stories
(3) Origins: Colliding Causalities
(4) Universe Horribilis
(5) Playing with Fire

Rhapsody of the Spheres

(6) Lost Worlds, Retraced
(7) Redshifted: Martian Stories
(8) Astronomical Odds
(9) Master Minds
(10) Abbreviated Epics
(11) The Time It Happened
(12) Only Disconnect
(13) Ain't Superstitious
(14) Third Flatiron's Best of 2015
(15) It's Come to Our Attention
(16) Hyperpowers
(17) Keystone Chronicles
(18) Principia Ponderosa
(19) Cat's Breakfast: Kurt Vonnegut Tribute
(20) Strange Beasties
(21) Third Flatiron Best of 2017
(22) Monstrosities
(23) Galileo's Theme Park
(24) Terra! Tara! Terror!
(25) Hidden Histories
(26) Infinite Lives: Short Tales of Longevity
(27) Third Flatiron Best of 2019
(28) Gotta Wear Eclipse Glasses
(29) Brain Games: Stories to Astonish
(30) Things With Feathers: Stories of Hope
(31) After the Gold Rush

THIRD FLATIRON
www.thirdflatiron.com